Vampire Wake
(Kiera Hudson Series One)
Book 2

Tim O'Rourke

ISBN:1475264127
ISBN-13::978-1475264128

Story Editor
Lynda O'Rourke
Book cover designed by:
Carles Barrios
Copyright: Carles Barrios 2011
Carlesbarrios.blogspot.com
Edited by:
Carolyn M. Pinard
carolynpinardconsults@gmail.com

For Lynda
Who puts up with me...

More books by Tim O'Rourke

Vampire Shift (Kiera Hudson Series 1) Book 1
Vampire Wake (Kiera Hudson Series 1) Book 2
Vampire Hunt (Kiera Hudson Series 1) Book 3
Vampire Breed (Kiera Hudson Series 1) Book 4
Wolf House (Kiera Hudson Series 1) Book 4.5
Vampire Hollows (Kiera Hudson Series 1) Book 5
Dead Flesh (Kiera Hudson Series 2) Book 1
Dead Night (Kiera Hudson Series 2) Book 1.5
Dead Angels (Kiera Hudson Series 2) Book 2
Dead Statues (Kiera Hudson Series 2) Book 3
Dead Seth (Kiera Hudson Series 2) Book 4
Dead Wolf (Kiera Hudson Series 2) Book 5
Dead Water (Kiera Hudson Series 2) Book 6
Witch (A Sydney Hart Novel)
Black Hill Farm (Book 1)
Black Hill Farm: Andy's Diary (Book 2)
Doorways (Doorways Trilogy Book 1)
The League of Doorways (Doorways Trilogy Book 2)
Moonlight (Moon Trilogy) Book 1
Moonbeam (Moon Trilogy) Book 2
Vampire Seeker (Samantha Carter Series) Book 1

Chapter One

"What about the nightmares, Kiera?"

"What about them?" I asked.

"Are you still having them?"

"Yes," I told her.

The doctor sat opposite me, her thin hands holding my case file across the lap of her tweed skirt. Her pale, grey eyes stared back at me from behind her glasses. She wasn't unattractive, but her fair hair was pulled too tightly into a bun at the base of her neck, which gave her face a pinched, almost angry look. She couldn't have been any older than thirty-five but the glasses and the way she fixed her hair made her look more like forty-five. She appeared very prim and proper – but I could see that there was more to her than that.

"Are they always the same?" she pushed, her eyes fixed on mine over the rim of her glasses.

"About my mother?" I asked, although I knew what she meant. "Yes they are mostly about my mother," I answered.

"Mostly?" she fired back, keen to pick up on every word that I said.

"Mostly," I repeated.

"What else then, if not about your mother?" she asked, opening my file and taking a pen from her desk.

"Doctor Keats, I've been coming to see you every week now for the last six months. You know what else," I replied.

"The vampires?" she asked.

"Yes," I said, not breaking her stare.

"Tell me about them," she pushed, pen poised above her notes.

"Why? What's the point?" I asked, trying not to get frustrated with her. "You don't believe me – no one believes me. That's why I'm here, isn't it? The force wants to know if I'm mad – wants to know if I'm fit to go back to policing the streets. Isn't that what this is all really about?"

"Can you blame your employer for doubting you, Kiera?" Keats asked with that patronising tone in her voice.

"Of course I blame them," I said. "They were the ones who sent me to The Ragged Cove."

Thumbing through my case notes, she said, "From what I can see, you volunteered to go, Kiera." Then looking up at me she added, "No one forced you."

"But if I'd known…" I snapped, then stopped myself from going on.

"Known what?" she said in that tone again.

"That the place was infested with vampires. I wouldn't have taken up the post," I explained.

Smiling at me, like a mother who knows best for her wayward child, Doctor Keats shook her head from side to side and said, "But Kiera, there were no vampires."

"How do you account for all those incinerated bodies in the church?" I asked, meeting her gaze again.

"A terrible tragedy. Those poor souls caught in a horrendous fire while celebrating an early morning mass," she said.

"Oh please," I groaned. "You don't really believe that, do you?"

"What else could've happened?" she asked.

Knowing that I was never going to convince her that those burnt remains were really the skeletons of vampires, I said, "So what about all the cops that went missing from that place?"

"Lots of people go missing from time to time, Kiera," she smiled. "It doesn't mean that they became vampires."

I looked around the blank colourless walls of her office and I didn't know for how many more days or weeks I could keep coming and going over the same old thing. She was never going to believe me and I was never going to change my story. So picking up my bag that rested against the leg of my chair, I stood up.

"I really can't keep doing this, so goodbye Doctor Keats," I said and turned towards the door.

"You know you can't just walk out of here," she said, and there was a tinge of smugness in her voice.

"Why not?" I asked, glancing back at her.

"Not if you want your badge back, Constable Hudson." Then staring me straight in the face, she smiled, "Not if you want to find your mother."

Lingering by the door, I said, "What do you know of my mother?" I breathed.

"Only what you've told me," she said. "But I know the only way you'll ever get your hands on her missing person's file will be to get back on the force. And the only way that's ever going to happen, is if I sign you Fit For Duty."

"That sounds like blackmail to me!" I hissed.

"No, it's not blackmail, Kiera," she smiled and pushed her glasses back onto the bridge of her nose. "It's called 'protecting the public.' They pay a lot of taxes for their police force and I'm sure they wouldn't want -"

"Want what?" I demanded.

"Somebody policing their streets and towns who -"

"Who was mad enough to believe in the existence of vampires?" I finished for her.

Holding out her hand towards me, I looked down at it as she ushered me back towards the chair. "Come Kiera, sit back down. Let's talk."

Taking my seat again, I asked, "Talk about what?"

"Luke Bishop," she half-smiled.

"We've' already been over this," I said, taking my seat again.

"Humour me," she said, pen poised over her notes again.

"What do you want to know?"

"He was a vampire, right?"

"A Vampyrus," I corrected her.

"So what's the difference?" she asked, peering at me over the rim of her glasses.

"You know what the difference is," I said, starting to feel frustrated again. "The Vampyrus are a breed of vampire bat. They're not like normal vampires – they don't have to kill -"

"But you said some of these Vampyrus did kill," she cut over me. "That they killed some of the townsfolk from The Ragged Cove."

"There are some Vampyrus that don't want to live underground anymore. They want to live above ground, like us," I started.

"But you've previously told me that some of these Vampyrus do live amongst us," she said thumbing through her notes as if to refresh her memory. "You told me that some of them have managed to work their way into some of the most senior positions in society."

"That's right," I told her. "But that isn't enough for some of them. Others want more than that…"

"So, Bishop, what does he want?" she asked, looking straight at me.

"He wants to live like us," I said.

"So how come we…I mean us *humans* aren't aware of these Vampyrus?" she asked as she scrawled some notes across the pad on her lap.

"Because they look just like us," I said, tired of going around and around in circles with Doctor Keats.

Then looking up at me she smiled and said, "But Kiera, you said that Luke Bishop had wings,"

"Look, I'm really bored of this…" I started.

"Did you have a relationship with this Bishop?" she asked, the tip of her pen hovering over her notes.

"What's that supposed to mean?"

"Were you in love with him?"

Looking away from her, I stared at the long windows behind her. The sky looked dreary and overcast and it reminded me of those wet and miserable days spent in The Ragged Cove. I thought of Luke, and it was hard sometimes to even recall his face in my mind's eye. All I could see was Potter lowering Luke's burnt body into Murphy's arms, then disappearing into the hole in the floor at the police station. Although it had only been six months since I'd left The Ragged Cove, it seemed more like a lifetime ago.

"Kiera?" Doctor Keats said.

"Huh?" I whispered looking back at her.

"Were you in love with this Luke…?"

"I thought I was," I said, my voice low, just above a whisper. "But now I'm not so sure. When I was with him – it was like he had me under a spell. I had feelings that I'd never known or experienced before. They were so intense at the time. But now that we've been apart, it's like those feelings have started to fade."

"Did you have a physical relationship with him?" Keats asked, her eyes fixed on mine.

"Oh please," I groaned. "Why does it always have to come back to that?"

"It's important," she said.

"How?"

9

"Kiera, you claim to have met and fallen in love with a species not known to mankind," she said, "a species of bat that looks human but has the ability to grow wings and fly. You also tell me that for hundreds, possibly thousands of years, these creatures have been sneaking from below ground to live amongst us. So isn't it possible that like you and Bishop, humans and these Vampyrus would have fallen in love and perhaps produced children? If that were the case, don't you think it would be worth investigating?"

"I'm not pregnant if that's what you're wondering," I snapped. "I'm not going to give birth to some mutant half-breed if that's what you're scared of!"

"You might not be," she smiled again, "but who's to say that others in the past haven't? How do we know that living right amongst us aren't the children born out of relationships between humans and these 'Vampyrus' as you call them?"

"Look, Doctor, I don't know anything about that," I hissed. "It's not like Luke and me sat around chatting all day long, we were too busy -"

"Doing what?" she jumped in.

"Fighting for our lives!" I felt like screaming.

Realising that she was pissing me off again, and I was close to getting up and leaving for good, Keats closed the folder on her lap and folded her hands.

"Okay Kiera, I can see that you find talking about Luke upsetting, so I'd like to talk about something else."

"Like what?" I sighed.

"The blood," she smiled.

"Blood?" I asked, but knew where she was heading.

"You've told me at length how you often *see* things," she said.

"Yes," I nodded.

"But you say you see more than...well more than I would, let's say."

"It's like I absorb every detail that I see," I tried to explain all over again to her. "It's like I see stuff that most people wouldn't even notice."

"But it's more than that now?" she asked.

Nodding, I said, "Sometimes I see things that I shouldn't be able to see. Things that haven't happened yet."

"Like a psychic?" she said, and I couldn't help but notice the smile tugging at the corners of her lips.

"No, not like a psychic," I cringed. "I can't explain it…"

"But you said that you've started to bleed from your left eye when you have these visions. Is that right?"

"I'm not sure if the two are connected," I said. "It could be caused by something else."

"A brain tumour?"

"You tell me, you're the doc, Doc," I grinned at her.

"Kiera, you had all the tests, there is nothing wrong with you," she said.

"I'm not lying," I insisted.

"How about another kind of test?" Keats asked.

"What sort of a test?"

"Okay, you say you can see things about people," she smiled again. "Tell me, what did I have for my breakfast?"

"Give me a break," I sighed. "It doesn't work like that."

"How does it work, then?" she said. "Go on, tell me something about me that you couldn't possibly know."

"You really don't want me to do that," I said, and looked straight at her.

"Why not?" she asked in that tone again.

I looked at her sitting across the room from me, back straight, legs together, hands folded on her tweed skirt. She looked like a headmistress who thought she was in some way superior to me.

"Are you sure?" I asked her, almost as a warning.

"I'm sure," she smiled, not believing for a moment that I would be able to see anything about her at all.

Without taking my eyes off hers, there was a small part of me that was going to enjoy this.

"You're married, but not happily and you don't have any children. You find your husband boring, and despite your sober appearance, you crave excitement and adventure. You find this in the affair that you're having with a male who is about ten years younger than you. He is tall, lean, and strong-looking. His hair is blonde and he has blue eyes, the complete opposite of your husband. Your lover isn't married and you want him to believe that you aren't either. But I don't think he really cares about that. He would probably like it if you were – he'd find it more exciting that way. You hide the fact that you are married from him, not to protect your husband, but there is a very small part of you that knows what you are doing is wrong, so you're not really deceiving him, you're tricking yourself. You just can't let go of the austere image that you like to promote."

I couldn't help but notice Keats shift uncomfortably in her seat, pulling the hem of her skirt an inch or two over her knee. "Kiera, please could you stop…."

"Oh, I'm sorry, I thought this was some kind of test. I really think I should carry on." Now it was my turn to smile.

"Kiera -" she started, but I cut over her.

"You spent your lunch hour today with your lover in a room in the Holiday Inn Motel, just two streets from here. Your sex was quick and rushed, but he had time to…let me see…yes restrain you…"

"Enough already!" Doctor Keats screamed, almost falling forward off her seat. Her face was flushed, and her hands trembled in her lap. "I think that's all for today Kiera," she said, sounding out of breath. "You should go."

"As you wish," I smiled to myself, gathering up my bag and standing.

"I think we've gone as far as we can go with our sessions," she said, not looking at me. "I'm going to refer your case onto another colleague."

"Whatever you think is best, Doc," I said, pulling open the door to her office. Then just as I was about to step out into the corridor, she called after me.

"How did you know all that?" she asked. "It was some kind of trick, right?"

Shaking my head, I said, "No tricks, no magic."

"But how then?"

"The picture of you and that man on your desk has got to be your husband. If you have a picture of your husband then you'd have pictures of your children, too. Seeing as there aren't any pictures of sons and daughters tells me the chances are you don't have any. Your bag is open on the floor beside you and on the top are your car keys, compact mirror and a key card with the words *Holiday Inn Havensfield* printed on it. Must have been used today or otherwise it would have been further down your bag. The fact that it's there at all, says that you were in a rush to leave the motel and forgot to hand it back in at Reception. The top two buttons of your blouse have been fastened incorrectly, I can smell aftershave on you and you're not wearing your wedding ring as usual. Again, all signs that you were in a rush getting back from lunch. It's not the only time I've seen you not wearing your ring. You always have it on during my morning appointments, but this is the seventh time I've noticed it missing during my afternoon appointments, suggesting that you often remove it during your lunch break; and why would that be? You don't wear bracelets, but today, like on four other occasions I've noticed red circular marks on your wrists. You forget, Doctor Keats, I'm a police officer, and I'd recognise the marks left behind by handcuffs anywhere."

"Okay, okay," she groaned at me. "You've made your point. But how did you know what he looks like?"

Smiling down at her, I said, "Why, Doctor, that was the easy part. Three weeks ago, I arrived early for my appointment with you, so I sat and ate a sandwich in the small gardens just across the road. I happened to look up and see you climbing from a taxi. But before you got out, you lent back inside and kissed a young blonde-haired man. He didn't look like the picture of the man in the photo on your desk, and the kiss wasn't like the kiss you give to a friend or a brother – your lips lingered just a little too long over his. He had to be your lover."

Without looking back at her, I stepped out into the corridor, closing the door behind me. The thought of never having to sit opposite her again and face another of her interrogations felt wonderful – it felt like freedom. And as I left the building and stepped out into the grey afternoon sun, I guessed that she was glad that she would never have to see me again, too.

Chapter Two

Despite the overcast sky, I made my way on foot through
Havensfield town centre. A cool breeze swirled litter along the
gutter and I pulled the collar of my jacket up about my neck. The
streets with their rows of Victorian-built shops were just beginning
to close for the day, and most of the shoppers had started to head
home for the evening. Being a coastal town, seagulls squawked
overhead and the mouth-watering smell of fish and chips wafted on
the air.

It was just short of five in the afternoon, and I was annoyed
that I'd wasted yet another afternoon being analysed by Keats. I
hadn't meant to hurt her, and there was a small part of me that felt
bad for saying what I had. *But hey, she asked for it right?* I told
myself. She wanted to know what I could *see* about her – so I'd
told her – but had I needed to be so smug about it? Whatever, it
was done now and so were my weekly afternoon sessions with her,
I hoped.

Quickening my pace, I made my way across town towards the
newsagents. I wanted to buy a copy of each of the national
newspapers before they closed up shop for the day. Since leaving
The Ragged Cove and my suspension from work, I'd taken to
buying as many newspapers I could each day. With the T.V.
permanently tuned to the news channel, I would sit on the living
room floor of my small rented room and search each of the papers
for news stories involving any sudden disappearances of people.
But what I was really looking for were any stories relating to
murder where the victims had been found with injuries to their
throats. I would spend hours shut away, my eyes scanning every
page looking for anything that might suggest the return of
vampires. If there were vampires, my belief was that the Vampyrus
would be somewhere close by, and that meant Luke might be with
them. Murphy had told me that they were going in search of Taylor
and the other Vampyrus that were like him, unable to resist the
taste of human blood. If I could find Luke, Murphy, or Potter
again, then they would lead me to Taylor and perhaps my old
trainer, Sergeant Phillips, if he were still alive.

I wasn't interested in finding Taylor and Philips in order to seek any revenge, or help my old colleagues destroy them – I hoped to be able to convince Luke, Murphy, and Potter to keep them alive long enough, at least, for Taylor and Phillips to tell me what had truly happened to my mother. Ever since leaving The Ragged Cove, the thought of finding out what had happened to her and that image of Henry Blake's grey, cold hand clutching a lock of her hair wouldn't leave me. Nights had become almost unbearable, as I lay awake on the sofa, staring blankly at the news channel, my dreams and thoughts consumed by images of my mother and the nightmare that I'd lived at The Ragged Cove.

Night and day I thought about her and I wanted so much to keep the promise that I had made to my father. I knew that she was still alive and suspected that Taylor and Phillips held the answers. When I wasn't thinking about my mother, I was thinking about Luke. I wondered if he were alright and if he had managed to survive the burns that he had received saving my life in the sky above St. Mary's Church. On my many walks to see Doctor Keats, I would look down at the paving stones and wonder if Luke were somewhere beneath me in The Hollows. Then I would get to thinking that perhaps he wasn't beneath me at all, that he had recovered and was already above ground tracking Taylor and Phillips like Murphy had said they would.

There was so much that I didn't know, and that was what was driving me mad. Sometimes, after my sessions with Keats, I would question my own sanity. Had I really seen the things that I had in The Ragged Cove? Had I really been working the night shift with men that claimed to be a race of vampire bats? If I had been told such a thing by anyone, wouldn't I have had the same reaction to them as Keats had towards me? I mean this was the stuff of fairy tales, horror movies, and books. But I knew that it had all been real, I hadn't imagined any of it. And in the darkness at night as I lay awake, the T.V. set flickering in the corner, I would think of Luke and the brief time that we had spent together. Those feelings that I had felt for him would come flooding back and they would feel as raw and intense as they had when he had held me close to him, when he'd kissed me and enclosed me in his wings.

Had I really felt love for him? Or had it just simply been my emotions freaking out due to the unimaginable situation that I had found myself in? Had it just been lust? The guy was a hottie. But when I thought of him, his jet-black hair, bright green eyes, and fit body, I knew it was more than those things that made my soul ache for him. Like everything else that had taken place it, was hard to explain to myself, so how would I ever get the likes of Keats to understand or believe me?

Within days, of leaving The Ragged Cove and returning to my room in Havensfield, the nightmares had started. It was strange, because although I could see more than I always wanted to when I was awake, my dreams were a blur; a mosaic of broken images, distant voices, violence and death. The result was always the same; I would wake in my bed, but more often than not on the couch, with my heart thumping in my chest and gasping for breath. Then one night, as I sat gasping in air, I noticed something warm and wet trickling down my cheek. Dabbing at it with the tips of my fingers, I was horrified to discover that I was bleeding from my left tear duct.

Leaping from the couch, I raced to the bathroom and looked in the mirror to find a crimson stream of tears running from my eye. Taking a piece of tissue, I wiped it away, leaving a red smear across my cheek. At first I didn't do anything, telling myself that I must have unknowingly rubbed my eye in my sleep and scratched it with one of my fingernails. But it happened again the next night, and the night after that, a stream of blood-red tears flowing from my eye. For weeks I didn't mention this to Keats, I kept it to myself.

Then the red tears came during the day, but it was more than that. I started seeing things. I mean more than *seeing*. Those flash-bulbs would go *pop* again inside my mind's eye. Fleeting glimpses of crime scenes, bodies lying dead and bleeding, their eyes turned towards me. The images became more horrific – terrifying – like waking nightmares. I would get snapshots of catastrophes; buildings reduced to rubble; iron girders twisted out of shape; planes falling from the sky; trains crashing, piles of bodies stacked as high as mountains, limbs entwined like a grotesque puzzle; row upon row of open graves for as far as my eye could see. These images, however quick, came without warning and when I least expected them, they hit me like a blow to the head. They left me feeling confused, dazed, and nauseous. Then the tears would come, thick and red – almost black. It was as if holes the size of pinpricks had opened in my mind and was bleeding the anguish and suffering of those who I saw in those flashes.

In the end, I had to tell Keats – I had to tell someone. At first I didn't tell her about the visions I saw, just about the tears. Immediately, she sent me for CAT and MRI scans, but they found nothing. Doctor Keats became suspicious and that tone crept into her voice again, whenever I mentioned the tears. So I told her about the pictures I saw in my head. How it was like being in the dark, then suddenly the blackness is lit-up with a flash of white light revealing the gruesome scenes hidden within.

Keats wanted more detail. "Kiera, who are these victims you see?"

"I don't know," I told her with a shake of my head.

"Where are these bodies that you see?" she pushed.

"I don't know that, either," I said.

"What about the planes? The ones you see falling from the sky?"

"What about them?" I asked.

"Why are they falling from the sky? Are these catastrophes that *have* happened or *yet* to take place?"

"I don't know!" I insisted.

"What causes them to crash?" she pushed harder, the gap between her questions getting less, and reminding me of being cross-examined in court.

I felt I knew the answer to her last question, but I just couldn't say it.

"Well? Who is responsible for these atrocities?" she came at me again.

All I wanted to scream was: *The vampires did it! The vampires made the planes fall out of the sky. It was the vampires that brought those buildings to the ground and it was the vampires that killed all of those people!* But I couldn't say any of that to her – because I didn't know if that were true myself.

With my world seeming to fall apart all around me, I knew that I needed to occupy my mind. It had to be kept busy. I needed a mental challenge – some stimulus, a puzzle to solve to take my mind off what was happening to me. I needed to be back at work where I belonged – but I didn't know when or if ever that was going to happen. So I placed a small add in the local paper, which read:

Got a problem that needs investigating?
I'll solve anything!
Email: Kierahudson91@aol.com

I soon realised that I should have been more specific in my advert, as the first email I received was from a guy who thought he was paying too much for his electricity and wanted me to find out why. The second was from a woman who had lost her cat and the third was from an old gentleman who…well let's just say it was more of a medical matter. The fourth was not a great deal more interesting, it was from an old woman who had misplaced her wedding ring. Mrs. Lovelace was seventy-eight-years-old and had been married for sixty of them. Her husband had died in the last six months. She looked frail and vulnerable so I agreed to help. During one long Sunday afternoon and over several cups of watery tea, I got her to work backwards in her mind exactly what she had done and where she had been on the day that she had misplaced it. Eventually she remembered taking it off and placing it on the kitchen windowsill the previous Thursday morning.

"My fingers are thinner than they used to be," she smiled. "I always take the ring off when I'm washing the dishes. Don't want it to slip off and lose it down the plug-hole, you see. But I get so forgetful these days and don't always remember to put it back on again. Frank was forever reminding me."

"Frank?" I asked.

"My late husband – his memory was sharper than mine," she said, a sadness overcoming her face as she thought of him.

"May I take a look in the kitchen?" I asked her, placing my teacup on the table that sat between us.

"Of course you can, my dear," she said, struggling out of her chair.

Taking her by the arm, I led her into the kitchen, and she pointed to the spot on the windowsill where she had last seen her wedding ring. The window was open and a breeze blew in and cooled the stuffy kitchen. I leant forward and inspected the area where she said she had left her wedding ring.

"Mrs. Lovelace, can you remember if the window was open last Thursday?" I asked her.

"Now let me see," she said, and scratched her grey wispy hair with her gnarled fingers. "Yes, it would have been. I always have the window open in the warm weather."

"Can I take a look outside?" I asked her.

"Outside?" she said, eyeing me with curiosity. "Whatever for?"

"Oh, I don't know," I smiled at her. "I'm just nosey like that."

"Go right ahead, my dear," she said, and shuffled behind me to the kitchen door.

Stepping into the small garden, I could see a pretty-looking flowerbed in the earth directly under her window. Kneeling down, I brushed my fingertips over the Lavender that grew there.

"You're an excellent gardener," I said, gently pushing the plants aside so I could inspect the earth.

"Oh it's not down to me, a local man comes in twice a week and does it all for me," she said. "He's a terrific chap."

I had seen enough, so standing straight, I asked, "When was your gardener last here?"

"Let me see," she said, and scratched her hair again. "Last week sometime, I think."

"Nice is he?" I asked her.

"He's a lovely man," she said.

"What's his name?"

"Dave-something-or-other," she smiled. "I can't remember, and I only spoke to him this morning."

"How come?"

"He telephoned to ask if I wanted him to get me some more Fuschias. Apparently they're on sale at the gardening centre," she told me.

"You don't have an address for him, do you?" I asked.

"It's written down somewhere," she said, shuffling back into the house. "Now let me see…where did I put it?"

Following her into the kitchen, I watched as she picked up a tatty-looking handbag. Pawing through it she said, "I'm sure it's in here somewhere – he gave me one of these little card things with his number on it. Oh dear, I can't seem to find it now."

"Don't worry, Mrs. Lovelace," I assured her, then walked into the hallway where the telephone sat on a small round table. Anyone else called you today?" I asked over my shoulder.

"No, I don't think so," she said back from the kitchen.

Lifting the receiver, I pressed the 'last caller' button and made a note of the number. Going back into the kitchen, the old woman was still rummaging through her bag.

"Don't worry, Mrs. Lovelace. It wasn't important," I told her.

"Why did you want it?" she asked.

"My garden is a bit overgrown and I could do with a gardener, that was all." Then changing the subject, I added, "Have you got a picture of your wedding ring?"

Trundling back into the living room, she took a picture from the mantelpiece and handed it to me.

"That's me and Frank," she said. "One of the last pictures we had taken together," and I noticed her pale blue eyes begin to water.

In the picture she had her arms around her husband, both of them frail-looking but happy. Her left hand rested against Frank's arm, and I could clearly see her missing wedding ring. It was gold, with a yellow transparent-looking stone set into it. I guessed that the stone was citrine. On either side of the stone sat a cluster of tiny diamonds.

"It certainly is a beautiful ring," I told her.

"Will you be able to find it?" she asked, her voice wavering.

"I'll do my best," I said, taking her hand. "Can I hold onto this picture for a couple of days?"

"Yes, but why?" she asked, giving me that curious stare again.

"Oh it's just a hunch."

"Ok, if you think it will help, although I don't see how," she said, easing herself back down into her arm chair.

"I'll be back in a day or two," I told her, heading for the door. "I'll see myself out."

Climbing into my beat-up old Mini, I headed straight into town. Parking, I went to the local pawnbrokers. With picture in hand, I peered in through the windows, and there sitting on display, was Mrs. Lovelace's wedding ring. Without my badge, I would never be able to seize the ring from the owner of the shop, so heading across the street to a nearby Starbucks, I called the only person that I had stayed in contact with since being *temporarily* relieved of my duties – while I was mentally evaluated by Doctor Keats.

Constable John Miles had joined the police force at the same time as me and not being the brightest of recruits he had soon acquired the nickname 'Sparky'. But John was a sweet guy, dependable, and a loyal friend. Whereas my other fellow recruits had given up on me, Sparky had stayed in touch. He had been my lifeline back to the police, just updating me with gossip really, but it helped me maintain some kind of contact with the job that I longed to go back to. Sparky had never asked me about the 'vampire thing' which had caused so many raised eyebrows, sniggers, and condemnation amongst my peers. In fact, John had been pretty cool, and on the odd occasion that I had needed some information regarding my own enquiries, he had put his job on the line and run checks on the police computers for me. I knew that John wanted more than friendship, but I didn't have those kinds of feelings for him. The only feelings that I had for anyone like that was Luke, and I couldn't even be sure what they were anymore. But in return for the odd piece of information that John gave me to assist in one of my cases, I would sometimes cook him dinner or take him to the movies. John was awkward-looking, gangly, and shy and there was a part of me that I hated because I knew deep down I kind of used him. But knowing this didn't stop me from calling him up and asking him for his help - again.

John was on a day off from work, and joined me in the coffee shop within half an hour of my phone call to him. Nervously kissing me on my cheek, he pulled up a chair and sat opposite me. For someone who was in their mid-twenties he still had a sprinkling of spots on his forehead and cheeks – giving him a constant flushed look. His eyes were a dull grey and his glasses always perched lopsided on the bridge of his nose, giving his whole head a slanted look.

"What is it this time?" he asked, almost sounding excited that I was including him on one of my cases.

"I need you to flash your badge for me," I told him, with a smile, knowing that I wouldn't have to work hard at getting him to help me out. I then told him about Mrs. Lovelace's missing ring and how I'd found it sitting in the front window of the pawnbrokers across the street. I explained to him that without a badge, I would never be able to convince the owner to hand it over and get a look at the CCTV to see who it was that had brought the ring into the shop.

After finishing our coffees, I followed John across the street and into the pawnbrokers. Flipping his badge from his pocket, John spoke coolly to the owner and said, "I'm Constable Miles and this is Constable Hudson from Havensfield Police." Without giving the owner the opportunity to ask to see my identification John had started to talk again. I was impressed.

"The ring in the window, the one with the yellow stone, we suspect has come from a burglary," John said.

The owner, a smartly dressed man in his fifties with combed-back greying hair, looked back at John and said, "How can you be so sure?"

Producing the photograph given to me by Mrs. Lovelace, I waved it under the man's nose and said, "This is how we know."

Pulling a pair of spectacles from his suit pocket, he put them on and studied the picture.

"Take a look at the victim," I said. "That could easily be your mother sitting in that picture. Is your mother still alive?" I asked him.

"Well, yes…" he started.

"Lucky you," I cut in. "So she's not alone then, like this poor woman. See the guy in the picture?"

The owner nodded.

"Well that was her husband. Married for best part of sixty years," I told him. "But he died just six months ago and someone steals the wedding ring that he gave her. Now who would do a thing like that?"

"I don't -" the owner said, but this time it was Sparky who cut in.

"So you don't keep records of who you buy from?" and without waiting for the man's reply, Sparky said, "That's very remiss of you."

Then looking around the shop at all the other display cabinets, I said, "So, if you don't keep records or receipts, how can you be sure that none of this other stuff hasn't be stolen? I guess we had better get a warrant and come back and seize the lot. What do you reckon, Constable Miles?"

"Gee, and there seems to be so many pretty items in this shop to go through," Sparky said looking at owner. "It could take months to work our way through all this stuff – I mean this place could be closed down for God knows how long!"

"Okay, okay," the man sighed. "He came in last Thursday with it."

"Who did?" I asked.

"Didn't give his name," he said.

"CCTV?" John asked.

The man nodded.

"We'll be taking that, and the ring," I said, and held out my hand.

We drove back to my rented room, and while John fixed us both up with a mug of coffee and a sandwich, I watched the CCTV disc on my DVD player. There was a camera right above the counter and it gave a clear view of anyone that approached it. I sped through the disc to the previous Thursday. At 15:22 hours that day, my man came into the shop and produced Mrs. Lovelace's ring.

"I have him!" I shouted over my shoulder at John.

After a quick call to the number I had taken from Mrs. Lovelace's phone, I sat back in my favourite chair by the window, with John sitting opposite me, and we waited. Within half an hour, the buzzer on the door below sounded. Pressing the intercom button, I told the caller to come up. Leaving my door ajar, I went back to my seat. Moments later, a plump-looking middle-aged man, wearing overalls and muddy boots, stepped into my room. His hands were rough and dirty-looking, with mud under his fingernails.

"Mr. David Evans?" I asked, not getting up from my seat. "Owner of 'Tidy Gardens' who can be contacted via Tidy Gardens dot com, whose business address is fifteen Hayfields Road, Havensfield?"

"Why, yes," he said, looking at both me and Sparky. "You called me about some gardening that you need done?"

"That's correct," I said, not taking my eyes from his.

"But I don't understand," he said, scratching his untidy hair, "you live in a flat – you don't have a garden."

"No, I just like watching people dig themselves holes," I said back at him.

Looking at me totally confused, Evans said, "Is this some kind of joke?"

Placing Mrs. Lovelace's wedding ring onto the small coffee table that sat between Sparky and me, I said, "I don't think stealing from a seventy-eight-year-old woman is a joke."

The gardener looked down at the ring then back at me, his face white – the colour of paper. He opened and closed his mouth like a drowning fish.

"What have you got to say about that?" I asked him.

"I-I don't know…" he stammered. "I've never seen it before."

Snatching up the ring, I said, "Have it your way, Mr. Evans, but this gentleman over here is a police officer and is ready to take you into custody."

Hearing this, Evans dropped to his knees at my feet and gripped my ankles.

"Please, I beg you!" he cried. "This will ruin me – my family and my business!"

Kicking him away, I shouted, "Pull yourself together, man. It's only yourself you have to blame for the situation that you now find yourself in. You have tears of pity in your eyes, now that you have been caught – but where were your tears for Mrs. Lovelace?"

Still on his knees, Evans looked at me and, through his tears, he said, "I'm so sorry. I have been a fool. These last few months or more have been difficult for me. What with the credit crunch, most of my business has dried up. People can't afford to have their gardens tended to by me. It's a luxury that most people can now ill afford."

Showing him no pity, I said, "And so it is hard for millions of people up and down the length of the country, but do they all take to stealing from the elderly to supplement their wages?"

Sniffing, the man wiped his eyes with his dirty hands. "No they don't – but you must understand, I was desperate. Never before have I stolen anything. But I am behind with my mortgage and the bank is close to repossessing my home. My wife and children will be thrown out onto the street."

I didn't doubt that what Evans was telling me was the truth. I could tell that he was no hardened criminal, but still, I was angry with him for what he had done to Mrs. Lovelace. I looked at him; he was pathetic and a very small part of me felt sorry for him.

"Get up!" I snapped at him.

Like an obedient child, Evans stood, while Sparky and me remained seated. Then wringing his hands together, he looked at me and asked, "How did you know I had taken it? What led you to me?"

"Mrs. Lovelace contacted me as I am in the occasional business of solving…how can I put it? Little problems for people. I got her to work backwards in her mind and remember exactly where she had last seen it. She led me to the kitchen windowsill, where she had removed it last Thursday so she could wash the dishes. After a very brief examination of the windowsill, I could clearly see one muddy fingerprint, which suggested that it had been taken by someone with dirty hands. It wouldn't have taken a genius to have worked out that someone who spent much of their time with their hands in soil had removed it. After examining the flowerbed beneath the kitchen window, I found boot prints in the earth."

"But of course my foot marks would be there, I'm her gardener," Evans sniffled.

"You do a lot of your work standing on tiptoe, do you?" I asked him. "There were a set of prints that showed you had been standing on tiptoe just beneath her window. This is where you stood and reached in and took the ring."

"But…but," he said sounding astounded. "How did you find the ring?"

"The fact that Mrs. Lovelace didn't report any other missing valuables, suggests to me that this was a crime of impulse. Just as you have told us, you are struggling financially and on seeing the ring, you saw a way of solving your problems – albeit a mere quick fix. But you weren't thinking of the long-term consequences or of the outcome should you be caught for your crime. I knew that this theft was a crime of impulse – to make a quick buck, dare I say. Therefore you would want to get rid of the ring as quickly as possible and convert it into some cash. You wouldn't sell it to friends – they would have wondered where you had come by it – no, you are an amateur – you don't mix in criminal circles and wouldn't know anyone to pass it to. So needing the money quickly, you took it to the only place in town that would be interested in buying such an item – the pawnbrokers. So that was the next stop and there was the ring. You were smart enough not to leave your details, but the CCTV proves that it was you." Then smiling at him wryly, I added, "The chain of events weren't very hard to follow."

"I see," said Evans, sitting slowly into an armchair by the door. "So what happens now? There has been no real harm done, don't you think? Mrs. Lovelace has her ring back."

"Thanks to me and my colleague over there," I snapped. "If Mrs. Lovelace had not contacted me then your hope was that she would believe that she had misplaced the ring. Then what? The following month when you were short of money – would you have helped yourself to her pension money – taken a few notes from her purse when she had her back turned?"

"No!" Evans said, his voice wobbling again as if on the verge of more tears. "I swear. You have to believe me."

"Why should I take the word of a man that would stoop so low as to take something so precious from an elderly woman such as Mrs. Lovelace?" I scowled.

"Please don't arrest me!" he begged, sitting on the edge of his seat. "Please don't make this official."

Looking at Evans, I could see that his face had drained of all colour and he seemed almost near to collapse. Standing, I crossed the room to him. Looking down at him I said, "You disgust me Evans, but I do believe that you lost your head that day in the garden. You saw the ring and believed you saw a way out of your problems. I believe that you have led a previously good life and it is not my wish to destroy what has, up until this point, been an unblemished life. If my colleague were to arrest you, it would only harm the very people you so foolishly believed you could protect – your wife and children. But my main concern is with my client, Mrs. Lovelace. She could well do without the trauma of having to provide a statement to the police, and perhaps take the stand in court. But would be the realisation that you – someone she speaks so highly of and believes to be her friend – could steal her most precious possession, which would destroy her. I have no wish to break that poor woman's heart, when it is still healing from the death of her husband. Therefore, I will not be taking this matter any further."

Dropping from the armchair, and clasping hold of my trousers, Evans sobbed. "Thank you! Thank you." Kicking him free, I dragged him to his feet and grabbed him by his dirty overalls. Unable to make eye contact with me, Evans said, "How can I ever thank you enough?"

"There is still the matter of the pawnbroker – he is still five hundred pounds out of pocket thanks to you. You will repay him the money. I will be calling him in the next day or two to see that you have. And you are never to go back to Mrs. Lovelace's home again. That is a customer you have now lost and by the sounds of it, you need as many as you can get."

"I promise," Evans snivelled. "I promise."

Releasing him, I shoved him towards the door and said, "Now get out of here!"

With his shoulders slumped forward and his head cast down, Evans skulked from my room. From behind me, I could hear the sound of clapping. Turning, I saw Sparky, still seated in the armchair and slapping his hands together. Smiling at me, he said, "I've got to give it to you Hudson – you're a class act."

"It was nothing," I said, crossing back to my chair.

"I could see how you followed each step of the case, but how did you know his website and home address? You only had his telephone number."

"That was easy. It's written down the side of the van that he arrived in." Then smiling to myself, I looked out of the window.

I returned the ring to Mrs. Lovelace that evening. Once again, I went back to the flowerbed beneath her kitchen window, and making out that it had been there all along, I handed it to her. Slipping it back onto her finger, she wept with relief at having her wedding ring again.

"Whatever your fee, young lady, it would never be enough," she sobbed. "How much do I owe you?"

Taking her by the arm and leading her back inside, I told her she owed me nothing. In the following days, I hired another gardener for Mrs. Lovelace, giving him my bank account details so he could charge me directly for his labour.

"She's is to have the prettiest garden in Havensfield," I told him.

I reached the newsagents just as it was closing.

"I didn't think you were coming today," the paperboy said, as he opened the door to me.

"I got delayed, Jack," I said.

"Want a copy of each?" he asked, taking the pile of newspapers from the counter.

"As always," I smiled.

"What I can't figure out," the young lad said, "is how come you need so many newspapers every day. They all pretty much say the same old thing."

"I don't have a social life," I said, taking the papers from him.

"Fancy going on a date then, Kiera?" he said, trying to make his offer sound like a joke.

"Maybe in a couple of years," I winked at him and left the shop. Taking one of the papers, I rolled the others up and tucked them under my arm. Then looking at the headline splashed in thick black letters across the newspaper, my heart almost stopped.

Passenger plane crashes over Atlantic Ocean!

Then, just like so many times before, those bright lights began to flash behind my eyes. And in those bright lights I could see an airline pilot screaming into his headpiece, *"Mayday! Mayday! They are trying to breach the cockpit!"*

As quickly as they had come, those blinding images had gone, leaving me feeling punch-drunk and dazed. Then I heard the pitter-patter sound of raindrops splashing down onto the newspaper in my hands. Looking down at the headline, expecting to see black ink running across the page, I was startled to see that it wasn't rain that had dripped onto it, but crimson-coloured tears from my eye.

Chapter Three

Placing the newspapers on the table along with all the other cuttings and clippings I'd amassed over the weeks, I went to my poky bathroom and ran a sink full of water. Cupping my hands, I splashed some of it onto my face, and wiped away the red streak that ran from the corner of my left eye and down my cheek. Some of it had splashed onto my top, and pulling it off, I threw it into the wash basket.

The dizziness that I felt after these episodes had begun to fade, and I was left with a dull thud throbbing away behind my temple. Rolling my head from side to side on my neck, I rubbed my forehead with the tips of my fingers and went to my bedroom. Pulling a clean top from the wardrobe, I pulled it on. Sitting in my favourite seat by the window, I eased myself into it and turned on the T.V. I would go through the newspapers once my head had cleared. It had become my nightly habit of sitting in my armchair, the news playing on the T.V in the background, and methodically going through every newspaper looking for stories, anything that might lead me to Luke, Potter, and Murphy. With scissors in hand, I would cut out anything of interest and pin them to the living room wall. There were so many cuttings now attached to the walls, that if you stepped back and at a glance, the room looked as if it had been decorated with newspaper. Faces of the missing and murder victims stared back at me. Sparky said that it freaked him out just a little and he once asked me why they were there. I told him that I was fascinated by serious crime, and that I was writing a study on offender profiling. If Doctor Keats had ever made a house call, then my chances of ever returning back to the force would've been something close to zero. But I didn't have to worry about Keats anymore and she didn't have to worry about me – if she ever had.

The T.V. flashed images of the ocean. Rescue boats were racing towards what looked like the fragmented and broken pieces of an airliner. Cushion seats floated on the waves, along with yellow-coloured life jackets. The strap line running across the bottom of the screen read:

Air Atlantis Flight 281 crashes into sea 80 miles off the coast of Ireland. All 232 passengers and 12 crew feared to be dead.

Leaning forward in my chair, I turned up the volume to hear the reporter speaking over the images being played out on the screen.

"The investigation is still on-going," the reporter said. "The cause of the crash is yet to be formally determined. A statement by the BEA says that the last verbal contact was made with the aircraft at 11:52 hours BST. It is unclear what was said during that last transmission."

Slumping back into my chair, I could hear the sound of that voice inside my head. It wasn't like I was hearing with my ears, but like a distant radio signal hissing and spitting inside my mind. Over and over I could hear a voice screaming, *"They've breached the cabin...they've breached the cabin!"*

Was the voice I could hear that of the pilot from the plane that crashed into the sea? It couldn't be. Why would it be? And who had breached the cabin? But as I sat and tried to make sense of the changes that were taking hold of me, the buzzer on my door hummed, waking me from my thoughts. Placing the newspapers on the floor and turning down the volume on the T.V., I got up from my chair and peered out of the window and down at the street below. It was starting to get dark outside. The long shadow of someone standing at the door stretched up the street like a deep crack in the pavement. The buzzer sounded again.

Pressing the intercom button, I spoke into it.

"Hello?"

"Ms. Kiera Hudson?" the voice asked, and it was female.

"Yes," I said back, wondering who it could be.

"I was hoping I could speak with you," the voice crackled through the intercom.

Peering over my shoulder at my room, the piles of old newspapers scattered across the floor and stacked beside my chair, and the news cuttings covering the walls, I turned back and said, "This isn't a good time for me at the moment. Couldn't you come back -"

"You've been recommended to me," the voice cut in. "I've heard you're good at...how can I put it? Solving little problems?"

"Erm," I stammered.

"Please, Ms. Hudson," the voice came again. "I've travelled a great distance to ask for your help."

Releasing the latch, I spoke into the intercom and said, "Okay, come on up."

Hurrying around the room, I kicked some of the scattered newspapers under the chair and sofa, and scraped my hair into a ponytail. Before I'd even had the chance of finishing my hair, there was a woman standing in my open doorway. Closing the door behind her, she stepped in.

Glancing at all the hundreds of newspaper cuttings, she said, "Thank you for seeing me, Ms. Hudson."

Knocking a pile of newspapers from an armchair, I ushered her towards it. "Please call me Kiera," I smiled. "Ms. Hudson makes me sound so old."

"Of course," the woman smiled back, not taking her eyes from me, "Someone so young and pretty but with a knowledge way past her years."

"I'm sorry?" I said sitting back in my chair.

'I've heard very good things about you, Kiera," she said, smoothing out her trousers with her hands and then pulling down the cuffs of her suit jacket. The woman was dressed all in black, apart from the grey-coloured blouse that I could see beneath her jacket. But that was all I could *see* – I mean unlike Doctor Keats – this woman gave nothing away. I guessed she was in her early to mid-forties, her skin was pale and in great condition. She had thick auburn hair that flowed onto her shoulders. Her eyes were clear blue and she wore little-to-no make-up, apart from a crimson lipstick she had daubed her full lips with. The woman wore no jewellery – no rings, necklaces, or bracelets.

"Can I get you something?" I asked her. "A cup of tea or…"

"No, thank you," the woman smiled. "Let me introduce myself. I am Lady Hunt – but I'm happy for you to call me Elizabeth. I find titles so stuffy, don't you?"

"I guess," I said, wondering what it was that she could possibly want me to help her with.

"My husband, Lord Hunt, is the owner of Raven Industries. I don't know if you have ever heard of them?"

Shaking my head, I said, "I'm not sure that I have. What's the purpose of his company?"

"It has something to do with renewable genetics," she said. "I don't claim to really have understood what it was that Michael did, but maybe I should have taken more of an interest."

"Did?" I asked.

"Michael...how can I put this? Went missing a few months ago," she started to explain. "He had gone on a business trip to New York and hasn't been seen since."

"I'm sorry to hear that," I told her.

"That's very kind of you, but I have been left with somewhat of a dilemma," she said, and stared straight at me. "Since Michael's disappearance, I have been left to manage the business and as I've explained, I know very little about it. There is a meeting of shareholders in New York two days from now which I must attend."

"I'm sorry, but is it the disappearance of your husband you want me to investigate?" I asked, somewhat confused. "I know very little about business and even less about the complexities of renewable genetics."

Covering her mouth to stifle a giggle, Lady Hunt looked at me and said, "Oh no Kiera, I've employed someone else to investigate Michael's disappearance. That's not the problem I require your services for."

"What then?" I asked her with a frown.

"My sixteen-year-old daughter, Kayla, she's the problem," the woman said.

"In what way?" I asked, wondering where this was heading.

Standing, the woman went to the window and looked out. Without looking at me she said, "How can I describe Kayla? Apart from being exceptionally beautiful, she is also very bright," then turning to face me she said, "and also out of control."

"In what way?" I asked her, wondering if this wasn't going to be a *my-daughter's-mixed-up-in-drugs-and-I-don't-like-the-guy-she-hangs-out-with* kind of problem.

"You have to understand, Kiera, that my husband and I have always given our daughter the very best – the very best of everything," she said. "No money has been spared. She has gone to the best private schools; she's had the best of holidays, the best of everything."

What about attention and love? I wondered but didn't dare say this.

"But over the last few years, she has become wayward – rebelled against me and her father. Much to her father's shame, Kayla has been expelled from every school we have sent her to. Even when Michael offered to pay double the tuition fees to keep her at one school, the headmaster refused, stating that it wasn't the money – it was for the wellbeing of the other students and the sanity of the staff, which was his main concern. The headmaster went on to explain that Kayla's behaviour had become so disruptive, that several parents had taken their child out of the school and he had a list of several other parents that were threatening to take their children elsewhere if Kayla was not removed. Finally, Kayla had built such a reputation for herself that no school – however much money we offered – would take her. Eventually, she became home-tutored and to my last count we have been through seven teachers in the last year."

Heading back towards the chair and ringing her pale hands together, Lady Hunt took her seat again. "I am at my wit's end."

"But how can I help?" I asked her.

"I heard that you were a police officer," Lady Hunt said.

"*Still* a police officer," I corrected her. "Let's just say I'm on an extended career break at the moment."

"Well that's even better, don't you see?" the woman said, and I detected a note of desperation in her voice.

"For once in my life, I don't see," I told her.

"As I've said, I've got to go to New York tomorrow, and I need someone to keep an eye on -" she started.

Guessing what was coming, I cut in and said, "Can't you take your daughter with you? She might like to…"

"You must be joking," she scoffed. "I couldn't possibly take Kayla with me – what would *they* think?"

"I don't know," I said. "But perhaps some time with just you – her mother – might be good for her."

"But I'll be so busy in meetings and conferences, I wouldn't be able to spend any time with her," she explained. "And I shudder to think of what she might get up to in New York while I was busy all day."

"So what is it you're asking me to do?" I said.

"Please come and stay at our home while I'm away and keep an eye on Kayla for me," she asked. "You're not too many years older than her and having a police officer around might be a stabling influence for her. You will be well looked after by my staff…"

"Can't they keep an eye on her?" I asked, not wanting to take up the job of babysitting some spoilt brat.

"The Housekeeper has enough to do keeping the house running without having to concern herself with Kayla. Then there is Marshal, the grounds man, he is quiet and aloof – not the slightest bit interested in some teenager's rebellion. If left to her devices, Kayla would escape."

"Escape?" I said, imagining a house with bars on the windows.

"Escape is probably too strong a word," Lady Hunt said. "But Kayla has run away from home on several occasions. She travelled to London. We spent hundreds – no thousands of pounds in private detective fees in tracing her. The last time she was discovered living like a homeless person by the Embankment Tube Station. It was all very stressful and upsetting for us." Then pulling a handkerchief from her suit pocket she dabbed the corner of her eyes.

"No wonder Michael vanished – maybe he just had enough and couldn't face coming home anymore. I don't blame Kayla, but she has caused so much stress over the last few years."

"Why do you think she behaves like this?" I asked her.

"I don't know," she groaned. "Like I said, we've given her everything."

And that's the problem, I thought to myself.

"I'd love to help, but…'" I started to make my excuses.

"Please Kiera," she said, moving to the edge of her seat. "I'll pay you well…"

"It's not the money," I started to assure her.

"Please, all I ask is for you to come to my home for a week and keep an eye on my daughter…"

"It's not really my idea of problem-solving," I explained. "And besides, there must be someone else, some family member better suited to watch over your daughter. Somebody she knows and trusts, unless…"

"Unless what?" Lady Hunt asked me.

"Unless your concerns run deeper than just your daughter's delinquent behaviour," I said, eyeing her. "Perhaps you haven't told me everything."

"Your reputation does you justice," she said, placing her hanky back into her pocket. "It seems that it is very difficult to get anything past you."

"To fool me, Lady Hunt?" I said, feeling resentful that she hadn't told me everything from the start.

"The problem is a little more complex than I first suggested," Lady Hunt said, her skin so pale that she looked as if she might just faint.

"How complex?" I said, my interest in this case suddenly heightening.

"There is someone watching my daughter," she said, her voice dropping to a whisper.

"Who?" I asked her.

"That, I do not know," she said. "But I have seen him, at night, beyond the grounds of our home. He lurks in the dark at night, spying up at my daughter's room."

"Grounds?" I asked.

"Yes, we live in a Manor House," she explained. "It's a wretched place, really. It's far too big for us and terribly hard to heat in the winter. Half of it is unused and has been for years, but it has been in my husband's family for generations and it was his wish to reside in the home of his forefathers. The grounds are surrounded by a moat and there is a drawbridge – this is the only way in and out of the grounds."

"A moat?" I gasped. "Sounds more like a castle!"

"I've probably talked it up far too much," she said. "It's not as grand as I've portrayed it to be. In fact, much of the manor is in disrepair and the whole place could do with tidying up. But Michael is a traditionalist and wants the manor to stay in the style that it had originally been built. He is very fussy about who he gets to work on the place. If it were going to be renovated, he was insistent that it be done just right. I lost count on how many builders we had visit the place and give quotes on the cost – but he never hired any of them. The whole place needs to be rewired and the plumbing – well don't get me started on that. The noise those pipes make is just deafening at times. But even in the short time since my husband has vanished, I have taken steps to have the work done. There are currently some workmen up at the manor carrying out some work for me."

"How do you know it's a man?" I asked her.

"Sorry?" she said, almost as if my question had surprised her.

"You said that the person watching your daughter is a man," I reminded her.

"Marshal, the grounds man, disturbed him one night as he stood hidden in the undergrowth and bushes on the other side of the moat," she said.

"Could Marshal give a description of this man?" I asked.

"No, it was dark. We live miles from anywhere, deep on the Welsh Moors. Save for the moonlight, the area is in complete darkness come nightfall. Marshal didn't get a good look at him and he was quick on his feet – disappearing over the rugged landscape and into the night."

"Do you have any idea who this person might be and why he would want to watch your daughter?" I asked her.

"I suspect that it's someone she has met on one of her many escapades to London," she said. "It scares me half to death, the thought of who she may have associated with while she was there. Perhaps she told him of her privileged upbringing and he has come to rob our home. Or maybe he has come to entice her back to London – for what reason I dare not wonder. But whatever the reason, Kiera, I feel that Kayla is at risk of much harm from him."

"Have you spoken to Kayla and asked her if she knows the identity of this stranger?" I asked.

"Yes, but she becomes evasive and then angry, throwing the most violent of tantrums," she said. "With the help of Marshal, we have had to lock her in her room until she calms herself."

"Tell me, did this stranger appear before or after your husband's sudden disappearance?" I asked her.

"Just after," she said, eyeing me. "Why do you ask?"

"No real reason," I said trying to brush off her question. Changing the subject, I said, "Why haven't you called the police to investigate this male?"

"As of yet, he has done nothing wrong," she said. "He has been seen loitering around at night, but as I've said, I wouldn't even be able to describe him. He hasn't committed burglary or harmed me, my daughter, or my staff. But you have to believe me, Kiera, there is something very wrong and although Kayla seems fearless, my heart is full of dread. We live miles from the nearest town, the manor is remote, and should this man gain access to our home in my absence, I'm terrified at the thought of what might happen to my daughter. So I beg you, Kiera Hudson, please accept my offer and come to my home and protect my dear Kayla– it will be a week at the most."

I looked into her eyes, and I could see the fear in them. What else did I have planned? Nights sitting in front of the T.V. cutting out news articles and tacking them to walls of my flat? A trip into the country would probably do me some good; take my mind off Luke, Potter, and Murphy and the search for my mother. But more than that, this was the most interesting case to come along since…since I was posted to The Ragged Cove.

"Okay, I'll come," I told her, and for the briefest of moments I thought she was going to faint to the floor with relief.

"Oh thank you! Thank you!" she gasped, clutching her hands together as if in prayer.

"You'll have to give me your address, so I can drive down tomorrow," I said.

Then springing to her feet, Lady Hunt said, "You must come tonight, Kiera, as I leave for America first thing tomorrow morning."

"But I'll need to pack some stuff together -" I started.

"My driver is waiting outside," she said, her voice sounding urgent. "We must leave now!"

Chapter Four

Within five minutes, I'd packed a rucksack with everything that I guessed I might need. If I'd had longer to think about Lady Hunt's offer, maybe I wouldn't have been so eager to go. But things in my life since returning from The Ragged Cove hadn't been the same. Luke had left a hole somewhere inside of me, my dreams were plagued with images of my mother, nightmares haunted me day and night, and apart from Sparky, no one believed what had happened in The Ragged Cove. As I looked around at the piles of newspapers and the thousands of cuttings pinned to my wall, I knew deep down that I had to get away; but more than that, for the first time since leaving the Cove, I had a problem – something to solve – and that to me was irresistible.

With my rucksack hung over my shoulder, I switched out the light in my bedroom and closed the door behind me. Lady Hunt was standing and peering at the newspaper cuttings. Hearing me entering the room, she turned and smiled at me.

"Ready?" she asked.

"I guess," I said.

"Let's get going then."

I locked the door to my flat and followed Lady Hunt down the stairs and out into the street. It was near dark, and parked by the curb was a sleek black Rolls Royce Phantom. Its body glistened like glass in the darkness and in it I could see my own reflection. Parked just in front of my Mini, or *piece of junk* as Potter had called it, the Rolls Royce looked like something from another planet. Lady Hunt was wealthier than I first realised. Oddly, the chauffeur stayed seated behind the wheel as Lady Hunt opened the back door for me to climb in. The interior of the car was upholstered in off-white leather, there were dark navy curtains at the windows, the glass in them was tinted, and a flat-screen T.V. hung down from the ceiling.

Lady Hunt closed the door shut behind me, walked round the rear of the vehicle and got in beside me. The vehicle purred into life
and crawled away from the curb. I looked back at my flat and my little red Mini, and as they disappeared into the distance, I got the

strangest feeling that I might not ever see them again. Telling myself that I was just scared of stepping out of the comfort zone that I had entombed myself in, I faced front.

"The cuttings?" Lady Hunt asked.

"What about them?" I asked back.

"Why so many?"

"I'm working on a project," I lied. "I'm doing a study on offender prof -" I started.

"I thought that perhaps you were searching for someone or some *thing*?" she cut in.

I knew by the way that she emphasised the *thing* that she was possibly referring to vampires. Trying to keep myself composed, I just stared back at her.

"You don't really think I would leave you in charge of my daughter without doing some research into your background first, do you?" she said.

"What did you find out?" I asked her.

"You tell me," she smiled.

"I guess it all depends on who you spoke to," I smiled back.

Glancing out of the tinted windows, Lady Hunt said, "I know about your tales of vampires."

Looking at her almost perfect profile, I said, "You must have believed my account of what happened to me."

"What makes you think I believe you?" she said without turning to face me.

"If you believed me to be a liar, you wouldn't have hired me to babysit your daughter," I said back.

Then turning to face me she said, "I haven't hired you for your storytelling abilities, Kiera Hudson. I've hired you to protect my daughter from whomever it is that lurks in the shadows at night and watches her."

"What makes you think I can offer your daughter any protection?" I asked.

"I take it you're not a liar?" she said, her eyes almost seeming to twinkle in the gloom of the rear of the car.

"Correct," I said, sounding defensive.

"Well then," she smiled. "Your account of what happened to you in The Ragged Cove must be true. And if that is the case, who better to look after my daughter than someone who managed to survive the odds against all those vampires!"

Before I'd the chance to say anything back, the car was slowing and pulling into the curb outside Havensfield Railway Station. Lady Hunt pushed open her door and started to climb out.

"We can't be here already?" I said, knowing that we had only been on the road ten minutes.

"This is as far as I go," she said, looking back over her shoulder at me.

"What, you're not coming back with me?" I said feeling confused. "What about your daughter, the staff at -"

"They're expecting you," she smiled back at me. "My staff will welcome you and provide you with anything that you need."

"How are they expecting me?" I said. "How did you know that I would come?"

"Like I said. Kiera, I've done my homework and I knew you wouldn't be able to turn down such a problem as I've got," she said.

"But where are you going?" I asked.

Standing on the pavement and looking back at me sitting in the huge car, Lady Hunt said, "I'm catching the next train to London where I'm meeting up with a business acquaintance, and tomorrow we fly out to New York. I'll see you in one week." Then closing the car door, she was gone.

Leaning across the back seat, I reached for the handle to open the door again, but the chauffeur was accelerating the car away down the street. Peering out of the back window, I was surprised to see that Lady Hunt had already disappeared from view. But at last, despite her immaculate but bland appearance, I had *seen* something about her. She wasn't going to New York, any more than I was. Turning front, I looked at the back of the head of the chauffeur. Sliding across the backseat, I tried to get a better look at him. The interior of the car was in darkness and only the glare from the headlights of passing cars offered any light. The chauffeur wore a grey peaked cap, which was pulled down low over his eyes, bushy white sideburns covered his cheeks, and a pair of glasses with black lenses covered his eyes. He gripped the steering wheel with a brown leather pair of driving gloves.

"So what's your name?" I asked him, slumping back into the soft backseat of the car.

He made no reply.

Okay, I thought to myself. "So where exactly is this place you're taking me to? I know it's on the Welsh Moors but what's -"

Before I'd the chance to finish what I was saying, he reached forward and pressed a button on the dashboard, raising a glass panel between us – sealing me in the rear of the car.

"What a jerk! So you're not the talkative type," I mumbled aloud. "Two can play that game." Reaching into my rucksack, I pulled out my iPod and turned it on. Listening to *'Give Me Everything'* by Pit-Bull and Ne-Yo, I settled back into the seat, and noted the time of my wristwatch – 20:07 hours. Staring out into the night, I couldn't help but wonder what lay ahead for me in the darkness. But that was exciting, right?

Chapter Five

I was driven through the night by the nameless chauffeur, and I could do little else but listen to my iPod and stare out the window into the dark. What was I getting myself into? Where was I being taken? And why had Lady Hunt lied to me about going to New York? Most people would be demanding to be let free of the car or to be taken home to safety. But I didn't feel anything like that. Yeah, if I'm to be honest, my innards felt like they were being gripped by an invisible fist, but that feeling of apprehension – of not knowing – made me feel alive, all of my senses tingled with the thought of what might lay ahead.

As I stared out of the window, I made a mental note of the route which I was being taken – just in case. We took routes, A390, A39, and the A30, reaching the M5 at 21:34 hours. We travelled along the M5 until we reached the M49 an hour and fifteen minutes later. After a further five minutes we took the exit onto the M4 and I noted we travelled this for a further twenty-nine minutes until we left the motorway and headed onto the A470 and to a place called Merthyr Jydfil. We reached Brecon twenty-one minutes later and this is where the chauffeur took a series of unmarked roads that led us away across the Brecon Beacon moors. The roads twisted and climbed, the chauffeur having to slow the car as he navigated his way via a series of slate stone lanes that were shielded each side by low, black slate walls. It was so dark outside, that all I could see was the pale shadow of my face reflecting back at me off the glass. We drove further and deeper across the moors. Every now and then, the barren landscape would be illuminated by the light of the moon as it appeared from behind passing clouds. It was bleak, rugged, and desolate. As I sensed the rest of civilisation disappearing behind me, that invisible fist drew tighter around my guts.

The vehicle climbed again, then the ground beneath us levelled out. In the distance, I could see the shape of a building set against the night sky. The sound of gravel crunching and breaking beneath the wheels of the car seemed almost deafening as the chauffeur headed towards this building – or castle?

The vehicle slowed, and I pressed the button set into the car door to lower the window. It made a buzzing noise, but the window refused to open. Cupping my hands together and pressing them against the glass, I peered out into the darkness, keen to find out why we had stopped. It looked as if we had come to a bridge that had only been half-finished. Then in the distance, I could hear a grinding and clanking sound, like heavy metal chains being dragged across concrete. Then I saw it, the drawbridge that Lady Hunt had told me about, coming out of the sky like a vast black wing. With an earth-trembling shudder, it fell into place in front of the car, and we slowly crept over it. No sooner had we reached the other side than the sound of those clunking chains came again. I looked back to see the drawbridge rising back into the sky, sealing access to the outside world. Ahead, there was a huge iron gate, and set into the ancient stone wall was what looked like a small gate house. Stepping from the shadows was what looked like some weird creature. But as it came towards the gate, I could see that it was, in fact, a man. In one of his hands he held an old fashioned-looking lamp. In the glow of the light, I could see that his back looked misshapen and twisted as he lurched from the gate house. Even though he was stooped forward, he was tall. He wore a long dark coat, which hung about his knees. The gates wailed as if in pain as he pushed them open. Sitting forward in my seat, I tried to get a better look at him. The chauffeur steered the car forward through the gates and as he did, I peered through the window at the gatekeeper. He wore a large-brimmed hat, which looked tattered and old. The brim was pulled low over his brow. Bending forward, I tried to get a look at the face beneath it and what I saw made me gasp and jump back in my seat. His face was partially covered in a grubby-looking bandage. Tufts of beard protruded from between the gaps, and only one eye and his mouth were left uncovered. His one eye swivelled in its socket as he looked at me. But it was his mouth. The top lip was twisted upwards and as he stared at me, I couldn't tell if he were smiling at me or snarling.

Looking away, the gates screamed as the deformed-looking gatekeeper closed them behind us. The chauffeur drove forward, and on each side of the car I could just make out the sheer vastness of the estate that the manor was set in. We followed the winding gravel path for what seemed like forever until we reached the entrance to the building.

Coming to a slow stop, the chauffeur killed the engine. I looked ahead, and although he wore those dark glasses, I knew that the chauffeur was watching me in the rear view mirror.

"What?" I said, staring back.

He said nothing.

Then I was aware of a light coming towards the car. I looked sideways to see someone approaching my door. Placing my iPod back into my pocket, I groped for my bag as the car door was swung open.

"Good evening, Ms. Hudson," said a soft voice.

I looked up into the face of an elderly woman. In the glow of the lamp, her face looked warm, friendly, and kind.

"Can I help you with your bags?" she asked, holding out a hand that was so wrinkled it looked as if it had been covered in papier-mâché.

"No, thank you," I smiled, as I got it from the car. "I only have the one."

"Very well," the old woman said, and I noticed that her silver hair was tied into a bun at the nape of her neck. She wore a plain, grey dress and white apron. "I'm Mrs. Payne," she said. "I'm Lady Hunt's housekeeper."

"Hello," I said back, feeling overwhelmed by the size of the manor house that loomed above me in the darkness. The Rolls Royce crept away, back down the gravel path.

Turning back to the old woman, I said, "Where am I, exactly?"

"Hallowed Manor," she said, turning away and guiding me with the light from her lamp to the front door. Following her, I glanced at my wristwatch. It read 00:13 hours. With a quick calculation in my head, I knew that the journey from Havensfield to Hallowed Manor had taken four hours and six minutes and that I was about two hundred and twenty-five-and-a-half miles from home.

The giant oak front door was open, and Mrs. Payne ushered me inside. The manor had a strange odour. It smelt musty but yet, almost kind of sweet. It wasn't the scent of flowers or mildew, and I couldn't quite place it. The hallway was lit with candles and I could just make out a wide set of stairs, which led up into the darkness. I glanced up to see a beautiful chandelier hanging from the high ceiling. What a shame it wasn't lit-up as I guessed it would have looked beautiful.

"No lights?" I asked as she shut the door behind us.

"Oh no," she sighed. "The house has been undergoing some repairs and the workmen have somehow managed to fuse all the lights. Marshal has contacted an electrician who'll be here in a day or two. They're very busy, apparently."

"Marshal?"

"The gatekeeper come grounds man," she said.

I pictured his twisted back and lip, and shuddered. "So all the electricity is out?" I asked her.

"No, no," she smiled at me, "just the lights."

Leading me to the foot of the staircase, she placed her lantern on a nearby table, plucked up two of the candles and handed one to me. Throwing my rucksack over my shoulder, I took the candle and followed the old woman up the staircase. With each step, the stairs beneath me groaned and creaked, and the candle flame bobbed to and fro, splashing the orange light into the darkness. The walls were covered in large oil paintings.

Mrs. Payne must have detected my sudden apprehension as she said, "Don't be scared Ms. Hudson. I know the old place can look a little creepy at night, but by day you'll see what a wonderful home this is."

"I'll take your word for it," I said, straining to see into the darkness ahead of me. "And call me Kiera. Ms. Hudson makes me sound like a school teacher or something. What about you?"

"I'm sorry, dear?" she asked, nearing the top of the stairs.

"Do you have a first name?"

Smiling at me from behind her candle, her eyes twinkled and she said, "Mrs. Payne, dear. Just call me Mrs. Payne."

"Okay, whatever you like," I sighed.

We reached what I thought was the top of the stairs, only to discover that we were on a small landing where the staircase divided left and right. Leading me to the left, I looked back over my shoulder in the direction of the right set of stairs that almost seemed to lead upwards into a black hole.

"What's back there?" I asked as we started to climb again.

"That's the right wing of the house, but it's out of bounds."

"How come?" I asked, my curiosity getting the better of me.

"Like I said, we've got builders working here. They're refurbishing that side of the house." Then stopping, she looked at me and that twinkle in her eye had faded. "Don't go into that side of the building – it could be very dangerous."

"Dangerous?" I asked her.

"The floors are unsafe as is the whole structure," she said fixing me with a cool stare. "The whole lot could come down at any time."

"So no one goes into that part of the house?" I said just wanting to make sure.

"No one," she said, turning away. "It is forbidden."

Now why did she have to go and say that? I mean that was like waving a red flag at a bull – my curiosity dial had just gone crazy. Smiling to myself, I said, "Okay, yeah – sure, it does look kind of creepy back there." In fact the whole house looked eerie, but perhaps like she said, in daylight it would look more welcoming and friendly.

Reaching the top of the second flight of stairs, Mrs. Payne – as she insisted on being called – led me down a narrow corridor. The walls on each side had doors set into them. I didn't know what lay behind these doors and guessed that perhaps they were bedrooms. Either way, if anyone were behind them, they were asleep, as I couldn't see any light seeping from around the door frames. At the end of the passageway, Mrs. Payne stopped outside a white-coloured door. Turning the handle with her frail-looking hand, she pushed it open. Standing outside the open doorway, she peered at me from the gloom and said, "This will be your room for the duration of your stay, Kiera. Please make yourself comfortable. I hope I've thought of everything for you, but if there is something that you should need, just ring the bell."

"The bell?" I asked feeling bemused.

"You'll find a bell cord beside your bed," she said. "Just pull on it should you require anything. The bell will alert me."

"Don't worry," I said stepping into the room, "I won't disturb you tonight."

"Oh don't worry your pretty head about me, dear," she smiled. "I don't sleep as well as I used to. You'll find that I'm awake most of the night."

"Still," I said, "I'm a grown-up, I think I can look after myself."

"Whatever you wish," Mrs. Payne said, and then seemed to almost curtsy at me before leaving the room.

Closing the door, I held the candle out before me and inspected the room. It was huge. Against the far wall, and seeming to take up most of the space, was the biggest bed that I'd ever seen. It was a four poster, with ornate pillars at each corner that reached up into the dark. What looked like drapes had been fastened with white ribbons to each post. Beside the bed was a wooden dressing table with a mirror. Placing the candle on it, I sat on the edge of the giant bed. The mattress felt wonderfully soft.

Getting up, I crossed the room, the single candle barely penetrating the darkness that seemed to wrap itself around me like a blanket. On the opposite side of the room to the bed was a set of windows, and as I made my way towards them, my boots sank into a soft white rug that was spread out across the floor. The windows were as big as a doorway, and they opened outwards onto a small balcony. Pushing them open, a chilly breeze circled me and made the curtains whisper. Standing on the balcony, I looked out into the darkness. In the distance, I could hear the sound of lapping water and I guessed it was the sound of the moat rushing around the grounds of Hallowed Manor. Closing my eyes, I tilted my head back and let the wind cool me as I enjoyed the silence. I felt a million miles away from my poky flat with its walls covered in clippings and its piles of newspapers. Then the silence was broken by the sound of gravel being crunched under foot. Leaning over the balcony, I looked down to see a dark figure crossing the grounds below me, a lantern held in the hand to light their way. From my hiding place, I watched, and as my eyes grew accustomed to the darkness and shadows, I could see the curved-shaped spine of the figure below and I knew it was Marshal. Then without any warning, Marshal stopped dead in his tracks, held the lantern above his head and turning he looked up at me. In the orange glow of the lamp, I could see his one good eye boring into mine.

"Whatcha looking at, copper?" he almost seemed to growl, his top lip rolling back in a snarl.

Without saying anything, and with my heart in my throat, I skulked back into my room. Shutting the windows, I pulled the curtains closed. Crossing back to the dressing table, I snatched up the candle. To be holding the candle made me feel safer somehow. But what was I scared of? And why did I need to feel safe? The poor guy had probably had years of people staring at him, pointing the finger and making fun. This place was probably his sanctuary against all that, and there I was staring at him.

There was a door leading from my room, just to the right of the window. Crossing to it, I pushed it open to reveal a large bathroom. There was a deep bath that stood on four metal legs. It looked big enough to take a swim in. There was a toilet, basin, and shower. Taking my rucksack from where I had left it on the floor, I rummaged around for my wash kit. Stripping to my underwear, I washed my face, cleaned my teeth, and got into bed. Pulling the blankets up under my chin, I suddenly felt tired. Blowing out the candle, I lay in the blackness, and listened to the sound of Marshal's feet crunching over the gravel as he paced up and down beneath my window.

Chapter Six

The door to my flat was pushed open. The male crept in, closing the door behind him, making himself feel secure, unable to be seen from prying eyes. Creeping across the room, he drew the curtain on the night and switched on his torch. Keeping the beam of light low, he swept it over the piles of newspapers that cluttered the room.

Kicking out with his foot, he knocked a pile over. Bending, he thumbed through them, his hands gloved, so as not to leave any fingerprints. Turning on another pile, he did the same, spreading the newspapers across the floor.

What are you doing? I wanted to ask him, but the words wouldn't leave my throat. In the darkness I couldn't see his face, although there was something about him that was vaguely familiar.

Who are you and what do you want?

From the shadows of my bedroom door, I watched him.

He stood and went to one of the walls. Casting the torchlight over it, he looked at the hundreds of paper clippings. Clawing at them with his gloved fingers, he tore them from the wall. Wisps of torn black and white paper fluttered to the floor. I wanted to go to him, to stop him, but my feet felt as if someone had snuck up on me while I wasn't looking and nailed them to the floor.

The male turned away from the wall and came towards me. I wanted to move, but I couldn't. With the glare of the light from his torch shining in my eyes, I couldn't see his face. I wanted to reach out and grab the torch from his hands. I wanted to know who it was that was ransacking my flat. He came closer and my heart began to thunder in my chest.

Get out of here! I tried to scream, but my throat felt raw and dry and nothing came out.

He came straight towards me and my stomach somersaulted. As if I wasn't there, he passed me and as he did, I caught the first glimpse of his face and I wanted to recoil in fear. It was a mask of hideous scars. And in that brief moment, I saw that not only was his face scarred, but it looked as if the left part of his face was missing. It was almost as if he had been attacked by some wild animal which had ripped that part of his face away. Running diagonally from above his left eye to the right side of his top lip, his face was twisted out of shape where the skin had grown over the gaping wound.

I wanted to run from him, to get as far away as possible, but I just couldn't move. He went to my bed and pulled back the covers. Taking hold of one of the pillows, he raised it to his face and inhaled. Once he had finished smelling it, he tossed the pillow to one side. Stooping over, he pulled open the drawers of the dresser that was next to my bed. The male rummaged through it, his movements quick yet precise, as if he knew what he was looking for.

But what could that be?

Tossing it aside, he pulled open the second drawer, searched it, then threw it aside, smashing it into the floor where it broke like matchwood. He did the same to the third and the fourth drawers. His breathing began to quicken as he raced about the room, knocking over my CD player and stack of CDs. He trampled over the cases, and I could hear the plastic snapping like broken bones.

What are you looking for? I wanted to scream, but nothing came out.

Once my bedroom resembled something close to a demolition site, he came back towards me, this time the torchlight sweeping over the mess on the floor, almost as if making sure that he hadn't missed anything. And as he came towards me, I got a clearer view of his face. Although it was hideously disfigured, he reminded me of someone. Again, he brushed past me as if I wasn't even there. He stood in the centre of the room like a dog and sniffed at the air. He froze, as if he had detected a familiar scent. Hunkering down, he crawled on all fours across the middle of my living room and towards one of the armchairs. His nose touched it. He paused, then was off again, the tip of his nose brushing up and over the seat, arms, and back of the chair. Whose scent had he detected – latched onto?

Mine? No not mine. I never sat in that chair; I always sat by the window so I could look out. Who then? Who had been the last person to have sat there?

Lady Hunt! I wanted to shout aloud, but my throat felt as if I were being strangled.

The male stood up as if he had been disturbed in some way. Maybe he had heard something that I hadn't. Some noise that suggested someone was coming or was close by. Then I heard the noise that had obviously disturbed him. It sounded like water dripping from a tap that hadn't been turned off tight enough. The sound was close by. I looked down and in the darkness I could see the black spatters of blood on the newspapers spread about at my feet. I looked up to see the male sniffing at the air again. He looked in my direction, as I felt the warm sensation of red tears leaking from my left eye. I wanted to wipe them away, to stop them dribbling from my chin, but my arms felt as if they had been tied to my sides.

The male came towards me again. He stopped, the tip of his nose almost touching mine. It was then that I knew how he had gotten those scars and who had given them to him. I stared into Sergeant Phillips' twisted and deformed face and remembered how Potter had attacked him and left him for dead in the graveyard at St. Mary's church in The Ragged Cove. He sniffed the air and smiled.

"Oh Kiera," he whispered. "So what they said about you was true after all."

Before I could say anything, he lunged forward and...

...I sat up in bed. I drew in deep lungfuls of breath as I tried to figure out where I was. My chest was rising up and down and sounded like a clapped-out steam train, sweat covered me in a fine sheen and my throat felt raw. I looked all around me, and it was only when I saw the four wooden posts protruding from each corner of the bed that I remembered that I was in my room at Hallowed Manor. Daylight glistened around the edges of the curtains. Slowly, it was all coming back to me.

But there was a noise – it sounded as if it were coming from miles away. It was music and it sounded hissy. Tilting my head to one side to listen, I realised I recognised the music that was being played. It was *'Party Rock Anthem'* by LMFAO, and I had that particular track on my iPod. Straining to hear where it was coming from, I realised the music was closer than I originally thought. Wrapping myself in my blanket, I crawled to the end of my bed and peered over the edge. Sitting crossed-legged on the floor was a girl. She was rummaging through my rucksack and was listening to my iPod.

Reaching out, I tapped her on the shoulder and said, "What do you think you're doing?"

Jumping with a start, the girl removed the earphones, looked at me and said, "Do you know that your eye is bleeding?"

Chapter Seven

Pulling the blanket around me like a shawl, I swung my legs over the side of the bed and went to the bathroom. Taking a piece of tissue paper, I dabbed the corner of my left eye and wiped away the crimson smear that ran down the length of my cheek to my chin.

"So you're a cop?" the girl said from the other room.

Flushing the bloodied piece of tissue down the toilet, I went back into the room and sat on the edge of the bed. Looking at the girl, who was still rummaging through my belongings, I said, "Do you mind?"

Ignoring me, the girl said, "Where's your gun?"

"I don't have a gun," I told her.

"Taser?"

"I don't have one of those, either."

"CS spray?" she asked, looking almost hopeful.

I shook my head.

"Cuffs?"

"Nope," I said, holding out my hand for my belongings.

Tossing the rucksack to one side and crossing to the window, she said, "What sort of cop doesn't have a pair of handcuffs?"

Smiling inside, I said, "I'm sorry, but I didn't realise I would need a full arsenal of weaponry to babysit you – you're not that bad are you?" It must have come out sounding all wrong because she turned back from the window and scowled at me.

"Listen lady, or whatever your name is, I don't need no babysitter."

Taking a T-shirt from the rucksack, I pulled it over my head and said, "My name's Kiera. I take it you're Kayla."

"Yeah, so?" she said taking a piece of gum from her jeans pocket and popping it into her mouth. Like her mother, she had stunning looks, with a mass of auburn hair that curled around her shoulders, an impish-looking face, and icy-blue eyes. Her skin was the colour of cream and she had a spattering of freckles across her cheeks and the bridge of her nose. She was already beautiful, but give it another couple of years, and most men will find her drop-dead gorgeous. I wondered if Kayla knew that, but her confident manner suggested that she already did.

Matching her stare, I said, "So what?" and smiled.

"I don't need this shit," she scowled and stormed towards the bedroom door.

"That's cool," I said. "I don't need this shit, either."

Reaching the bedroom door, she turned and looked at me, and I couldn't help but notice the slight look of surprise on her face. Maybe she was expecting some kind of rebuke for swearing and going through my rucksack without permission. I knew she was testing me. Perhaps Kayla had been expecting some hard-nosed copper who was going to lay down the law, but that wasn't me. I had a week with her and I'd already made up my mind that I wasn't going to spend it fighting. She glanced down at my iPod that lay on the floor where she'd left it. Music hissed from the speakers, sounding faint and far off.

"Can I borrow that?" she asked, her voice still sounding stubborn and cold. "Mine's broken."

Snatching it up off the floor, I tossed it at her. "Knock yourself out," I said.

Catching it out of the air, she turned away, back towards the door. But before she had a chance to disappear, I asked, "What time's breakfast around here? I'm starving."

Without looking back she said, "I'll wait down the hall for you." Then she was gone.

I went to the bathroom, stripped off my T-shirt and underwear, and jumped in the shower. That ever-so-deep bath looked so inviting but I'd just have to try it out later. I didn't want to leave Kayla waiting. Getting on her good side was going to be difficult enough. The water was warm and I hoped it would help wash away the images that I still had in my mind from the nightmare that I had woken from.

Why had I dreamt of Phillips ransacking my flat? It wasn't the first time that he had made a guest appearance in my nightmares since leaving The Ragged Cove, but they had never seemed so vivid – so real. And why did my eye keep bleeding? Like the visions of the plane crash I'd *seen* yesterday – had the pilot really been screaming that the cockpit had been breached by *them* before it had fallen out of the sky and nose-dived into the sea? I wanted to keep telling myself that it was my imagination working overtime – that perhaps what had happened in The Ragged Cove had disturbed me more than I first had thought, and the nightmares and visions were a consequence of that. Maybe Dr. Keats had been right. No, she thought I was raving mad but I knew I wasn't.

If the nightmare had been some kind of vision, then had Philips really been to my flat and ransacked it? But why? What had he been looking for? If it had been some sort of premonition, that would mean Phillips was still alive and Taylor would be close by. And if they were together, Luke, Potter, and Murphy would be hot on their tail. After all, didn't they say they were going to track them?

Stepping from the shower and towelling myself dry, I wondered if coming to the Hallowed Manor had been such a good idea after all. For months, I'd been looking for – *searching* – each and every newspaper and news report for anything that might suggest their return and as soon as I turn my back....

Kiera, what are you thinking of? I scolded myself. It was just a dream. It had been the first night away from my flat since leaving The Ragged Cove and somewhere deep inside I was probably feeling insecure. That was all I was feeling – I was being paranoid that now I had left Havensfield behind, Luke was going to put in an appearance and I wouldn't be there. I was two hundred and fifty-five-and-a- half miles away staying on some godforsaken moor. How would he ever find me?

"Stop it!" I groaned to myself as I pulled on a pair of jeans, boots and jumper. "Stop torturing yourself."

But I couldn't stop. I needed to know if the nightmare I'd had about Phillips burgling my flat had been some vision or just a dream. How would I know? I still had a whole week down here. So taking my mobile phone from my bag, I went to 'contacts' and scrolled down to 'Sparky'. Hitting 'message' with my fingernail, I wrote the following text:

> **Had to go away 4 wk can u check on flat?**
> **Thanx. Kiera. x**

After hitting the send button, I tucked the phone into my jeans pocket and left my room in search of Kayla.

Chapter Eight

As soon as I stepped into the passageway outside my room, there was that smell again – the sweet-musty odour that I had noticed last night. Even though it was nearly nine a.m., the corridor was very dark as all the doors leading from it were shut, and there wasn't any windows. I could see a grey patch of light ahead of me where the daylight shone up the staircase from below. I could see the silhouette of a figure sitting further down the passageway. To guide myself in the gloom, I trailed my fingertips along the wall. It was then I noticed that they felt sticky, as if someone had covered them in some kind of varnish which hadn't yet dried. I brought the tips of my fingers up to my nose and it was the strange varnish that was making the manor smell so odd. Perhaps it had something to do with the renovation of the manor. Maybe the builders had been tasked to varnish the entire place. But who had ever heard of varnishing wallpaper?

Wiping my hands against my jeans, I walked towards the light and the figure sitting at the end of the passageway. As I drew closer, I could see that Kayla was sitting on the top stair waiting for me.

Looking down at her, I said, "Thanks."

"For what?" she asked, taking out the earphones and offering me back my iPod.

"For waiting for me," I smiled, then added. "You can keep hold of my iPod for the time being, I'm in no rush to have it back."

"Thanks," Kayla mumbled, as if saying those very words caused her pain.

"So what's for breakfast?" I asked.

"Dunno," she replied, and headed down the stairs.

I followed her to the next landing. Just before we headed down to the hallway, I pointed to the staircase that led into the *'forbidden'* right wing, as Mrs. Payne had liked to call it. Although the light wasn't great, it was better than the candlelight from the night before. Despite Mrs. Payne's warning that the right wing was a no-go area, I could see that someone had been up there this morning. I looked at Kayla and could see that it hadn't been her. Whoever it had been was male, was right-handed, and had carried something heavy in their left hand, probably a breakfast tray, which they'd had difficulty balancing. But why would they have been taking a tray load of breakfast into an area that was *forbidden* and who had it been for?

"What's up there?" I asked Kayla.

Hearing my question, Kayla almost seemed to falter on the stairs and she gripped the banister as if to steady herself. "Oh, we don't go up there. No one does," she said without looking back at me.

Really? I thought to myself. "Why not?" I pressed, as I followed her down to the large circular hallway.

"Mother says it's too dangerous," she said. "It's structurally unsafe or something like that."

"Have you ever been up there?" I asked her, not wanting to let the subject drop.

"Not since I was a kid," she said. "It's been like that for a long time now."

"Never been tempted to take another look?" I asked, but before Kayla had had a chance to reply, Mrs. Payne had appeared in the hallway.

"Kayla," she said, her voice sounding frustrated rather than cross. "You know you should be at your chores by now and you still haven't had any breakfast. What would your mother say?"

"I don't know and I don't care," Kayla shrugged as she passed Mrs. Payne without even looking at her.

"Kayla!" the old woman snapped. "That's no way to speak -"

"It's not Kayla's fault she's running late," I cut in.

"Whose is it then?" Mrs. Payne asked, eyeing me up and down. As she did, I noticed white flecks of something in her hair.

"It's mine I'm afraid," I smiled. "I've been talking to her in my room – just getting to know her."

Kayla turned back and looked at me with suspicion.

"Well, Kiera, Kayla has rules that she must -" the old woman started.

"I'm sure Lady Hunt wouldn't have minded just this once. I was keen to get to know Kayla," I said. "After all, I think it's what her mother would have wanted."

Offering me a smile that looked like a crack in a plate, Mrs. Payne said, "Yes, you're probably right. Lady Hunt did ask you here to keep an eye on Kayla."

"I am right here, you know!" Kayla snapped. "You don't have to talk about me as if I wasn't. And besides, I'm sixteen for Christ's sake, I don't need anyone looking out for me!" Then, staring in my direction, she added, "Especially not some stressed-out cop!"

I took her spiteful comment on the chin. After all, I'd been called worse, so I smiled at her.

"Kayla, that's no way to speak to Ms. Hudson. She's a guest in this house, so you show her some respect!" Mrs. Payne scolded her.

"She's getting paid, isn't she?" Kayla came back.

"Don't you dare be so ill-mannered!" Mrs. Payne said, her voice sounding cross. "You apologise right this minute young lady!"

Kayla just looked at me, huffed, and then putting in the earphones, she switched my iPod back on.

Cheeky-little-cow, I smiled inwardly.

"I'm so sorry about this, Kiera," Mrs. Payne said, and she looked genuinely embarrassed.

"No worries," I said. "I'm sure Kayla and I will become the bests of friends."

"We'll see," Mrs. Payne said, and tutted in the direction of Kayla.

Changing the subject, I said, "I was wondering if I could get some breakfast? I'm starving."

"Of course, my dear," she smiled. "Come with me."

The kitchen was, like the rest of the manor, huge. Down the centre of it ran a giant wooden table that would have been big enough to seat an entire football team, coaches and all. Around the far wall stood grey metal sinks and stoves, the kind you would see in the kitchen of a large hotel. There were too many cupboards to count and the three of us looked lost in the vastness of such a great room. How many people could be fed here? Hundreds I guessed, except there was only Mrs. Payne and as far as I could gather she did the cooking, cleaning and if I hadn't of been around, keeping an eye on Kayla as well.

Pulling back a chair, I sat down at the table and Kayla sat opposite me. The table was so wide that even if we had stretched our arms out as far as possible, our hands still wouldn't have touched. Mrs. Payne placed a large bowl of fruit on the table, some bread, butter, and several different types of cereal.

"Would you like me to cook you something?" she asked us. "Some kippers, perhaps?"

Taking a bowl and filling it with some corn flakes, I waved my hand at her and said, "No this will be just fine."

Without even acknowledging the housekeeper, Kayla took an apple from the fruit bowl and took a bite. She still wore the earphones, and she rocked in her seat as she listened to the music.

"So how do you manage looking after such a big place?" I asked Mrs. Payne as I splashed ice cold milk onto the cereal.

"Oh, it's not so bad," she said, pouring me a mug of coffee and setting it before me. "There is only Lady Hunt, Kayla, Mr. Marshal, and James to worry about."

"James?" I asked her.

"The chauffeur," she said, placing a glass of orange juice down in front of Kayla. Again she was ignored, there was no 'thank- you.'

"Oh, is that his name?" I said. "He wasn't very talkative last night. I did ask him, but he wouldn't tell me."

"James is a little deaf, perhaps he didn't hear you," she tried to explain.

He heard me alright, I thought. Mrs. Payne must have sensed that I wasn't convinced, because she added, "We don't really know him that well."

"How come?" I asked around a mouthful of cornflakes.

"After the disappearance of Lord Hunt, Lady Hunt let the last chauffeur go and hired James," she explained. Then looking at me, she added, "In fact, she let all of the staff go except me."

"Why did she keep you on?" I half-smiled.

"No one knows this house or The Hunts like I do," she said with some pride.

"So why the new driver?" I asked her.

Mrs. Payne stared at me and said, "Why so many questions? Are you on duty?"

"Nope," I said, matching her stare.

"I thought police officers were always on duty," she said with a wry smile.

"Not this one," I said back.

"Lady Hunt wanted a change I guess. The last driver could be very cantankerous at times and Lady Hunt never got on very well with him. Besides, Lady Hunt is very much into her charity work."

"Charity work? What's that got to do with hiring herself a new chauffeur?" I asked feeling bemused.

"James can't walk," she said, as if I should have already known this. "Lady Hunt has done a lot of great work for the disabled and believes that everyone should have an equal chance of employment."

"Apparently he had an accident or something years ago and hasn't walked since," Kayla cut in.

I looked across the table at her to see that she had removed the earphones and turned off the iPod.

"Really?" I said, somewhat bewildered. "But he drove me all the way here," and I pushed my empty bowl to one side and took a banana from the pile of fruit.

"Lady Hunt had the Rolls Royce converted so it could be driven by a disabled driver," Mrs. Payne cut in.

It was hearing this that I understood why the chauffeur hadn't got out of the car last night for Lady Hunt and me. He'd stayed in the vehicle when she'd gotten out at the railway station and again on our arrival at the manor. All off a sudden, I felt incredibly guilty and wondered perhaps if I had judged him unfairly. I regretted calling him a jerk.

"So what about Marshal?" I asked them.

"What about him?" Mrs. Payne said.

"Is he new here too?"

"Yes, he was hired by Lady Hunt after Lord Hunt disappeared," she explained.

Then raising my hand to my face, I said, "So what about…you know…the bandages?"

"The bandages?" Mrs. Payne said, and I couldn't help but notice her glance at Kayla. There was a pause – it lasted only a fraction of a second – but long enough to be noticeable. "Oh, them," she eventually said. "Marshal was born with a facial deformity and a twisted spine."

"Yeah, his face scares the shit outta me," Kayla cut in.

"That's quite enough of that, thank you very much," Mrs. Payne glared at the girl.

"Another one of Lady Hunt's charitable works?" I asked.

"Lady Hunt came across him by chance on a visit to a homeless shelter. Marshal had been living on the streets since he was not much older than Kayla is now. He had fallen foul of the law and because of his deformities, he had never been given the same opportunities in life like the rest of us. Lady Hunt therefore took it upon herself to give him sanctuary here, and in return, Marshal tends to the grounds and he has become quite an accomplished handyman. Lady Hunt has even provided the funds for him to have reconstructive surgery. The bandages are covering the scars while they heal," she said.

Looking at Kayla, I said, "Gee, your mother sounds like a real saint."

"She can be okay, I guess," Kayla said thoughtfully.

"Only okay?" Mrs. Payne cut in. "After everything that your mother has done for you?"

Pushing her chair back from the table, Kayla jumped up. "What would you know about anything!" Kayla shouted at Mrs. Payne. "You're just the housekeeper, so keep your nose out of my business!"

"Don't you dare speak to me like that!" Mrs. Payne snapped back, her face flushing scarlet.

"Or what?" Kayla spat back.

"You wait until your mother gets home," the housekeeper warned her.

"And then what?" Kayla snapped. "What's she gonna do, pack me off to another boarding school? Well if you didn't already know, there isn't a school in the country that will take me. So it looks as if you and mother are stuck with me."

"Right, young lady," Mrs. Payne said, "get to your room and don't come out until you've learnt to keep a civil tongue in your head!"

"You can't tell me what to do, so why don't you just do us all a favour and piss off!" Kayla yelled, snatching up the iPod. She stormed out of the back kitchen door and onto the grounds of the manor.

"Well, that couldn't of gone any better," I sighed.

"You don't know what she's like," Mrs. Payne complained.

"So what *is* she like?" I asked, raising an eyebrow and getting up from my seat.

"There's something wrong with her," she said, her voice sounding angry.

"She's not the only one," I whispered to myself as I went after Kayla.

It was cold outside, so I was glad I'd put on a jumper. A strong wind blew about the eves of the old manor as I passed down the side of it and towards the front of the building. I went around the front and down the gravel path. Ahead of me, there was a wide open grassy area and in the distance, I could see Kayla propped against a tree, her knees drawn up under her chin. I walked towards her and as I did, I looked back at the house and up towards the *'forbidden'* right wing. I hadn't noticed it the night before, but the right side of the building was hidden by scaffolding and thick sheets of tarpaulin, which kept most of it hidden from view. On the ground, just beneath the scaffolding, were four large yellow skips and each of these had been filled with rubble and masonry. Perhaps that part of the manor was being renovated after all, but I couldn't see any workmen or builders.

Turning front again, I headed towards Kayla. "Want to show me around?" I asked her.

She just shrugged her shoulders.

"You might as well," I said. "You've got my company for a whole week, so we should try and be friends."

Taking the iPod and placing it in her pocket, (I guess it was hers now, at least until I left) Kayla said, "Why did you cover for me back there?"

"I don't know what you mean?" I said, helping her to her feet.

"You told that old bag that it was your fault I'd been late for breakfast."

"Oh, that. Aren't friends allowed to cover for each other from time to time?" I smiled and looped my arm through hers.

"You're not what I expected," she said, leading me through the trees and away from the manor.

"What were you expecting then?" I asked her.

"I dunno," she said. "Somebody a bit older to start with. And not so…easy going, I guess. I thought coppers were meant to be serious all the time."

"Why don't you just forget I'm a cop for a while – I'm a person too, you know," I smiled.

"Okay," she smiled back.

"I know you're pissed off that your mother asked me -" I started.

"To come down here and spy on me," she said.

"Is there a reason to spy on you?" I asked her, ducking down to avoid a low-hanging branch.

"You tell me," she said. "My mother's told me you have a bit of a reputation for being a smart-arse – like you have this knack of working out things real quick."

"Did she?" I said. "What else did she tell you about me?" I asked.

"That you had been suspended from the police, but she didn't tell me why," Kayla said. Then looking at me with a twinkle in her eyes, she added, "Are you like one of those rebel cops who's always breaking the rules and getting into trouble with their superiors?"

"No," I told her. "I don't think I am."

"So why were you suspended then?"

"I haven't been suspended…I've been…"

"What?"

"Given some extended leave," I told her.

"What you're telling me is that your boss thinks you're a pain in the arse, but he doesn't know what to do with you," she said, leading me out into a wide open area with the most wonderful flowerbeds I'd ever seen. *Mrs. Lovelace would love it here*, I thought to myself.

"How did you figure that out?" I asked Kayla.

"It's exactly what happened to me at school," she explained. "If you're different or you speak out, people think you're a pain and it's easier for them to either pretend you're not there or better still, just get rid of you altogether. People like me and you, Kiera, don't fit in."

"Why didn't you fit in at school?" I asked her, the smell of the flowers a break from the musty stench that permeated the manor. "Your mother told me that you can be disruptive."

"She would say that," Kayla said, sounding angry again. "I was just sticking up for myself, that's all."

"Why would you feel the need to stick up for yourself?" I asked.

"Mother didn't tell you did, she?" Kayla said her eyes wide.

"Tell me what?" I asked her.

Letting go of my arm, she quickly looked back over her shoulder in the direction from which we had come, as if to make sure that we hadn't been followed. Then quickly, she pulled her top from over her head and let it flutter to the floor. She stood before me, the pale morning sun reflecting off her round shoulders and glinting off her auburn hair. Then slowly, she turned around. Raising a hand to my mouth, I gasped, as poking around the white straps of her bra were two small, black wings.

Chapter Nine

As quickly as she had taken it off, Kayla pulled her top back over her head and covered her wings. They weren't like the giant sized wings I had seen grow from Luke's back; Kayla's were smaller and trailed halfway down her back. They didn't have that leathery look either; they seemed finer, like those of a butterfly's. Although they were black, the wings had looked like they had been splashed with liquid silver. They had almost seemed to shimmer in the light of the hazy sun.

"Do they fold away?" I asked her as she stood looking at me, her arms now folded across her chest. "What I mean is, can you make them disappear into your back?"

"No," she said, shaking her head. "But they are so soft, they lie flat against my back, just like an extra layer of skin."

I couldn't think of anything to say, so I said, "Okay." I was still reeling inside from what she had shown me. It wasn't like I hadn't seen this sort of thing before, but finding out that Kayla was a Vampyrus was like being hit with a sledgehammer. It was the last thing I had been expecting.

"So you can see now why my mother asked you to come here," she said turning away and heading back towards the shelter of the trees.

"What do you mean by that?" I asked, catching up with her.

"Your mother said that someone was stalking you. That someone was coming to the manor and watching you. She wanted me to find out who it was."

"That's only half of it," Kayla said, weaving her way through the trees. "She wants you here because of what happened to you in that other place."

"The Ragged Cove?" I asked.

"Yeah, that's the place," she said glancing at me. "Don't you get it? You've seen people like me before – and survived. Now that my father has vanished, my mother doesn't know what to do."

"But if you're a Vampyrus, your mother must be one, too," I said.

"That's the problem, Kiera," Kayla said, leading me towards the iron gate that I'd been driven through the night before. "I'm not

65

a true Vampyrus. My father *is* one – but my mother is human. So I don't really know what that makes me – and my mother doesn't know either."

I looked at Kayla and all I could hear was Dr. Keats voice in my head. *"How do we know that living right amongst us aren't the children born out of relationships between humans and these 'Vampyrus' as you call them."* And here I was looking at the result of one of those unions.

"Did your mother know that your father was a Vampyrus?" I asked her.

"No, not at first," she said, as we reached the ancient stone wall that circled the grounds of the manor. On the other side of it, I could hear the sound of the water from the moat lapping against the wall.

"For years, it seems that my father lead a double life," she started to explain. "On one hand, he was this successful businessman, the head of a multinational company developing renewable genetics. He was married with a daughter, but secretly he was a creature from below ground who could grow wings, fly at incredible speeds, and had almost invincible strength."

Before I'd the chance to say anything, Kayla disappeared up a stone spiral staircase set into the wall. I followed her. At the top, the stairs levelled out onto a narrow ledge that ran around the top of the wall. I peered over the top, and for miles all I could see were the barren and featureless moors, stretching out into the distance. The ground seemed almost black, with a spattering of green where some vegetation had sprung up between the huge, jagged rocks. The sight had a prehistoric feel to it, like we were the very first humans to encroach upon this land.

Kayla hoisted herself up onto the lip of the wall and I joined her. The wind raced all around us, forcing bruised-looking clouds over the sun, turning the day overcast and bleak.

"How my father kept it from my mother for so many years, I don't know," Kayla continued. "I understand now that like vampires, he would often crave blood - human blood – but to quench his thirst he would have to go beneath ground, to where he came from, his home."

"The Hollows," I said, looking at Kayla, her thick auburn hair billowing out in the wind like a mane.

"Yeah, that's what he called it," she said, looking ahead over the moors. "He would tell my mother and me that he had to go away on business for a week or two, but really he was going back home, to his real home. He'd go on one of his *business trips* three or four times a year."

"Were you or your mother never suspicious?" I asked her, now understanding the complications of being in love and sharing your life with one of these creatures. My mind couldn't help but turn to thoughts of Luke.

"I wasn't, but I don't know about my mother," she said. "It was just the way it was for as long as I can remember. But things started to change – *I* started to change."

"In what way?" I asked.

"When I was about fourteen, I had these lumps appear on my back, just between my shoulder-blades. They were small at first, like pimples. But they never burst or went away, they just gradually got bigger. My mother was concerned, but my father just kept brushing it off as something to do with puberty and that they would go away. But they didn't. Then, one day at one of those boarding schools, I was in the showers and one of the other girls started screaming and pointing at my back. All the other girls looked at me then started screaming too."

"What had they seen?" I asked her.

Reaching up and rubbing her left shoulder, Kayla said, "Just about here, a little black lump had started to poke through my skin. It was hard and felt like a piece of bone. I didn't know what it was and to be honest, I was so scared at the sight of it that I started to scream, too. Anyway, I was taken to the nurse's room and she covered it with a bandage, not because it was bleeding or anything, just so she didn't have to look at it, I guess. The headmaster called my parents and they brought me back here. My mother was almost hysterical when she saw that little piece of black bone sticking out of my back. I remember her screaming, 'Michael what is it? What's wrong with our baby?'

"Without being able to take his eyes off my back, my father whispered, 'Leave it to me, I'll get a friend of mine to look at it.'

'What friend!' my mother hollered at him, as she wrung her hands together.

'He's a doctor I know,' my father tried to comfort her. 'He'll know what to do.'

'But why can't Kayla go to see our doctor?' my mother begged him.

'Just leave it to me,' he said, taking her in her arms.

"I remember my mother sobbing against his chest. But I caught her peering at me, Kiera, and it was fear that I saw in her eyes. It was like my own mother was scared of me," Kayla said. Sitting listening to her, I could see a kind of sadness in her eyes so I took one of her hands in mine. She didn't flinch or pull away, but just let it rest there on her lap.

"So what did this doctor friend of your father's say?" I asked her.

"We didn't go to him, he came to us," she told me. "He was a thick-set man, with a pale complexion and glasses perched on the end of his nose which drooped down like a beak. I remember lying there on my bed, looking up at him thinking how much he looked like an owl. After rolling me over onto my front and gently prodding the piece of black bone, I heard him whispering to my father from the corner of the room. But I could hear some of what he said.

'The Terminal Phalanx is coming through,' the doctor whispered.

'What can you do about it?' my father asked him, and like my mother's eyes, I could hear the fear in his voice.

'This is uncharted ground, Michael – you know that, don't you?' the doctor said to my father, in an uneasy-sounding voice.

'But we can't risk them growing,' my father almost seemed to plead with him.

'All I can do is cut it off, stitch up the hole, and pray that it doesn't grow back,' the doctor said.

"Then looking back over my shoulder, I saw the doctor coming towards me with a needle.

'This might sting a bit,' he smiled

"The next thing I knew I was waking up in my room," Kayla said. "My father was sitting on the edge of my bed and stroking the hair from my brow.

'My precious Kayla,' he whispered, and for the first time in my life I thought I could see tears in his eyes. 'I'm so sorry.'

'I love you daddy,' I smiled and drifted back into unconsciousness.

"What had the doctor done?" I asked her, alarmed by her story.

"He had removed that piece of bone and sewn up the hole that it had left behind," she said, rubbing her shoulder with her free hand, almost as if it still hurt in some way.

"But it came back, right?" I asked.

"Not straight away. About six months later, I guess," she explained, again staring out across the cracked and boggy wasteland before us. "When I returned to school, my once good friends had started to keep their distance. They called me 'Stickleback' and other stupid names. Although I pretended it didn't bother me, it did. I was miles away from home and I was scared."

"What of?" I asked her, my heart aching.

"Those words that I'd heard the doctor whisper into my father's ear – Terminal Phalanx – I couldn't get them out of my head. So one afternoon after class, I went to the school library and Googled those two words. And do you know what they meant?" she asked me.

I shook my head and shrugged.

"They are the bones located at the tips of the fingers and toes," she said and grimaced. "I couldn't believe what I was reading. I mean, how could I have fingers or toes growing out of my back? What sort of a monster was I turning into? I was so scared, Kiera."

I thought of the three bony fingers that I had seen at the tip of Luke's wings and knew exactly what they were. I only had to come to terms with a sprinkling of acne as a teenager – and I thought that had been horrific enough. How I would have coped with fingers growing from between my shoulder blades I did not know.

Knocking her fringe from her eyes, Kayla said, "One morning, I woke up and it felt as if something was sticking out of my mattress into my back. After inspecting the bed, I could see that none of the springs had come through, so with my stomach feeling as if it had been tied into knots, I went to the communal bathroom at the end of the dormitory and took off my nightdress.

Peering over my shoulder, I looked at the reflection of my back in the mirror. To my horror, not only had that piece of black bone returned, but there were now six of them poking out of my back, three above each shoulder blade. But that wasn't the worst of it, Kiera. Those pieces of black bone didn't look like bone, they looked like fingers and they wiggled back and forth as if clutching at the air.

"I dropped to my knees in front of the toilet and puked my guts up and didn't stop until my stomach felt bruised and raw and my throat felt as if I'd swallowed a pint of battery acid," she said.

"Did you tell anyone?" I asked her.

"Are you kidding me?" she scoffed. "And put up with more piss-taking from my class mates? No way. I packed up a few of my belongings and fled. I ran away as far as possible."

"Didn't you come back here?"

"What? And have that quack operating on me again? No way! I never wanted to see this place again or my mother and father for that matter," she said, sounding spiteful and angry.

"Why not?"

"Because I knew that they understood more than they were letting on. And I feared that they would just send me back to school again to face my tormentors," she said.

"So how did you come to be back here?" I asked.

"My father hired these two guys," she said. "They were some kinda cops or something. One of them was young, in his early twenties, I guess. He was a real arrogant jerk and loved himself. The other one was older- but he was okay."

I knew straightaway who she was talking about, and the fact the Kayla's father had known Potter and Murphy made me feel kind of strange. I didn't know how I should feel – but it gave me a connection to Kayla, her father, and this place. Perhaps I'd done the right thing in coming to Hallowed Manor after all. Maybe they would come here too?

"Can you remember these guy's names?" I asked her.

"The jerk's name was Potter – I don't think he ever told me his Christian name – not that I wanted to know it. The other guy – the older one – his name was Jim Murphy I think."

"The jerk's name was Sean," I said.

"You know them?" she said, sounding surprised. "How?"

"They were on my shift in The Ragged Cove," I told her.

"Where are they now?"

"I wish I knew," I said, looking out across the moor.

"They were real cops then?" she asked.

"I guess. Did you ever meet a guy called Luke Bishop?" I asked, wondering what had happened to him and why he wasn't with his friends. "You couldn't forget him – he's a real hottie."

"Yeah, I've met him," Kayla said and my heart raced.

"Where? When?" I blurted out.

"The last time I ran away. He came in search of me."

"How long ago was that?" I asked her, keen to know what information she had about Luke.

"Two months ago – just before my father went missing," she said.

Only two months ago! I thought to myself. *Then that means Luke is out there somewhere and connected to the manor. Maybe he will come here after all?*

"He was a really nice guy and very kind to me, but he didn't look cute like you say he does," Kayla said.

"What do you mean?" I asked confused.

"He looked as if he had been in some kinda accident or something, because the left side of his face was all scarred," and she looked sad as she thought of him.

I remembered how Luke had looked the last time that I had seen him, his face blistered and charred from the fire at St. Mary's Church. I felt sick inside at the thought that by rescuing me, he had been left disfigured.

"Are you okay?" Kayla asked me. "You've gone really pale."

"Hmm?" I muttered. "No I'm okay. I was just remembering something."

"What?"

"It doesn't matter now," I said just above a whisper.

Then from nowhere Kayla said, "You've got a text on your phone."

"Sorry?" I said, still feeling dazed by what Kayla had told me about Luke.

"You've got a text on your phone – or you're gonna get a text any moment now," she said, her head tilted towards me as if listening to something.

"I haven't got a text," I told her, rummaging for my phone in my pocket. Pulling it out, I looked at the screen and it was blank. Holding it up to her, I said, "See, I haven't got a text come through." And just as those words left my lips, the phone vibrated in my hand. I looked at the words *'New Message'* flashing on the front of the screen.

Tapping the screen with my fingernail, the message opened and it was from 'Sparky'. It read:

> ***Bad news Kiera – your flat has been burgled.***
> ***It's a real mess here. Where are you?***
> ***Sparky. x***

Looking back at Kayla, I said, "How did you know I was going to receive -" But before I'd the chance to finish what I was about to say, I felt myself falling off the wall and everything went black.

Chapter Ten

The tube train doors closed. It was hot and stuffy – way too many people were in the carriage. It smelt of bodies and sweat. The train rattled out of Euston Road Station and into the tunnel. The lights flickered above me, sending the carriage into a moment's darkness. The lights came back on and with it, a scream. It was ear-splitting and I covered my ears with my hands. The train lurched over a set of points, and with my hands covering my ears; I stumbled into the male standing next to me. My face came to rest against his sweaty armpit. He didn't notice, he was too busy, like all the other passengers wedged in beside me, the guy was straining to see who had screamed. Gripping the handrail above me, I regained my balance and looked through the mass of bodies to see what was happening further down the carriage.

There was another scream – this time it was different. It sounded more like a roar.

"What's happening?" a plump, middle-aged woman asked, fear and confusion brimming in her eyes.

Another scream. This time nearer. Then those passengers lucky enough to have grabbed themselves a seat started to stand, so they too could see what was going on.

Another scream but this time it sounded like whoever had made it was gurgling on something in the back of their throat. Then there was chaos. Those at the opposite end of the carriage started towards those of us at the far end. Bodies began to enclose tighter around me as people tried desperately to get away from whatever was at the other end of the carriage.

"Let me out!" Someone screamed, their voice bordering on hysteria.

"It ripped her fucking throat out!" Some cried. "Did you see that?"

Passengers rushed towards me in a blur of panic, their eyes bulging from their sockets with terror.

Another scream!

Standing on tiptoe, I frantically tried to get a glimpse of what was happening at the other end of the carriage. Then a jet of crimson liquid sprayed across the walls.

"Jesus!" the man with the sweaty armpits screamed and his voice was shrill like that of a little girl. He turned to look at me and I could see that his face was speckled with little red drops of blood.

More screams and blood, as I was pushed back into the side of the carriage and crushed against the door. Then I saw a familiar face in the crowd – how would I ever forget his piercing blue eyes? Those sunken cheeks and the way he wore that black wide brimmed hat.

"What's happening?" the plump woman squealed, clutching her handbag to her chest as if were going to offer her some kind of protection.

"A priest just ripped some woman's throat out with his teeth!" a spotty-looking youth gasped as he started to hoist himself on to the shoulders of those near him in an attempt to get away. I watched as he fought his way over the heads of other passengers, knocking some of them to the ground who then became trampled underfoot by those that stampeded through the carriage. As he came closer, I could see that his face wasn't covered in spots but in lumps of bloodied flesh.

Taking hold of the handrail, I tried to pull myself up, desperate not to be pulled under with the tide of people that now trampled over the seats and each other. I strained to see back down the carriage at the face that I had recognised. His eyes met mine, and his lips turned up in a smile. No, not a smile, a snarl.

"Taylor," I whispered.

"Open the door! Open the fucking door!" someone squealed.

"I'm being crushed!" yelled another.

"I can't breathe!" someone gasped.

Turning, I looked at the knot of bodies pressed against the interconnecting carriage door. But the door opened inwards and with so many bodies pressed against it, it was impossible to open.

"Move back! Move Back!" A guy with glasses was screaming. But then he was gone, drowning beneath the sea of frantic passengers. I tried to reach down for his hand to pull him free, but his fingers slipped from my grasp, and I was suddenly grateful for the deafening screams all around me, as his fingers

74

were snapped beneath somebody's boot. I didn't want to hear the sound of those fingers being crushed.

More screams from the opposite end of the carriage – where Taylor stood, blood running from his chin like crimson gravy. A fair-haired woman seemed to suddenly pounce from the floor of the carriage as if being launched from a springboard. Her eyes rolled in their sockets and they burnt orange as if on fire. Her face was as white as soap but her neck was…was open. I could see her windpipe opening and closing like a fist as she gasped for air. Her torn open throat made a sucking and burping noise. Then she opened her mouth and revealed a drooling set of fangs.

Those passengers still unfortunate enough not to have been able to press themselves into the opposite end of the carriage looked at her, their mouths open in shock and terror. Then she was on them, her arms pin wheeling at the speed of motorboat blades as her claws sliced through those around her. Lifting them from where they'd fallen as if they were rag dolls, she buried her face into their necks.

"Please! Please!" I heard somebody sob from close by. I looked down to see a young woman, not much older than myself kneeling on one of the cushioned seats. She had removed one of her stilettos and was smashing the heel against one of the carriage windows.

"Please let me out! Please!" she cried, as she slammed the heel of her shoe into the glass. But the reinforced glass didn't even chip and the heel of her shoe snapped loose, bouncing back and striking her across the forehead. A gash appeared, seeping blood down into her eyes. The victims of the fair-haired woman must have smelt the blood running from the girl's forehead, because they sprung-up from the carriage floor, newly awakened, their own throats open and sucking in air.

The girl dropped her broken shoe and frantically rubbed the blood from her eyes, but in her moment of blindness, the vampires took their chance and dragged her to the floor kicking and screaming.

I could feel the tube train begin to slow and I looked up to see that we were pulling into Kings Cross underground station. Before the train had even come to a stop, the passengers that crushed against me were trying to pry the doors open with their fingers. The people on the platform were unaware of what was awaiting them. I opened my mouth to scream at them to run – to get off the platform. But I was unable to form the words – it felt as if something had got lodged in the back of my throat and I was gagging on whatever it was. The train stopped. The doors were forced open and the frantic passengers spilled on top of each other onto the platform. Some of those passengers waiting looked stunned and bewildered as they were trampled underfoot.

Those that had been bitten on the train sprang with lightning speed from the carriage and launched themselves at the unsuspecting commuters. Within seconds the platform had become a scene of complete panic and confusion. People fell, collapsed and collided with one another in sheer terror. Their screams echoed through the tunnels and maze of passageways beneath ground.

The carriage had emptied and I found myself alone, unable to move, my arm stuck in the air, gripping the safety rail. I looked right and I could see that I wasn't alone after all. Taylor stood at the opposite end of the carriage. He was now stripped to the waist. His body was white, almost opaque, and his ribs seemed to poke through his skin like rungs on a ladder. His mottled black wings hung from his back like a tattered cape. His eyes were fixed on mine, but he didn't come forward. He just stood there. I couldn't bear the sight of his eyes; it was as if they were boring into me – looking inside of me.

Turning away, I looked through the open carriage door and out onto the platform and watched the girl with the bleeding forehead, hobble up the platform in her one remaining stiletto as she sought out her first victim. Looking back at Taylor, he smiled at me and whispered, "Wake…"

Chapter Eleven

"…up!" someone was saying. "Wake-up!"

"She's bleeding," I heard a gruff male voice say above me.

"Get her up and into the house," a female said.

I felt myself being lifted into the air and held by a strong set of arms. My face was resting against some kind of rough material. Opening my eyes, I looked up to see a single eye looking down at me. Why couldn't I see the other eye? I blinked and looked again. The other was covered with a dirty bandage. My eyes closed again, and I felt sick and disorientated.

"She fell from the wall," someone said. "She fell like a stone."

The voice sounded familiar and it took me a moment to realise that it was Kayla who was talking.

"Is she going to be okay?" someone else asked, and it was Mrs. Payne.

I opened my eyes again, and this time they focused to reveal the covered face of Marshal looking down at me.

"Will she be alright?" I heard Mrs. Payne ask again, but I couldn't see her.

"How should I know?" Marshal grunted from above, his top lip curling upwards. Twisting my head slightly, a bolt of pain sliced through my skull and down into my neck.

"Where am I?" I murmured.

I felt someone touch my hand, the fingers were soft and gentle. "You're going to be okay," Kayla said, and I looked around to see her beside me. I couldn't help but notice the concern in her eyes.

Rolling my head back, I could feel that rough material against my cheek again. I looked and could see that my face was pressed against Marshal's chest as he carried me in his arms back towards the manor. That sweet-musty smell lingered on his clothes and it made me feel sick. Screwing up my nose, I looked up into his face again, those filthy-looking bandages concealing most of him. Tuffs of unkempt beard poked through the gaps around his chin and neck. His hat covered his hair, but I could see straggly black lengths sticking out from underneath. He saw me study him and he looked away. I couldn't help notice that although his arms felt muscular beneath and his chest as hard as rock against my face, he seemed to tilt forward and it was then that I remembered his misshapen back.

"I think I will be okay to walk," I told him, but without looking down at me, he grunted and continued to carry me back towards the manor.

Despite his back, Marshal carried me up the two flights of stairs and down the corridor to my room, where he gently laid me on my bed. Without looking back at me, he turned and left my room. As he did I looked at his long black coat, the sleeves and his boots. Kayla bounded onto the bed, and crossing her legs she came and sat next to me.

Mrs. Payne appeared in the bedroom doorway with a tray which had a glass, bowl, and jug of water balancing on it.

"Kayla, don't just sit there gawking at Kiera, go to the bathroom and get me a flannel!" Mrs. Payne snapped.

Without argument, Kayla scuttled from the bed and returned moments later. She handed the housekeeper the flannel, who then poured some of the water from the jug into the bowl. Moistening the flannel with some of the water, Mrs. Payne began to gently dab at the corner of my left eye.

"Your eye has been bleeding, Kiera,' she explained. "But I don't seem to be able to find a cut or where the blood is coming from."

Taking the flannel from her, I said, "It's okay, it happens sometimes."

"Does it?" She asked, sounding alarmed.

"There's nothing to worry about," I tried to assure her, and I noticed Kayla staring at me from the foot of the bed.

"You should see a doctor, dear," Mrs. Payne said, plumping up the pillows beneath my head.

"I have, but they tell me there's nothing wrong with me," I said.

"Well, whatever, but you need to get some rest. You've had a nasty fall," she told me. It was then that I remembered getting the text message on my phone from Sparky, and then…everything had just gone black.

"How many times have you been told not to climb up on that wall, Kayla?" Mrs. Payne snapped.

"I'm not six-years-old anymore," Kayla muttered.

"I don't want to see you up there again," the housekeeper said, staring at Kayla. "Do you understand me?"

"Whatever," Kayla sighed, flopping down on the bed.

"And what do you think you're doing?" Mrs. Payne snapped at her again.

Poor Kid, I thought to myself. *Wings or no wings – I'd want to run away from this place and never come back.*

"I'm going to sit with Kiera and make sure she's okay," Kayla said.

"You'll do no such thing," the housekeeper sighed. "Kiera needs to get some rest. She doesn't want you -"

"It's okay," I said. "I feel fine – honestly."

"Don't talk such nonsense."

"No, I'd like Kayla to stay -" I started.

Ignoring me, Mrs. Payne, glared at Kayla and said, "Come on, you have some chores to do."

Swinging her legs over the side of the bed, Kayla shrugged at me and headed towards the door, following the housekeeper.

Just as she was about to disappear into the corridor, I called after her, "Have you got my phone?"

"Huh?" Kayla said looking back over her shoulder at me.

"My mobile phone?"

Staring at me, Kayla said, "I don't know where it is. Maybe you dropped it into the moat as you fell from the wall." Then she was gone, swinging the door shut behind her.

"Not my phone," I groaned, punching the mattress with a clenched fist. I closed my eyes and tried to recall the text message Sparky had sent me. I remembered looking at my phone, and behind my eyes those flash-bulbs popped on and off again and in those flashes of light, the words from the message that Sparky had sent swam about in front of my closed eyes. Like I was solving some word puzzle I put the words in order so that they made sense. Then, as clear as if I were holding the phone in my hand, I read the words that seemed to have appeared on the inside of my eyelids.

> **Bad news Kiera – your flat has been burgled.**
> **It's a real mess here. Where are you?**
> **Sparky. X**

Opening my eyes, the words shot away, like the pieces of a scrabble game being tossed around the inside of my skull. So my nightmare about Phillips ransacking my flat had been true. He'd really been there, going through my stuff. But why? And what had he been looking for? But more than that, the message from Sparky proved that my dream had been more than just a nightmare, it had been a vision – premonition – of some kind. Realising this, my body turned cold and gooseflesh crawled up my arms and legs. If the nightmare that I'd had about Phillips had somehow been a window to what was happening outside the grounds of Hallowed Manor, then perhaps the nightmare I'd experienced while unconscious might also be….

Could that have really happened? I asked myself as I sat bolt upright on my bed. Could vampires have really gone berserk on the London Underground and killed all those people? And if it were true – if that had really taken place – what about the plane crash? And the voice of the pilot screamed inside my head: *"Mayday! Mayday! They've breached the cockpit!"* The pilot's voice seemed almost deafening inside my head. Covering my ears with my hands, I lay back down on the bed and rolled onto my side. Pulling my knees up under my chin, I cradled myself like a baby.

What is happening to me? And what is happening out there beyond the walls of Hallowed Manor? If the world was coming under attack by vampires, why was I seeing it? I didn't want to see it! I needed to make contact with the outside world – I needed to speak with Sparky, but without my phone how would I? This place would surely have a phone. Perhaps Kayla would have a mobile that I could borrow – all teenagers had a mobile phone these days, right? But what was his number? I had it stored in my phone, sure, but I couldn't remember it. That was the whole point of storing it in my phone – so I wouldn't have to remember it. Perhaps I could get his home number by ringing directory enquires – yes that's what I would do. Sparky would be able to tell me if any vampires had been found on that plane, if there had been a massacre on the Underground. Something like that would be all over the news and in the papers. God how I wish I had access to some newspapers right now. I wouldn't be able to stop myself from cutting and pasting. I pictured my flat in Havensfield covered with the news cuttings of vampires at forty thousand feet above ground and two hundred feet below ground.

My head started to pound and it felt as if someone or something was chipping away at my brain with a pickaxe. I didn't know if the pain was due to my fall or the realisation that I was somehow *seeing* what had happened, what was happening, or had yet to happen. Closing my eyes, I thought about the show-and-tell session Kayla and me had shared that morning. There were still questions that I wanted to ask Kayla – there was stuff I needed answers to. Some I could provide myself, like I now knew that it had been Marshal who had been up to the *'forbidden'* wing. Why had he taken a tray up there and for whom? That I didn't know. But there was someone else living at the manor other than Kayla, Mrs. Payne, Marshal, and the chauffeur. I also knew that Lady Hunt hadn't gone to New York like she claimed she was going to. She was definitely going somewhere – but it was closer to home than that or she would have taken suitcases with her. She didn't even have a handbag when she got out of the car at the railway station.

I now understood the true reason why she had asked me to come and watch her daughter – but where was she, and what was she doing? And what of Murphy, Potter, and Luke? Where were they when I needed them? What about Luke? Kayla had said that the last time she had seen him, he had looked disfigured – burnt. But there was one thing that I just couldn't work out. Sitting on that wall with Kayla, she had known that I was going to receive a text message on my phone – some seconds before it had arrived. How had she known that? I would have to ask her, I thought as my eyes drooped shut and I drifted into sleep.

Chapter Twelve

I didn't dream – I just slept – and when I woke my room was in semi-darkness. Someone had lit candles and placed them around my room. The curtains were open, and through the window, I could see that it was night and a crescent-shaped moon hung in the sky like a piece of cheese rind. Glancing at my wristwatch, the little luminous hands told me it was just before 9 p.m. Rolling onto my back, I propped myself up onto my elbows. My head still ached from my fall, but the pain had eased. Then in the gloom, I spotted Kayla sitting in the chair in the corner of the room. Noticing that I was awake, she removed the iPod's earphones, picked something up from the dresser, and brought it towards me.

"I made you a sandwich," she said, handing me a plate. "I thought you might be hungry." Taking the plate of neatly-cut sandwiches from her, I looked at them and she added, "They're ham. You do like ham, don't you? I wasn't sure."

"I love cheese," I said, taking a bite. "Mmm. These are good."

"I fetched you a glass of milk, too," Kayla smiled and took a glass from the dressing table.

"You're too kind," I smiled and took a gulp.

"Are you okay?" she asked, and I could see the concern in her eyes that twinkled in the candlelight.

"I'll be fine," I said, putting the glass to one side.

"You had me worried for a bit," she said.

"Don't worry about me. I'm as tough as an old pair of boots," I told her, and she laughed. There was an awkward silence that fell between us, so I broke it by saying, "So what have you been doing while I've been out of it?"

"Not much," she sighed. "The old bag has had me mopping the kitchen floor and then I had to go and wash the Rolls Royce for James." Then holding out her hands, she said, "See, look my hands have gone all wrinkly. Then I made you a sandwich and have just been sitting up here in the corner listening to music."

"Anything good?" I asked her.

" 'Rocket Man' by Elton John. I love that song," she said.

As we were on the subject of listening to things, I said, "So tell me, how did you know I was going to get that text earlier? I mean, you knew it was coming even before it showed up on my phone."

Making herself comfortable on the edge of my bed, Kayla looked at me and said, "I hear things."

Swallowing a mouthful of ham and bread, I said, "How do you mean?"

"I don't know – it's hard to explain," she sighed. "Remember how I told you I heard that doctor whisper in my father's ear? Well they were right on the other side of my room but I could still hear them."

"It could just have been good acoustics," I said, but didn't really believe that. And to hear myself doubt her like that reminded me of how Doctor Keats disbelieved me. The girl had wings for crying out loud – I should be able to believe anything.

"Come with me," Kayla said, climbing from the edge and taking one of the candles. Pushing the plate aside, I took a candle for myself and followed her.

"Where you taking me?" I asked her.

"C'mon," she said over her shoulder. "I want to show you my room."

Following Kayla down the passageway, that smell hit my nostrils again. I tried not to get too close to the walls in an attempt to avoid getting that sticky stuff on my clothes. Just before the stairs, Kayla stopped outside a door and pushed it open. Looking back at me, she stepped inside. With my candle held out before me, I followed her. The room that I'd entered was lit with so many candles that it could have easily been mistaken for some kind of chapel. There were tall ones, short ones, fat and thin ones. The smell of melting wax was almost overwhelming. Apart from the candles, Kayla's room could have been mistaken for any other teenage girl's room up and down the country – apart from the four-poster bed, Ensuite bathroom, sheer size, and the balcony outside. Her room was covered with pictures of Enrique Iglesias, Robert Pattinson, and Katy Perry. Clothes spilled from the half-open wardrobe and across the floor, a Kindle lay on her bed.

"Reading anything good?" I asked.

Looking back over her shoulder, she said, "'*Atlas*' by Sienna Rose."

"Any good?" I asked, turning to look at her dressing table.

"Awesome," she said. "You should read it sometime."

"Perhaps I will someday," I smiled, noticing how her dressing table was littered with lipsticks, half-empty bottles of perfume, face wipes, hairgrips, and nail polish.

Kicking some of her clothes under the bed, Kayla smiled and said, "Sorry about the mess."

"Hey, this looks like paradise compared to the state of my flat," I said. Then I thought of how Phillips had left it and dreaded going back there to face it.

"Right. You lay down there," she said. "I want to prove something to you."

Playing along with her, I lay on her bed. Looking up I could see the bell pull hanging from the ceiling. It was frayed all down one side and at its end. Glancing away, I watched Kayla cross to the far side of the room. "Right now, close your eyes so you can't lip read. Go on, close your eyes," she urged me.

Smiling to myself, I closed my eyes and lay back. All I could hear was the sound of my own breathing.

"Ok, so what did I say?" she asked.

Opening my eyes, I looked at her standing across the room from me. "I couldn't hear what you said," I told her.

"See!" she exclaimed coming back towards me. "I was standing exactly where my father and that quack were that night, but I still heard them. That would be impossible, right?"

"I guess," I said sitting back up. "So you have extra-sensitive hearing?" I asked her.

"It was like that at first," she started to explain. "But now it's different."

"How?" I asked, crossing to the window to look out onto the balcony.

"I don't know how to explain it – but it's not like I hear voices, words, or sounds – it's more like vibrations," she said. "And it's those vibrations that create noises inside my head. Like today, when we were sitting on the wall. I couldn't have heard your text arriving because I heard it before it arrived on your phone. So how could I have heard it, if it hadn't made a sound?"

"I don't know," I said, stepping away from the window. I'd seen enough so I went to her bathroom and glanced inside.

"I heard the vibrations of that text message travelling towards your phone through the air – does that makes sense?" she said.

Sitting on the edge of her bed, I looked at Kayla and said, "I think so."

"That's why I like to listen to music," she said, coming to sit next to me.

"How come?"

"There is always noise going on inside my head – it can kinda drive me nuts at times," she said. "It's like just sitting here next to you, I can hear your heart beating, I can hear the blood surging through your veins, I can hear your hair and nails growing. It's like there is this constant background noise."

"How do you cope with it?" I asked her.

"Sometimes I don't," she explained. "That's one of the reasons I was distracted at school. It was so hard to concentrate when I could hear the lunch that the girl sitting next me had eaten being broken down by her stomach acid inside her. It wasn't very nice and very distracting!"

"I know how you feel," I told her. "I can see things."

"See things?" she asked, then with an excited glint in her eyes, she added, "What, like ghosts and stuff?"

"No," I laughed. "I'm not psychic." But then I thought of how I'd seen Phillips burgle my flat in a dream and wondered if I was. God, Doctor Keats would have enough material to keep her busy for the rest of her life!

"How do you mean then?" Kayla asked.

"Okay," I said. "How many people live in this house?"

"Well, including you and my mother when she's here -" she started.

"Apart from us," I cut in. "How many staff are there?"

"Why, just three," she said, looking confused. "Mrs. Payne, Marshal, and James."

"Wrong, there's another," I said looking her straight in the eye.

"But that's impossible!" she gasped. "Who are they, and where are they? I haven't seen anyone!"

"But I have," I said. "I don't know who they are, but I know that they are probably living in the other wing."

"How can you be so sure?" She asked, sounding breathless.

"Marshal took them breakfast this morning," I assured her.

"Marshal? How do you know that?"

"The stairs leading up to the 'forbidden' wing, as the good housekeeper likes to call it, are covered in dust. Thick dust which I guess has been created by the renovations that have been taking place there. It looks reddish in colour which probably makes it brick dust," I said.

"So?"

"There aren't any builders here – not that I've seen," I said.

"No, they stopped work last week," Kayla said. "They can't continue until some more supplies have been ordered. Well, that's what Mrs. Payne told me anyhow. Apparently, they'll be back next week."

"Okay, so if there haven't been any builders in the manor since last week, why are there fresh boot prints in the dust on those stairs? The prints looked to me to be about a size twelve – far too big to be Mrs. Payne's or yours. The chauffeur can't walk, so that only leaves one other person…"

"Marshal!" Kayla breathed, her eyes growing wide. "But how do you know that he was taking someone their breakfast?"

"Halfway up the banisters, there is a handprint where someone gripped hold of it. It wasn't because they slipped or fell, having to suddenly take hold of the banister, the footprints didn't show any sign of this. The fact that there isn't a matching handprint on the opposite banister tells me that they were carrying something else in their hand. Something that they were trying to balance and something that they couldn't drop for fear of bringing unwanted attention to themselves," I explained. Then holding my arm up with my hand out flat, I pretended that I was holding a tray. "See, a tray would contain plates, cutlery, or a teapot and a cup at the very least. Imagine the noise that would have made if it had gone clattering down the stairs."

"But what makes you think it was breakfast?" Kayla asked, looking intrigued.

"What else could someone possibly be carrying on a tray at such an early hour in the morning?" I said.

"How do you know it was in the morning?" she asked.

"I passed those stairs at gone midnight last night and even though I only had the aid of a candle to guide me, it was adequate enough for me to have noticed any great big boot marks if they'd been there."

Looking at me, Kayla blew out her cheeks and said, "That was pretty neat. But how can you definitely be sure it was Marshal? I know what you said about him being the only -"

"When he placed me on the bed after my fall today, I couldn't help but notice a trail of the same coloured brick dust along the right sleeve of his coat. And as he walked away, I could see it on the soles of his boots," I explained.

"You really do *see* things, don't you?" Kayla said. "But if you are right - and I don't doubt you – who was Marshal taking breakfast to and what are they doing up there?"

"I don't know," I said. "But it would be nice to find out."

"If you go up there, will you take me with you?" she asked.

"I don't know," I said shaking my head.

"I used to go up there as a kid," she told me. "I could show you the way."

"I'll think about it," I said getting up from the bed and heading for the door.

"You know what?" Kayla said, as I reached for the door handle.

"What?"

"My mother was wrong about you."

"In what way?" I asked, looking back.

"She said you were going to be tough – that you wouldn't put up with any nonsense and that you would keep me line," Kayla said.

"But your mother was right about one thing," I said lingering by the door.

"Oh, what was that?"

"You do have someone watching you," I said, but I didn't tell her that I knew she knew who he was. I didn't tell her that despite the moat, the walls, the drawbridge and gate, he somehow gained access to the grounds. That she sends him messages to let him know the coast is clear. That he waits for her below until it is safe for him to come up to her balcony, but he is not her boyfriend. But nevertheless, he is someone she trusts and feels comfortable with. I didn't tell Kayla that I had seen all of this since entering her bedroom.

"Do you know who it is?" Kayla said, springing from the edge of her bed and I could detect fear in her voice.

"Not yet," I told her, closing the bedroom door behind me.

Chapter Thirteen

Instead of going back to my room, I crept down the stairs to the next landing. With the candle flickering in my hand, I looked at the stairs leading up into the *'forbidden'* wing. Crouching forward, I looked only to see that the stairs and banisters had now been cleaned. Any trace of Marshal's footsteps had been wiped away.

"Have you lost something?" a voice said from behind me.

With a gasp of fright, I leapt up and spun round. Peering through the flame of the candle that she held in her hand, Mrs. Payne gave me a distrusting look.

"Erm, no...well yes," I said, sounding flustered.

"Oh, yes?" Mrs. Payne said without taking her beady eyes off me. "What have you lost"'

"My earrings," I blurted out.

"Really?" Mrs. Payne said. "Well, you couldn't have lost them here."

"How come?" I said, looking down, pretending to be searching for them.

"You weren't wearing any earrings today as Marshal carried you back into the house after your fall," she smiled through the candlelight at me.

"That would be it then," I said sounding relieved. "They must have come off when I fell."

"Perhaps," the housekeeper said, moving around me so as to block the stairs leading up into the blackness. "I'll get Marshal to have a look for you tomorrow."

"No, it's okay," I said. "They weren't very expensive – just forget about it."

"Whatever you wish," Mrs. Payne smiled, but it was false. For a moment we just stood and looked at each other in the gloom.

"Any idea on when the lights are going to come back on?" I asked her.

"Very soon," she said her fake smile fading.

"When would that be exactly?" I pushed.

"In a day or so – when the builders return. Why? Is there a problem, Kiera?" she asked.

"No, no problem," I said, turning away and heading back up the stairs to my room.

"Goodnight then," Mrs. Payne's voice echoed up from the darkness.

"Goodnight," I said, and climbed the stairs.

Back in my room, I closed the door and went to the bathroom. The bath looked inviting; so, taking off my jeans and jumper, I put my hair up and ran myself a bath. While the water was tumbling from the taps, I lit a few more candles and went to the windows, opening them just enough to let the cool night air into my room.

Turning, I went back to the bathroom, took off my underwear, and climbed into the bath. I sunk right to the bottom of it and the warm water almost came up to my chin. Leaning my head back I closed my eyes. I wished that I had my iPod with me; to be able to listen to Adele while I relaxed in the bath surrounded by candlelight would have been perfection. But Kayla still had it and I guessed her need was greater than mine. I liked Kayla and she was nothing like her mother had portrayed her. Sure she could be a little cocky, but she had a lot to deal with. Not only had one of her parents recently disappeared (and I knew how that felt), she had been left knowing that she was different from everyone else. Although she knew that her father had been a Vampyrus, had he ever really talked to her about that? Had she ever seen his wings? Surely he would have tried to have comforted her, made her feel as normal as possible. No wonder she was bitter and angry at times. And where was her mother now? Why had she really gone away? Was it in search of her husband?

I could understand Lady Hunt believing I might be able to protect her daughter; after all she told me herself that she knew I'd managed to survive in The Ragged Cove. But who was I protecting Kayla from, and did she really need protecting? I knew that Kayla was in contact with someone on the outside of the manor, I could *see* that when I looked out of her bedroom window onto the balcony. There was a torch hidden in the corner. If she had a torch available to her, why wasn't she using it to light her way through the house at night instead of a candle? No, she was using the torch to send a signal to someone at night on the moors. She flicked the torch light on and off to send messages to him. A candle would be no good; the wind would blow out the flame. There was also a sprinkling of earth on the stone floor of the balcony and some had dirtied the windows. Directly below her balcony was a flowerbed, and this is where the man stood and threw earth up at her window to get Kayla's attention. How did he get up onto the balcony? Kayla would unfasten the bell pull. She would tie a knot in one end to secure it between the balcony railings and the male would hoist himself up. He wasn't a Vampyrus or he would have flown onto her balcony and there would have been no need for the mud-slinging or frayed looking-bell pull.

Whoever it was, he was just a friend to Kayla. There was no romantic interest as she wasn't trying to impress him. Any young girl wanting to grab the attentions of a young man wouldn't dare let him into such an untidy room, where used face wipes were discarded on the dresser, and dirty clothes and underwear sprawled across the floor. But this did show that whoever it was, she felt comfortable with him – comfortable enough not to put on a show.

My head spun with so much information. So splashing some water onto my face to waken myself, I climbed out of the bath. Wrapping a towel around me, I peered into the mirror fastened to the wall above the basin. With the forefinger of my right hand, I touched the tear duct of my left eye. I couldn't see any blood and my eye didn't even look bloodshot. I still didn't understand why my eye bled when I had those – visions – when I *saw* things.

What, with me *seeing* things and Kayla *hearing* things, nothing would ever get past us. What a team we would make! Then as if being punched in the face, I staggered backwards – nearly stumbling back into the bath. How had I not *seen* it? Kayla had been going through changes since the age of fourteen. And since that age she had been *hearing* things. I tried to remember at what age I had started to *see* things – probably about the same age I guessed. But just like her hearing, which over the years had started to develop – *change* – so had my sight. No longer was I just able to *see* things that anybody else would if only they looked for them, but now I was *seeing* stuff that either had yet to happen or had happened. But Kayla had gone through other changes too – she had started to grow wings. Although small at the moment, they were sure to develop into full-sized wings as she grew older.

With my heart pounding in my chest, and my mouth turning dry, I lowered the towel that I had wrapped around me. Glancing back over my shoulder, I looked at my back in the mirror.

"What am I doing?" I shouted aloud. "Kiera Hudson, you need to get a grip!"

Then I started to laugh, there was no way I could be some kind of half-breed human-slash-Vampyrus. One of Kayla's parents had been a Vampyrus; mine had just been plain old –

...then I screamed in horror and pulled the towel tight about me. Reflected in the mirror was my bedroom window, and in its reflection was the bandaged face of Marshal staring back at me.

Chapter Fourteen

Tying the towel around me, I turned around and raced towards the windows on the far side of my room. Throwing them open, I went out onto the balcony.

"What's the big idea?" I shouted, expecting to see Marshal standing there, but the balcony was empty. There was no one there. Suspecting that he might have seen me coming and climbed off the balcony, I peered over the edge, but couldn't see him. How had he disappeared so quickly? It only took me moments to get from the bathroom to here. My mind then started to tell me that perhaps he hadn't been there at all. Maybe I hadn't seen him spying on me through the windows. But I knew he'd been there watching me. But for how long had he been standing on my balcony, and why?

There was a squeaking noise from below and I wondered if it were Marshal trying to make good his escape. Peering down into the darkness, I could hear the squeaking noise but couldn't see anything. Running back into my room, I blew out the candles. Returning to my balcony, I crouched down and peered through the concrete railings, hiding myself in the darkness, hoping that whoever was below might reveal themselves if they thought that I had gone back to my room, and gone to bed.

The squeaking came again and I couldn't work out where it was coming from or what was making the sound. Then, peering to my right, I saw James come from around the side of the manor house in his wheelchair. With every turn of the wheels, they let out a high-pitched squeaking sound. Staying hidden in the darkness, I watched him make his way down the gravel path towards the gatehouse. I sat there until the squeaking faded into the distance and he disappeared from view. I stayed hidden in the darkness and wondered why he would be out at such a late hour and heading for the gate house. Was he going to see Marshal? Deciding that there wasn't anything that odd about this, and suspecting I was just being jittery because I thought I saw Marshal watching me, I decided to go back inside and lock the windows behind me.

But just as I was about to crawl out from the shadows I saw a light blinking on and off out across the moors. The light flashed once, then again but this time longer. Then again, and again.

Staying hidden, I peered along the side of the building and could just make out Kayla's balcony in the distance. Lying as flat as I could, I watched her balcony windows swing slowly open. Within seconds, I watched as Kayla came crawling out on her hands and knees. Just like I knew she had been, she took the torch that she had been hiding, switched it on then quickly off again. The torchlight on the moors flashed again in recognition of her signal. Kayla switched her torch on and off in rapid succession and whoever she was signalling to on the moors signalled back with a quick flash of torchlight.

Scrambling back into my bedroom, I rummaged around for a pen and a scrap of paper in my bag. Searching in the darkness with the tips of my fingers, I pulled out a pen and an old mini-bank statement. Hurrying back onto the balcony, I waited for the flashes of torchlight to come from the darkness of the moors. At first there was nothing and I hoped that I hadn't missed the last of it. Then, out of the night came two long flashes followed by two short bursts of light, followed by one long flash, and then a pause which was quickly followed by a further two long flashes and one short burst. I frantically made a note of this on the scrap of paper and waited. Nothing more followed and I looked to my right and watched Kayla disappear back into her room, quietly closing the windows behind her.

Hurrying back into my room, not knowing if I had any time to lose, I struck a match from the box on the dressing table and lit a candle. In the dim light I tried to make sense of what I'd written. This is what I'd scrawled on the back of the bank statement:

-- --/-/-/--
-- --/-

How I wished I'd learnt the Morse code, as I sat looking at the lines and dashes I'd drawn. Trying to work as fast as I could, I knew that the top line made a four letter word and the second line consisted of a two-letter word. But what were they? I tried to think of as many two letter words that I could, but there were too many. Then I remembered reading once that the most commonly used letter in the English alphabet was the letter 'E'. So I hoped that maybe either word started with the letter 'E' or at least had the letter somewhere within them.

Then I noticed that the first word had two short dashes in the middle. So under them I wrote:

-- --/-/-/--
e/e

The two-letter word also had one of these short bursts as its second letter, so I wrote:

-- --/-/-/--
e/e
--/-
/e

I couldn't think of too many two-letter words that ended with 'E' and the first that came to mind was the word 'ME'. I looked at my scribbles and could see that the first letter of the first word was identical to that of the first word in the second word, so I wrote:

-- --/-/-/--
M/e/e/--
-- --/-
M/e

Looking down at the piece of scrap paper there was only one four letter word that I could think of which started with the letters M.E.E and that was the word *meet*. So placing the letter 'T' at the end of the cipher, I read the message that the person on the moors had sent Kayla. It read:

Meet me!

Fearing that Kayla was going to go and meet this stranger, I pulled on my clothes, and blowing out the candle I'd lit, I crept to my bedroom door. Opening it just an inch, I peered out and could just make out Kayla heading away from me down the corridor. Sneaking out, I suddenly stopped. Kayla could hear things? If she could hear my heartbeat just sitting next to her, wouldn't she be able to hear me following her? Closing the door behind me as quietly as I could, I knew it was a risk I'd have to take if I were to ever find out who it was she had been meeting. After all, that's what Lady Hunt was supposedly paying me to find out.

I waited until the top of Kayla's head had disappeared over the brow of the stairs, then as quickly and as quietly as I could, I set off down the passageway after her. At the top of the stairs, I looked around the banister to see her cross the hall beneath the giant chandelier. Hunkering down and peering through the gaps in the banisters, I watched as she reached the front door. Sliding back the bolts, she stole one quick glance back over her shoulder then disappeared out into the night.

Running down the stairs on tiptoe, I raced across the great hall and slowly opened the front door just a fraction. Pressing my eye against the gap that I'd created, I watched Kayla run across the open grassy area in front of the manor, heading towards the shelter and utter darkness beneath the trees. Not wanting to lose sight of her, I pulled the front door closed behind me, and headed across the lawns. Ahead of me, Kayla disappeared into the darkness and I lost her from view. With my heart racing in my chest, I prayed that she couldn't hear it and I headed towards the tree line.

Shielding myself behind the trunk of an ancient oak tree, I spied into the darkness that filled the gaps between the tree trunks like black ink. Then to my left and a short distance away, I saw a light weaving back and forward across the ground. Believing that she was a safe distance from the manor and hidden by the trees, she must have turned her torch on. Following the torch light, I crept after her. Gradually my eyes grew accustomed to the darkness, and everything around me looked grey and dull as if the colour had been sucked out of it. In the distance I could see the torchlight bobbing up and down. Then I heard a sound in the silence which made me quicken my step and close the gap between Kayla and me. It was the hissing sound of my iPod that I could hear, and if she was listening to that, then maybe she wouldn't be able to hear me following her.

Weaving between the tree trunks, I continued after her, until some way ahead, the torchlight went out. Stopping where I was, I listened, but there was only silence now, even the hissy sound of my iPod had stopped. Placing one foot carefully in front of the other, I made my way towards the area where I'd seen the torchlight go out. As I drew near, the trees thinned out into an open circular area. In its centre was a small summerhouse. It was white in colour and the roof was pointed, giving it the appearance of a medieval chapel. At the front of it there was a small covered porch and a swinging couch. The porch was raised off the ground, and to get to it there were several wooden steps. Surrounding the summerhouse was a white picket fence. From my hiding place and lit by the light of the moon, the tiny little house looked like something from a fairy-tale.

Kayla stood to one side of the summerhouse. I watched her wind the earphones around my iPod then place it on the ground next to her jacket which she had taken off. She was dressed in jeans and a black gym top, which was tight-fitting, stopped an inch above her navel, and was low-cut at the back. Arching her shoulders and hanging her arms loosely by her side, Kayla's small looking wings unfolded from her back. The tips of them peeked just above her shoulders and I could see the three bony fingers at each end of the wing wiggling open and closed in the moonlight.

Then I heard the sweetest sound that I think I'd ever heard. Kayla started giggling to herself and it sounded like the happiest sound in the world. As she giggled, she fluttered her wings and ever so slowly her feet began to lift off the ground. Watching from the darkness beneath the trees, I felt kind of weird as if I were intruding on a very private moment. But, however much I guessed that I should walk way, I couldn't; I was mesmerised by her beauty. She looked like an angel.

Kayla's feet rose about a foot off the ground, before she dropped again. Raising herself on the tips of her toes, she held her arms out on either side of her slender frame and with a gentle flap of her wings, she rose off the ground again. At first I wasn't sure what she was trying to achieve by doing this, but then she hovered a few feet off the ground, twisted her body to the right and fluttered in that direction. Seeing this, I knew that she was getting used to having wings – she was practising flying. I could tell that her wings were too underdeveloped to reach the heights and speeds that I'd seen Luke, Potter, and Murphy achieve, but one day – one day she would and what a sight she would make, soaring, racing, and diving through the sky with her flame-coloured hair billowing out behind her. As I thought of this, there was a very small part of me that was envious of her.

My thoughts were broken by the sound of gentle applause. Looking towards the sound I could see that someone had appeared on the porch of the summerhouse. I'd been so caught-up in the spectacle of Kayla that I hadn't noticed him arrive and neither had Kayla. Hearing the sound, she fluttered the few feet back to the ground and went racing towards him, her wings glinting in the moonlight behind her. Racing up the steps, she threw her arms around this man and they held each other. Even though it wasn't a lover's embrace, I could tell that Kayla felt deeply for him. From my hiding place, I watched the man plant a soft kiss on her forehead and she ran her hand gently down the length of one side of his face. The overhang of the porch cast such deep shadows that it was impossible for me to see the identity of this man. Letting go of each other, the male led Kayla by the hand into the summerhouse and closed the door behind them.

I waited several minutes, and when I was sure that they weren't coming out again, I tiptoed from beneath the shelter of the trees and made my way across the open area towards the summerhouse. Passing the porch, I crept around the side of the tiny structure. Set in the side of it, there was a window. Drooping low so I was almost crawling, I positioned myself below the window. Holding my breath and trying to calm my racing heart – I didn't want Kayla to hear it – I slowly pulled myself up and peered through the window.

Chapter Fifteen

The inside of the summerhouse was in semi-darkness. There was an oil lamp on the table and it cast an orange glow. There was a small wooden table in the centre of the room and Kayla and the male sat at it on two white-washed chairs. Kayla was sitting to one side, and I had to strain my neck to see her. That was good though, because if I couldn't see her without making some effort, then she wouldn't be able to see me. But the male was who I really wanted to get a good look at, but he had his back to me. What little I could see of him was cast in shadow. I could hear them talking, but their voices were low and muffled as if they were speaking in whisper, not wanting anyone else to hear what it was they were saying to one another.

Lowering my head, I pressed my ear against the thin wooden wall of the summerhouse and listened.

"I think I'm close," the male said, but that was all I got as his voice faded.

"How long now?" I heard Kayla ask, and from what I could tell, her voice had an urgency to it.

The male replied but the first part of what he said was incomprehensible. All I heard him say was, "...if all goes well."

"That soon?" Kayla gasped, her voice rising as if excited in some way.

"Shhh," I heard the male gesture. "You need to be ready, Kayla," he said, his voice just a little clearer.

"I'm practicing – but it's difficult now that..." and her voice faded again.

"Do you think she knows?" I heard the male say.

"...don't know," was all I got of Kayla's reply.

"She didn't miss a trick in The Ragged Cove," he said, and my stomach somersaulted as I suspected the male was referring to me.

The first part of Kayla's response was missing but I caught the last few words, "...don't like Marshal."

You're not the only one, I thought to myself.

"...not long now," the male said and I sensed he was trying to be reassuring. "Be ready."

"I'll try and...." her voice trailed away again.

"...got to be ready for what's coming," the male said. "We've all got to be ready."

Then I heard the sound of chairs scrapping against the wooden floor boards of the summerhouse as they stood up from the table, their secret meeting over. With my heart in my mouth, I crawled away, back towards the trees. I didn't look back until I was hidden once again out of the moonlight, and in the shadows. Tucking myself behind the trunk of a tree, I watched as Kayla and the man left the summerhouse. Leaning over her, he kissed Kayla softly on the cheek and silently walked towards the trees on the opposite side of the open area to where I was hiding. I watched Kayla pick her jacket up off the ground and put it on, concealing her wings beneath it. Unwinding the headphones, she placed them in her ears and switched on the iPod. With the sound of *'Rocket Man'* by Elton John hissing away in the darkness, I turned and raced back towards the manor house. Several times I stumbled in the darkness, tripping and falling over bracken and broken branches. I came to realise that lending Kayla my iPod was one of my better moves. With the noise I'd been making, I was surprised that I hadn't woken the whole manor. Reaching the tree line, I raced towards the front door, hoping that I could get inside and out of view before Kayla reached the clearing and saw me. With my feet crunching on the gravel path, I reached the door. Just as I was about to sneak inside someone said from behind me, "Did you enjoy your evening walk?"

Spinning round on my heels, I looked back to see the chauffeur sitting in his wheelchair just feet behind me.

Where in the hell did you spring from? I wanted to ask him, but I bit my tongue instead. How had I not heard him? I mean his wheelchair wailed like a set of fingernails being dragged across ice.

"I didn't mean to scare you," he said, looking at me from beneath the rim of his peaked cap. His unkempt sideburns glistened silver in the darkness and covered both sides of his face like wire wool.

"No worries," I said, just wanting to be back inside the house. I knew that if Kayla saw James and me she wouldn't come out from beneath the trees, but I didn't want her to see me at all. If she asked me tomorrow where I'd been, I really didn't want to have to lie to her or tell her the truth.

"What did you say?" the chauffeur said, raising a hand to his ear. "I'm a bit deaf."

"I said it doesn't matter," I told him. "You didn't scare me."

"What was that?" he asked again.

"It's ok – you didn't scare me!" I said, raising my voice but not wanting to shout.

"Where you been?" he asked.

Trying to be as casual as I could, I ignored his question and asked one of my own. "What happened to the squeak?"

"The what?" he asked, holding his hand to his ear again.

"Your wheelchair was making an awful squeaking noise earlier," I said in a raised voice which sounded more like a stage whisper.

"Oh, that," he said. "Went down to see Marshal at the gatehouse, I did. He put a bit of oil on it for me. As good as new now!" then he rolled the chair backwards a few inches as if to prove the point. The squeaking had gone.

"Oh, well that's good," I smiled. "If you don't mind, I should really be getting to bed now."

"What was that you said?" he asked, leaning forward in his chair.

"Goodnight," I said, stepping inside the manor.

"So long," he said, and I looked back to see him trundling away down the gravel path.

Then, just before I closed the door, I said just above a whisper, "vampires." If I'd blinked, I would have missed it, but as that word left my lips, the chauffeur seemed to falter as if suddenly stung. But then he was off again, wheeling himself down the path.

Shutting the door behind me, I wondered if the chauffeur was really as deaf as he claimed to be. After all, I could *see* that he didn't need the wheelchair. He could walk.

Taking two of the stairs at a time, I raced up them, wanting to be in my room before Kayla returned. As I passed the landing and the stairs leading to the *'forbidden'* wing, I couldn't help but wonder if Marshal was up there in the darkness. Leaping up the next flight of stairs, I ran down the corridor, through that musty-sweet smell and back to my room. Closing my door, and in the darkness, I went to the windows. Peeling back the curtain I peered out to see Kayla suddenly appear from beneath the trees. Jerking her head left and right to make sure the coast was clear, she snuck back across the lawns and to the house.

Closing the curtain, I flopped onto my bed. I didn't even bother to light a candle; all I wanted to do was sleep. And as I closed my eyes, I couldn't help but wonder what was going on at Hallowed Manor. Why was Marshal creeping around at night, staring at me through my window? Why was the chauffeur pretending to be deaf and wheelchair bound? Who was the man Kayla was secretly meeting? But what troubled me most of all was what I'd overheard him telling Kayla.

"…got to be ready for what's coming," the male had said. "We've all got to be ready."

Ready for what? I wondered, as I drifted off to sleep.

Chapter Sixteen

*My heart was racing and the smell of smoke was suffocating.
Everywhere I looked there was chaos. People ran screaming in
fear, but I didn't know from what. My heart raced inside me and
every one of my senses was telling me that I should run – but run
where and why?*

*The smoke cleared and I could see that I was standing in a
deserted street. Where had everyone else gone? It was dusk, and
for as far as I could see, the streets were lined with burning
buildings and cars. Had there been some kind of riot while I'd
been sleeping? What had happened to the world?*

*There was a noise above me, a high-pitched squawking.
Looking up I could see great black shadows soaring across the sky.
There were hundreds of them – no thousands. There were so many
that they almost turned the sky black, blocking out the last rays of
a dying sun. Shielding my eyes with my hands, I tried to make out
what they were; in my heart, I already knew, but my head was
telling me that it couldn't be possible. Their black wings rumbled
like thunder as the thousands of Vampyrus swooped above me.
From street level, it looked as if I'd woken back in time and the
world had been overrun with pterodactyl dinosaurs. Although they
looked terrifying as they raced above me, the sound of their
screaming and squawking hurting my ears, I couldn't help but also
notice their beauty. Beneath each set of prehistoric-looking wings,
was the body of a god. Their bodies, male and female, toned,
muscled, and as white as alabaster. They looked like perfect
sculptures. Their eyes burned like stars and their sharpened teeth
gleamed. Some looked old, others young and some were children,
but all of them were stunning.
Humans could only dream of such perfection, I thought to myself,
as I stared up at them.*

*They almost seemed to flock together, banking right,
swooping up, down, and then banking again. Then there was a
sound behind me, like a drum beating. Spinning round, I saw two
of the Vampyrus land, their wings rustling in the wind like sails.
They came towards me, and as they approached through the
burning smoke and flames, I could just make out that it was Taylor*

and Phillips. Even though their faces were a blur, distorted by the
ripples of heat that wafted up from the burning tarmac, I knew it
was them.

They came towards me, their strides purposeful and quick. I knew
that I was in danger. So turning, I ran between the burnt-out cars
and busses that littered the street. My boots crunched over broken
glass and my eyes stung from the smoke that billowed all around
me like fog. Finding an open doorway, I ran inside. The windows
of the building were frosted with cracks and splinters. I pulled at
the door but it was stuck fast.

"Please!" I groaned as I banged against it with my fists.
Glancing back over my shoulder, I could see Taylor and Phillips
coming closer. Running out from the doorway, I headed down an
alley. Bins had been overturned, their contents rotting in the
gutter, maggot-infested and being gnawed at by rats. Water ran
down the walls of the buildings that loomed above me on either
side and they felt as if they were closing in on me. The other end of
the alley seemed as if it was miles away, just a pinprick of grey
light in the distance. And however hard and fast I ran towards it,
the light never got any closer.

Peering back over my shoulder, I could see that Taylor and
Phillips were gaining on me. Desperate, I spun around and around
looking for any place to hide. Then I saw a rusty-looking fire
escape zigzagging up the side of the building. Kicking out at some
scrawny looking rats that had their heads buried in a nearby bin,
they scurried away. Turning the bin over, I climbed on top,
reached out for the bottom of the fire escape and hoisted myself up.
Placing one hand over the other, I climbed up. I swung my legs out
so they came to rest on the first step of the ladder. Then with the
little energy that I had left, I raced up the fire escape to the roof of
the building. Halfway up, I realised what a stupid thing I'd done.
Why was I climbing up, when the sky was fall of the very creatures
that I was trying to run from? But I had committed myself and had
nowhere else to go. Reaching the roof of the building, I looked out
across the horizon and screamed.

I was in London. In the distance I could see Big Ben; its
four clock faces were broken and leaking red flames into the fast-
approaching night. It looked like a giant candle lighting up the
horizon. Around it swooped the black-winged Vampyrus. Looking

to my right, I could see the giant dome of St. Paul's Cathedral, which looked as if half of it had crumbled away onto the streets below. Clouds of black smoke pumped from the huge hole. To my left, on the opposite side of the Thames, the London Eye looked broken and bent out of shape, like a bicycle wheel that had been run over by a truck. For as far as the eye could see, tendrils of smoke poured up into the night from the buildings which had been reduced to mountains of rubble. Vampyrus swooped and soared over the devastation, their squawks drowning out the sounds of collapsing buildings and raging fires.

"Kiera," a voice said from behind me. Whirling around, I gasped at the sight of my mother. She stood by the fire escape that I had climbed only moments before. "Kiera," my mother said again, and this time she held out her hands towards me.

"Mum," I stammered. "What are you doing here?"

I looked at her and she smiled. Her black hair curled around her neck and shoulders like velvet, and her blue eyes shone.

"Kiera, I'll explain later," she said, her voice soft and soothing, just as I remembered it to be. "We don't have time. You have to come with me now," and I noticed that her hands were smeared with blood.

"Mum – your hands," I breathed. But when I looked again, I could see that she was clutching a length of blonde hair between her fingers, just like Henry Blake had been clutching a length of hers under that tree in The Ragged Cove.

"She's one of us," somebody answered for her. Turning, I saw Taylor and Phillips standing behind me. I looked at them and covered my mouth with my hands to stifle the scream that was racing up my throat. I couldn't bear the sight of Phillips' mutilated face. It looked raw and infected. Why didn't he cover it with bandages or something?

"Mum," I whispered, moving towards her.

Taylor came towards me, his limp worse than I had previously remembered. He was having difficulty walking. "Don't trust her Kiera. Don't listen to what she says."

"But she's my mother," I said, feeling confused.

"Don't listen to him," my mother cried from over my shoulder.

Then, before I'd the chance to tell my mother how much I loved and missed her, the building began to shake like it was made out of children's building blocks. It tilted left, then right and I swayed towards the edge. I heard a tearing noise as the fire escape came away from the side of the building. Dust and brick flew into the air and the world seemed to spin all around me.

"Help me!" I cried, clutching at the air as I teetered backwards.

My mother reached for me, panic in her eyes, but then I was falling backwards, cartwheeling through the air until I....

...sat up in bed. Shards of grey daylight cut through the gaps in the curtain, dust moats caught within them. My face felt wet and warm. Touching my cheek with the tips of my fingers, I pulled them away to see the now familiar sight of blood. I felt woozy and sick as if I'd spent the night partying and now I was paying for it with a thumping hangover.

Climbing from my bed and heading to the bathroom, I couldn't help but notice the sense of urgency and panic my nightmare had left me feeling. Was the dream another premonition of what was going on in the world on the far side of the walls that surround the manor and its moat? Without a phone and no access to newspapers or television, I had no way of knowing. I thought of how similar a situation I'd found myself in while working in The Ragged Cove.

How does the same shit happen to the same girl twice? I wondered to myself.

Flushing the toilet, I took a flannel and washed away the blood that had leaked from my eye. But things didn't have to be like they had been for me in The Ragged Cove. The manor must have a T.V. and I wondered if Kayla had a mobile phone that I could borrow. I was no longer going to be a passive observer. The words of the man that had met up with Kayla kept going around and around in my mind and I wanted to know what it was that Kayla had to prepare herself for. But more than that, before the day was over, I was going to investigate the *'forbidden'* wing.

So after a quick shower, I changed into some fresh clothes and I made my way from my room. And that was another thing – *I am going to find out what that awful smell is!* I thought to myself as I passed down the stinky passageway.

In the great hall, I looked at the door which led to the kitchen, but where did the other doors lead to? What lay behind them? There must be a T.V. set or telephone in one of them. Heading in the opposite direction to the kitchen, I came to a double set of doors. Heaving them open, I went inside. Like most of the other rooms at the manor, it was huge, with a high ceiling that towered above me in a series of criss-crossing wooden beams. The floor was tiled, but huge rugs covered much of it. Along one of the walls was the centrepiece of the room. I'd never seen such a big fireplace – it looked as if you could've almost walked into it. Thick stone pillars stood on either side of it and along the top ran a marble shelf. I weaved my way between the luxurious-looking sofas and armchairs that were scattered about the room and headed towards the fireplace. All along the marble shelf were pictures and photographs, ornaments and candlesticks. I looked at the photographs in their silver frames and picked up one of the Hunt family. It couldn't have been taken that long ago because Kayla sat in the foreground in front of her parents and she looked pretty much identical to the way she looked now. Behind her and to her right was Lady Hunt and even in the picture, her beauty was startling. Then I studied the picture of her father. He was handsome, with thick jet-black hair swept back off his brow. It was longish and touching the collar of the white shirt he was wearing in the picture. He had the clearest green eyes I'd ever seen, full lips, and a square jaw line. But as I stared at the picture, there seemed something vaguely familiar about him. I was sure I'd never met him before but there was something; I just wasn't sure what.

"Can I help you?" Mrs. Payne's voice came from behind me.

Surprised at her sudden appearance, I nearly dropped the picture, sending it crashing to the floor. Placing it back onto the marble shelf, I turned to face her.

"What are you doing in here?" she asked, her beady eyes fixed on mine.

"Why? This isn't another area of the house that is *forbidden* is it?" I smiled.

"This is the family's private sitting room," she said. "Now if you would kindly -"

"I was looking for a T.V. set," I told her glancing about the room. Then, spying one of those big flat-screen T.V.'s sitting in the far corner, I crossed the room towards it.

"What do you want the T.V. for?" she asked, and I could hear her coming after me, her plain black shoes clacking against the tiled floor.

"To watch, of course," I said over my shoulder.

"It doesn't work!" she almost shouted at me.

"How come?" I asked, leaning forward and switching it on.

"The builders took the satellite dish down while they were repairing the house," she explained. "You won't be able to get a picture, I've tried."

Ignoring her, I pressed the 'ON' button. The screen flickered momentarily, then hissed with white snow.

"See, I told you so," the housekeeper said, snatching the T.V. controls from my hand and turning it off.

"What about a newspaper?" I snapped, placing my hands on my hips and staring at her. "Surely you must have a newspaper?"

"Never read them," she smiled. "Full of doom and gloom and a pack of lies, usually."

"A telephone?" I asked, doing everything in my power to control my ever increasing frustration. "This place must have a telephone?"

"We have several in fact," Mrs. Payne said.

"There's a *but* coming though, isn't there?" I said.

"It's the builders you see," she started. "They cut through the telephone cables -"

"And the electric cables and removed the satellite dish," I cut over her. "How convenient!" I shouted, storming from the room.

Mrs. Payne followed me, and quickly closed the living room door behind us.

Kayla appeared at the foot of the stairs and although she was dressed, she still looked half asleep. I wasn't surprised after her flying practice and secret meetings during the middle of the night. Crossing the hall towards her, I said, "Kayla, you must have a mobile phone that I can borrow?"

"Sure," she blinked at me and rubbed sleep from her eyes. "What's all the shouting about?"

"Ah, it's not important," I said, holding out my hand.

Kayla reached into the back pocket of her jeans and pulled out a mobile. "There you go," she smiled.

Snatching hold of the phone, I glanced at the housekeeper who had that knowing smile on her face. I looked at the screen and to my relief there was a full signal bar across the top of it.

Now that I had the phone in my hands, I couldn't think of one person to call. I couldn't remember Sparky's number and I didn't know his home number. He was my only contact with the outside world.

Come on Kiera – think of something! I screamed at myself inside. *You have your hands on a telephone now – make good use of it.* Then coming to my senses, I telephoned directory enquiries. I gave the operator Sparky's address.

Please don't be ex-directory! I prayed.

To my relief, the operator came back with Sparky's number. With my hands trembling, I entered his number into the phone and pressed the dial button. Holding it against my ear, I looked at Mrs. Payne as she hadn't been able to take her eyes off me. Kayla was now sitting on the bottom stair, yawning.

"Hello?" Sparky said from the other end of the line. To hear his voice made me want to jump in the air and start cheering.

"Sparky, it's me, Kiera," I said.

"Kiera!" he almost shouted down the phone. "Where in the hell are you?" I've been receiving your texts -"

"Sparky, I don't know how long I've got, I'm in a really remote place here so I don't know how long the signal will last," I gabbled down the phone at him. "What happened to my flat?"

"It's been badly trashed," he said. "Whoever did it has made a right mess, Kiera. I got scenes of crime to come round and -"

"Don't worry about that," I cut over him. "What I want to know is, have there been any problems on the London Underground?"

"What, with delays you mean?" he said, sounding confused. "I don't know, I mean London is like six hundred miles from Havensfield. Why would I know if there has been any disruption to the service -"

"I'm not talking about the bloody timetable!" I snapped, remembering why he was called Sparky. "Has there been, like, any major incidents? You know, like loads of unexplained deaths, rioting..."

"No, nothing like that," he said and his voice began to crackle on the other end of the line.

What I really wanted to ask him was had there been any sightings of vampires, but I didn't want to ask such a thing in front of Kayla and Mrs. Payne. So instead I said, "So there hasn't been anything out of the ordinary happening? You know, anything weird that can't be explained?"

"Well, there has been something," he said, his voice fading in and out.

With my heart starting to race, I said, "What is it, Sparky? What's happened?"

"Well, apart from the burglary at your flat – which really wasn't a burglary because I don't think anything was -"

"Just tell me, Sparky!" I shouted at him.

"Well, remember that old lady you helped?" he asked. "You know, the one who had her ring stolen?"

"Mrs. Lovelace?" I said, my heart getting quicker. "What about her?"

"Well her house got ransacked, too," he told me. "But worse than that, she's gone missing – like just disappeared off the face of the earth."

"But how...?" I mumbled, my confused mind trying to conjure up the right words.

"But it gets weirder, Kiera," Sparky continued. "Remember the guy who stole her ring – Evans?"

"Yes," I whispered.

"Well, he's gone missing too," he explained. "Not only that, remember the guy who owned the pawnbrokers? Well, he's gone missing and that doctor you used to see..."

"Keats," I said, filling in the blanks for him.

"Yeah, well she's gone – just vanished," he said, sounding bemused. "It's like anyone that you've come into contact with since returning from that creepy place you told me about has disappeared. Now you've gone missing and the police are wondering if you're not in some way involved. Kiera, they're looking for you – they've seen your flat and all the cuttings and newspapers. They found traces of blood in your bathroom and they think you've gone mad – they think you've…I don't know how to tell you this…but they think you've murdered them all. CID is even re-opening your mother's case, because she went missing too, didn't she?"

My brain felt as if it had been scrambled and I couldn't make sense of what he had told me. Then as if I'd been struck, I shouted down the phone at him, "Sparky, you're not safe – you've got to -"

"What do you mean I'm not safe?" he half-laughed down the phone at me.

"Don't you see, Sparky?" I said, my voice brimming with fear for him. "They're taking everyone that I've been in contact with since coming back from the Ragged -"

"Hang on a moment," he said, sounding far away. "There's someone at my door."

"No Sparky!" I screamed so loud down the phone that Kayla jumped up off the bottom stair and Mrs. Payne flinched. *"Don't open the door!"*

But the sound of the receiver clunking down onto the table in his hallway back in Havensfield told me that I was too late. Pressing the phone to the side of my head, I listened, but the line was so fussy and broken I couldn't hear what was happening. Then I had an idea. Turning on the speakerphone function, I held the phone towards Kayla.

"What can you hear?" I asked her, my voice and hand trembling.

"What?" she asked looking startled.

"Just Listen!" I hissed at her. "Tell me what you can hear!"

Kayla came towards me and lent her head towards the phone. She closed her eyes, and her face seemed to take on a calm and tranquil expression.

"Your friend is opening the door," she said. "There is a bolt and a lock with a key. He is turning it. His breathing is calm, but there are another two on the other side of the door. They are excited. I can hear their hearts – they're racing."

"Kayla, stop this at once!" Mrs. Payne shouted coming towards us.

Looking at her, I whispered, "Don't even think about it, lady!"

Seeing the grim expression on my face, the housekeeper skulked away.

"Your friend is opening the door, and he's saying 'Hello'," Kayla continued. " 'Are you John Miles?' one of them is asking. 'Yes' he says." Then Kayla stopped. Her eyes flickered open and she stared at me. I didn't need her to tell me that Sparky was screaming – I could hear it for myself. Then the phone line went dead.

Chapter Seventeen

I handed Kayla her phone, and slumped onto the bottom stair. What was I to do? For the first time that I could remember, I had no plan – I couldn't see a way forward. I couldn't *see* what to do. Pushing the mobile back into her pocket, Kayla came to sit next to me, wrapping her arm around my shoulder.

"I'm sorry, Kiera," she whispered.

"You don't have anything to be sorry for," I told her.

"I'm sorry for your friend."

"Me too."

"How about a nice cup of tea?" Mrs. Payne chipped in.

Glancing up at her, I could see that she felt as dumbfounded as we all did. I don't think any of us knew what to do or say after hearing Sparky scream like that. I guess we all felt helpless.

"A cuppa would be great," I smiled weakly at her.

"I'll be in the kitchen when you're ready," she said walking away, leaving Kayla and me on the stair alone.

"What's going on?" I said aloud, I don't know if I really meant for Kayla to have all the answers.

"What do you mean?" she asked.

I looked at Kayla and wanted to tell her I'd been watching her last night with that man. I wanted her to know what I'd heard them discussing together. But I couldn't, because it might cause her to distrust me, to become more secretive than she already was. But worse than that, she might warn her secret friend – tell him not to come back and then I might never know his identity. But there was other stuff, too. I wanted to know if Kayla was as suspicious of Marshal and James as I was. She had told her friend last night that she didn't like Marshal and I couldn't disagree with her about that. The guy was a creep – perhaps he spied on her too?

The whole set-up at the manor was wrong. But was Kayla a part of it? Did she know more than she was letting on? I didn't know who to trust or believe anymore. I'd made that mistake before – I'd put my trust in my friend Sergeant Phillips and it had nearly got me killed. For now, I would have to keep my suspicions to myself and unravel what was really going on at the manor in my own way.

"Do you know what?" I said, looking at Kayla.

"What?"

"Tell Mrs. Payne to put a hold on the tea, I'm going for a walk," I told her.

"Can I come?" she asked.

"I'm sorry Kayla, I just need some time on my own," I said heading for the door.

"Okay see you later alligator," she smiled at me.

Hearing those words, I froze. "What did you say?"

"I said, see you later, alligator," she said. "Is there a problem?"

"No. No problem," I half-smiled. "It's just that's the last thing I ever said to my mother before she disappeared." Then closing the door, I left the manor house.

It was cold, I tucked my hands into the pockets of my jeans and headed towards the tree line in the distance. I thought I would take the opportunity to go and have a look at the summerhouse in the daylight. It might give me a chance to clear my head and see what I could *see* there.

I followed the route that Kayla had taken the night before. Again, it was dark beneath the trees, and the air felt clammy and damp. It was so quiet and still that not even the branches or leaves stirred in the trees that towered above me. What was I to do about Sparky? What had happened to him and to the others that I'd had contact with. Had they gone missing or had...? I couldn't bring myself to think of the other possibility, but Sparky's screams sounded like his last. Shuddering at the thought, my skin turned cold. Should I contact the Police and give them what little information I had? But what information did I have?

I suspected that it was Phillips and Taylor who were behind what had happened to my friend and the others. But I was solely basing that on a series of nightmares that I'd had. Nightmares that I thought might perhaps be premonitions, but Sparky said that none of that other stuff had happened. Vampires hadn't gone berserk on the London Underground, feeding on everyone they came across. London didn't look like an apocalyptic wasteland with thousands of Vampyrus soaring through the sky and blocking out the sun. None of that had happened. But my flat had been turned over. I dreamt about that and Phillips had been responsible. But what did that prove? My superiors already thought I was nuts – they'd cart me straight off to the loony bin if I bowled straight into the nearest police station and started telling them about my nightmares. And besides, Sparky said that my colleagues suspected me of being involved with the disappearances of those people and possibly murder. If I showed my face at any police station I was bound to be arrested. What good would that do? No – I had more chance of finding out the truth of what was going on from the manor, not from a prison cell.

I knew that Luke, Potter, and Murphy had connections to the manor. Kayla had told me that her father had sent them in search of her when she'd gone missing in the past. Her father had known them. Perhaps that was what Lady Hunt was really doing – looking for the three of them? After all, she said that she already had enlisted help in search of her missing husband. Perhaps it was they who were helping her, and if so she might well return with them. The thought of seeing Luke again after all this time made my stomach flutter with anticipation and nerves. Would he feel the same way about me? Would my feelings be the same for him? There had definitely been a connection between us – but had those feelings been real? Had we not just been thrown together by circumstance? I knew deep down that I still had feelings for him – but what, I wasn't sure. I guessed I wouldn't really know until I saw him again and fell under his spell.

Reaching the clearing, I stepped out onto the grass and headed towards the summerhouse. In the light of the silver sun that hung above, it still looked magical. The small structure was white in colour and looked like somewhere a princess would live in a Disney film. Climbing the steps, I crossed the tiny porch to the door. Taking hold of the brass door handle and twisting it, I wasn't surprised to find it locked. Cupping my hands against the window, I peered inside. Just like it had been the night before, the room was in semi-darkness. The small wooden table sat in the centre of the room with two chairs placed on either side. The lamp was on the table. But then I noticed something I hadn't seen as I'd peered through the window the previous night. I wouldn't have because it was directly above the window I'd been peeking through. On the wall, just above the window, was the faded outline of where a crucifix had once been. It had left a mark against the wall similar to that when taking a painting down from where it had previously hung for many years. A clean patch had been left on the wall in the shape of a cross. But why had it been removed and by who?

I could see that it had only been taken down recently by the light colour of the wood left behind. Stepping away from the window, I made my way back down the steps and headed around the rear of the summerhouse. Leaning against the wall were three large cans and a pair of stepladders. Lifting one of the cans off the grass, I pulled open the lid with my fingernails. Looking inside I could see the traces of white paint in the bottom. Tucked behind the empty cans of paint, I found a large brush, its bristles stiff with dried paint.

Guessing that Marshal had probably recently given the summerhouse a new coat of paint, I placed the cans back where I'd found them and made my way back around the front of the summerhouse. Standing with my back to it, I looked left, then right. Heading right, I made my way from the summerhouse and headed in the direction that I'd seen Kayla's friend take the night before.

I made my way through the trees, leaving the summerhouse behind me. I'd been careful to enter the woods at the exact same point that I'd seen the male disappear the night before. Hunkering down, I scanned the ground for any tracks that he might have left behind. To my surprise I found several, and all of them different. I identified Kayla's friend's prints straightaway. It was easy to do so as it was only his that had ever ventured out from beneath the shadows of the trees, the other tracks stopped before leaving the clearing. Whoever these people were, on one occasion they had tiptoed away from the edge of the clearing and back into the dark. Then after inspecting the footprints left in the soil again, I slapped my forehead.

"How could you be so dumb, Kiera?" I whispered to myself. Whoever they'd been, they had run away – not tiptoed. The gap between each mark was too far apart for them to have been tiptoeing away. No, they had been running and fast, leaving only toe prints behind. But why? Who had they been running from?

Standing, I followed their tracks through the maze of trees. Ahead I could hear the rippling sound of the moat and realised I was heading towards the wall that surrounded the manor. I continued to follow the footprints left behind by Kayla's secret friend and whoever the other happened to be until they came to an abrupt end in front of a large bushy area that scaled the wall before me. Pulling the branches aside, I lurched backwards at finding a black iron door set into the ground. The last time I'd seen anything like it had been the grate in the floor at the police station in The Ragged Cove.

"A hatch to the hollows," I whispered, bending down to inspect it. There was a black metal ring pull and taking hold of it, I yanked as hard as I could. But like the summerhouse door, it was locked fast. Beneath the ring pull there was a lock.

"But where is the key?" I said, standing and brushing soil from the knees of my jeans. "And why are the Vampyrus coming in numbers from The Hollows, going only as far as the tree line surrounding the summerhouse then running away again?"

Covering the door with the brambles and bushes, I wondered where I might find the keys to the summerhouse and the door leading below ground.

"The gatehouse!" I said aloud, and palm-slapped my forehead again.

But that creep Marshal might be there. I could ask him what he was doing on my balcony last night. What did I have to lose, I thought to myself, heading for the gatehouse.

I walked for about ten minutes or so, when I came across a circle of weeping willows. Their branches hung so low that they made a curtain of leaves. Pulling them apart, I stepped into the circle and gasped. Hidden behind the branches was a small circular graveyard. There must have been sixty or so gravestones. Closing the gap on the branches behind me, I stepped slowly between the graves, looking down at the inscriptions written upon them.

In loving memory of Joshua Edwards
1704 – 1716

There was another, and the inscription upon this headstone read:

Karen Turner - Sadly missed
1833 – 1848

And another:

Richard Baker
Gone too soon
1927 – 1935

The dates on the graves spanned the centuries and the most recent I could find was dated from 2009. This one read:

Our precious Lucy
May your wings give you flight now
1996 – 2009

Standing in the centre of the tiny graveyard, gooseflesh ran up my back and the hairs at the nape of my neck stood on end. Although each of the gravestones and graves had been immaculately kept, and the whole setting hidden behind the branches of the weeping willows was tranquil and serene, I couldn't help but feel spooked. It was the dates carved into the blocks of grey stone that upset me so much. All of the people buried here hadn't lived passed the age of sixteen – they had all died as children.

Being careful not to stand on any of the graves that had been so tightly laid next to one another, I made my way out of the tiny surreal graveyard and back into the woods. Closing the branches over just how I'd found them, and my heart aching for all those poor children, I couldn't help but wonder why they had all died so young. And of what? Why be buried here, hidden away in the grounds of Hallowed Manor?

With my heart feeling like a lump of stone in my chest, I made my way towards the gatehouse.

Chapter Eighteen

Passing the front gate to the manor, I could see that the drawbridge was up. Glancing through the iron bars of the gate, I could just make out the moat. The water looked dark and choppy. I wondered how deep it was, and whether my phone lay at the bottom of it. In the distance I could just see the sun setting low over the moors and it looked like a thin strip of silver ribbon on the horizon.

Turning away, I crossed the wide, gravelled drive and approached the door to the gatehouse. It was a single story building constructed out of black slate, with a thatched roof that looked as if it could do with some urgent repairs before winter arrived. There was a stone chimney and a column of black smoke spiralled up into the sky. The door was made of wood, which had faded almost to grey and was warped at the bottom. Clenching my fist, I rapped on the door with my knuckles. There was no answer or sound from inside.

"Marshal?" I called out, knocking on the door again.

Nothing.

Looking over my shoulder at the manor way off in the distance, I gently pushed the door with my shoulder and to my surprise, it swung open. Making sure that I wasn't being watched, I slipped inside, closing the door behind me. There was one main room, and two smaller ones that led off it. One of these was a kitchen and the other, a poky-looking bathroom. Making sure that the gatehouse was deserted I said, "Marshal, are you here?"

The only sound was a fire snapping and crackling in the fireplace that was set into the wall. Crossing the room, I held my hands out and warmed them over the flames. Peering around the room, I could see that it was sparsely furnished with a worn-out sofa that had the stuffing sticking out of it like a string of spongy guts. There was a small cabinet and on this there was a lamp which hadn't yet been lit, even though the day had been grey and overcast. There was a table which was cluttered with what looked like nothing more than junk. Turning my back on the fireplace, I began to rummage around the stuff that had been strewn across the table. Snatching my hand away almost at once, I grimaced at the dirty bandages that had been left there. Picking up a pair of scissors which lay amongst the mess, I used them to turn the bandages over. Apart from being grey and dirty looking, I could see no signs of blood on them. But there was something. Holding the bandage towards the light from the fire, I used the scissors like a pair of tweezers to remove several hairs that seemed to be stuck to it. The hairs, if that's what they were, appeared to be made of some man-made fibre, similar to acrylic.

Placing these fibres on the table, I inspected the bandage again and noticed that parts of it were covered in a yellow gum that had crystallised. Turning-up my nose, I sniffed the filthy-looking bandage. The yellow crystals smelt of solvent – like some kind of glue. Putting the bandage to one side, I rummaged through the other clutter on the table and found a small bottle of liquid latex. Turing it over in my hands I read the label on the front.

Great for Halloween make-ups
Scare all your friends!

Beneath the writing there was a picture of some kid whose face had been covered in a load of fake scares and cuts.

"What the hell is going on here?" I whispered to myself. Placing the bottle back on the table, I found a false beard and a small bottle of Spirit gum to attach it with and a case containing blue-coloured contact lenses. Looking around the room in disbelief, I noticed what appeared to be a dead snake hanging from the back of the front door. Snatching it from the hook it had been hung from, I inspected it. The snake was nothing more than a woman's stocking that had been stuffed with torn-up pieces of cloth and knotted at both ends. Realising what it had been used for, I slung it over my shoulder and tied both ends of the stocking beneath my arm. Looking back over my shoulder, it appeared that I now had a hump. If I covered it with a jacket and lent forward, anyone would believe that I had a twisted spine – just like Marshal was supposed to have.

Taking off the fake hump, I looked at the make-up, fake beard, and contact lenses and knew that Marshal – if that really was his name – was trying to hide his true identity. But why? Who was really hiding beneath that disguise? And what did they have to hide?

Then I remembered what Kayla had told me yesterday as we sat on the wall together. Kayla said she had once met Luke and that his face was disfigured. It had looked scarred as if he had been in some kind of accident.

"Marshal is Luke!" I said aloud as if I'd just struck gold. Realising who Marshal really was, I didn't know if I should feel angry or relieved. But everything seemed to be fitting into place. He had tricked me into coming to the manor so he could protect me – that's why he was on my balcony – he had come to make sure that I was safe. Then wanting to kick myself for not seeing it before, I said aloud, "That's how he disappeared so quickly – he flew from my balcony!"

But why the disguise? I wondered. Then I thought again about his disfigurement. Perhaps he wasn't ready for me to see him like that. Did he really believe that I would be so shallow as to run from him? Be scared by him? There was only one way to find out his true reasons and that was to ask him.

"What are you doing in here," a gruff-sounding voice said from behind me.

Spinning around, I gasped as I saw Marshal standing in the open doorway. He stood, stooped slightly forward, one blue eye staring back at me from behind the grubby bandages.
With my heart racing in my chest, I said, "You don't have to hide from me any longer."

"I don't know what you're talking about, copper" he said back in that gruff voice.

Moving slowly towards him, I trembled and said, "I don't care what you look like under those bandages. You're still the same person that I met in The Ragged Cove."

Holding his hand out as if to stop me from coming any closer, he turned his head away and said, "Don't come near me."

Taking his hands in mine, I could feel that they weren't the hands of a workman – they were strong – but soft. He almost seemed to flinch at my touch. So wrapping my arm about his shoulder, I pulled him close to me and said, "I've missed you."
Then gently turning his head to face me, I leant forward and kissed him gently on the mouth. My heart was racing so hard and fast, I wondered whether Kayla could hear it in her room back at the manor.

He didn't respond to my first kiss, so I kissed him again, this time allowing my lips to linger over his. Then without warning, he was kissing me back, his strong arms wrapping themselves around me and pulling me against him. He smothered my lips with his and just like the kiss we had shared outside the Crescent Moon Inn all those months ago, they were frenzied – almost hungry. I matched his keenness, entwining my fingers in his hair as he ran his hands down my back. Without our mouths parting, he eased me down onto the crumpled sofa and ran his hands up my legs where they came to rest on my hips.

Being with him like this released all those feelings that I'd bottled up since leaving The Ragged Cove. It was like we had never been apart. And like they had been in the Cove, my feelings and senses seemed to be ablaze when with him. He kissed my face and neck, his hands running over me and pulling at my clothes. In an attempt to match his passion, I wanted to kiss his face, I wanted to show him however scarred or disfigured he may be under those bandages, I didn't care – my feelings wouldn't change for him. So working the tips of my fingers through the hair at the nape of his neck, I found the knot that held his mask together, and pulled it free. The bandage fell away, revealing his face beneath it. Staring wide eyed up at him, I screamed, "Oh my god! You disgusting pig!"

Chapter Nineteen

"Easy, tiger!" Potter smiled down at me.

Swiping at him with my hand, I tried to slap his face. I couldn't believe who I'd been kissing. But he was too quick for me, and had taken hold of my wrist in his hand. "Don't get so excited!"

"*Excited!*" I screamed, pushing him off me with my knees. "I'm not excited! You disgust me!"

"Could've fooled me," he said, standing by the table and tugging fake bits of beard from his cheeks. "You couldn't keep your hands off me a minute ago."

"That's because I thought you were someone else!" I roared at him, straightening my hair and clothes. "I should arrest you for indecent assault!"

"Indecent assault? Me?" he said with mock surprise on his face. "It was *you* who assaulted *me!* You threw yourself at me! You couldn't tear your lips off me!"

"You took advantage of the situation," I hissed. "You knew that I must have thought you to be somebody else. But oh no, you just had to be a jerk – you just couldn't resist -"

"Don't flatter yourself, sweet-cheeks!" he scowled.

"Don't call me that!" I hollered. "My name's Kiera!"

"Oh, I'm sorry *Kiera*," he said.

"Why do you have to make things so difficult for me?" I said, trying to get a grip of my anger.

"Difficult for you?" he said, sounding genuinely surprised. "Do you have the faintest idea how difficult it's been for me, skulking around this place night and day with bandages wrapped around my face and a pair of stockings stuffed up my jacket?"

"Don't you go blaming me for that," I snapped at him. "And why have you been disguised as the hunchback on Notre Dame ever since I got here?" Before he had a chance to answer, I added, "And that's another thing – why were you spying on me through my bedroom window the other night?"

"Making sure that you were safe – that's what this whole goddamn thing has been about!" he said, pulling out the stocking from beneath his long dark coat and throwing it down onto the table with the rest of his disguise. "And what thanks do I get, huh? I thought you were kissing me out of gratitude for saving your bacon."

"Saving me from what?" I asked.

"That's another thing," he said ignoring my question and removing something from his eye. "These contact lenses hurt like a bitch and then there's the cigarettes. I haven't been able to smoke since you got here."

"I haven't stopped you from smo -" I started.

"Oh no?" he sneered, pulling a packet of cigarettes from his pocket and lighting one up. "Knowing what you're like, the slightest sign of a discarded cigarette butt and you would've been crawling around on your hands and knees trying to figure out how tall the smoker was, how old he was, what zodiac sign he was, whether he'd taken a crap that morning, and Christ knows what else."

"So why put yourself through all of this for me if it's been such a nightmare for you?" I said.

"Why don't you ask *him*?" Potter said, pointing over my shoulder and blowing smoke through his nostrils. "He's the brains of the operation, sweet-cheeks."

Spinning round I saw James sitting in his wheelchair by the open door to the gatehouse. He looked at me from behind his tinted glasses, then at Potter. "I don't believe you Potter," he growled.

"Don't start having a moan at me, Sarge," he said. "She already had it figured out."

Looking at the chauffeur sitting in the wheelchair, I said, "Sergeant Murphy – I might have known. I guess you couldn't have walked around as I would have noticed your limp? But I'd already figured out you could walk."

Taking off his cap, glasses and pulling away his fake bushy sideburns, he sprang out of the wheelchair and said, "You mean I've been trundling around here for the last few weeks like that guy out of the X-Men and you knew it was me all the time?"

"I didn't know it was you, Sarge, but I figured out last night that you could walk," I told him.

"How?" he said, staring at me.

"Don't wear shoes that are clearly scuffed on the soles and covered in gravel dust and earth," I smiled at him.

"Oh great," Potter sighed in disbelief. "All this sneaking around and you go and blow it because -"

"I needed to take a leak, okay?' Murphy snapped. "You try wheeling yourself around this place – it aint easy you know! I was only out of my chair for a couple of minutes – long enough to sneak into some bushes and take a whiz. Anyway, you can't talk. What was with all the bandages? 'I said a beard, and a few scars and stuff,' and you end up looking like the invisible bleeding-man!"

"You try putting this crap on everyday – it ain't easy you know!" Potter snapped, waving the bottle of liquid latex under Murphy's nose. "I didn't think you would be back so soon the other night. There I was sticking on the beard and you arrive at the drawbridge with sweet-cheeks. What was I meant to do? I wasn't in character – so I grabbed the nearest thing that came to hand and covered my face with it. Got a problem with that?"

"Yeah, I got a problem with it," Murphy barked, pulling the last of the fake white whiskers from his chin.

"At least I came up with a fake name," Potter snapped back. "I mean Marshal's a cool name. What did you come up with? James! That's your real name for Christ's sake!"

"My name's Jim!"

"Whatever!" Potter said. "I'm glad she's found out. I was getting bored of all this sneaking around."

I looked at the pair of them and said, "You couple of amateurs. Call yourselves cops."

"Listen here, tiger," Potter hissed, "we had everything under control until you came in here and threw yourself at me."

"Threw herself at you?" Murphy said, looking and sounding confused.

"I thought he was Luke," I told Murphy. "Not for a second did I think it was Lon Chaney standing over there."

"Lon Chaney?" Potter said, confused. "Who in the bloody hell is Lon Chaney?"

Ignoring him, I turned to Murphy and said, "Where's Luke?"

Looking in my eyes, Murphy said, "He's not in a good way."

"Where is he?" I said.

"The burns didn't heal as well as we might have wanted them to," Murphy sighed.

"Where is he?" I said again. "I want to see him."

"He doesn't want to see you," Murphy said, coming close with that awkward limp that he had.

"Why not?"

"He's very badly burnt," Murphy explained. "He doesn't want you to see him like that."

"I thought the girls all loved a guy with a scar," Potter laughed.

"Put a sock in it, Potter," Murphy growled without looking at him.

"*Please* tell me where he is?" I said, my voice softening. "I just want to see him. I don't care what Luke looks like. It doesn't matter to me."

"Ain't that sweet," Potter smiled.

"I won't tell you again, Potter," Murphy said over his shoulder. "I promised him, I wouldn't say -"

"He's in the forbidden wing, isn't he?" I asked.

"Where?" Potter scoffed.

"The wing of the house that Mrs. Payne has forbidden me to enter," I said, staring at Murphy and then at Potter. "That's who you've been taking food to, isn't it?"

Before Potter could confirm or deny my accusation, Murphy turned on him, and chucking his tinted glasses across the room, he shouted, "I can't trust you to do anything without screwing up!"

"Don't you go blaming me for this!" Potter moaned. "It wasn't me who wanted to bring her here. I told you she would only go poking her nose around -"

"Look, I'm not interested in whose fault this is," I cut in. "I just want to see Luke."

Then from the doorway someone said, "I don't believe what I'm seeing!"

Turning, the three of us looked towards the open doorway of the gatehouse to find Kayla standing there.

"What you doing here?" I asked her, not knowing how long she'd been listening to our conversation.

"I thought you were my friend, Kiera," she said, sounding angry.

"I am," I told her, feeling confused.

"So why have you been keeping secrets from me?" she seethed. "Why have you been spying on me with them?"

"I don't understand," I said, going towards her.

"Those are the two guys who came looking for me when I ran away. The ones I told you about," she said. "And all the time they've been disguised as my mother's chauffeur and handyman, when really, she's had them down here watching me – *spying* on me - and you've known about it all along!"

"No Kayla," I said, reaching for her. "You don't understand."

Pushing my hand away she looked at me and I could see the hurt in her eyes. I could *see* that she thought I had in some way betrayed her. "I understand, Kiera. Everything I've shared with you – everything I've shown you – told you – you've been secretly telling them."

"I haven't," I insisted. "I promise you, Kayla. It's not what it looks like."

"They work for my mother and so do you," she said, her voice flat, just simmering with anger and hurt. "Why have they been in disguise if they haven't been here spying on me? I trusted you, Kiera, I really trusted you."

Before I had the chance to explain, she was gone, running back across the grounds to the manor. I went to go after her, but Murphy gripped my arm and pulled me back.

"Leave her be for now," he said. "She's confused and angry at the moment and not in the right frame of mind to listen or understand what you have to tell her."

"What is it I have to tell her?" I said, eyeing him.

"I'll let Luke explain," he said. "It will sound better coming from him."

"What will?" I asked.

"He's in the 'forbidden wing' as you like to call it," Murphy said. "First room on the right." I turned to go and as I did, he pulled me back again and said just above a whisper, "Nothing will be the same for you, Kiera, after you see what's in the forbidden wing."

Turning away, I started back towards the manor and as I did, Potter called after me and said, "Don't worry, sweet-cheeks, I won't tell Luke how happy you were to see me again. It will be our secret."

Jerk! I thought as I headed into the darkness.

Chapter Twenty

Taking a candle from the table in the enormous hall, I made my way to the foot of the stairs and began to climb. Knowing that Luke hid above in the darkness made me want to run up them, but another part of me wanted to hold back. Murphy's warning that nothing would ever be the same for me made me nervous. Why would everything be different for me after my visit to the 'forbidden' wing? What secrets could it possibly be hiding? And if those secrets were so bad, what was Luke doing hiding amongst them? Biting my lower lip, I continued to climb.

Reaching the landing where the staircase split left and right, I turned and shone the light from my candle up into the darkness at the top of the right-hand staircase. Even with the candle flame flickering before me, it did nothing to penetrate the blackness that lurked at the top of the stairs like a monstrous fog. Taking a deep breath, I started to climb. The stairs seemed to go on forever, each step taking me further away from the world below. With my heart racing in my chest like a trip hammer, and my stomach somersaulting, I stepped onto the landing. With my arm outstretched, I stared into the wall of blackness ahead of me.

Then there was a brilliant flash of white light and I closed my eyes. Those flashbulbs popped on and off inside my head like a thousand cameras and in those sparks of light, I could see the twisted shapes of people cowering in the darkness ahead of me, their bodies bent out of shape as if not properly formed. But these visions didn't scare me or make me want to run. The sight of these hideous creatures overwhelmed me with sadness. I wanted to seek them out in the darkness and tell them that everything would be alright – that I would save them. But who and what were they – they looked half human and half…

As soon as they had come they had gone again – those flashbulbs blinking out and leaving me to the blackness that clung to the walls on either side of me. Brushing the tips of my fingers against the wall to feel my way, I was aware of that tacky substance that coated the walls. Then my hand brushed against something cold, and at first I just wanted to snatch my hand away. But after shining my candle in that direction, I could see that I had come across a big brass door handle. The door that it was attached to was white – nondescript – and if what Murphy had told me was true, than Luke was hiding behind it. Against the wall next to the door was a chair and on it was a silver tray. Casting my candle over it, I could see the remains of a half-eaten fried egg sandwich. Remembering back to The Ragged Cove and how I had first spotted egg on Luke's tie, I smiled to myself. In my mind's eye, I could see him standing in the front office at the police station, his thick black hair dripping rainwater all over his coat, his boyish grin and those green eyes staring at me. As I remembered him, he looked almost kind of vulnerable. But then I thought of him racing through the night sky, his sturdy arms gripping me, his naked chest cold like iron against me, and he didn't seem vulnerable at all – he was like a god. Twisting the door handle, I pushed the door open.

If I thought the passageway was dark, then the room was a vast open hole of blackness that seemed to reach out and grab for me. With the candle shaking in my hand, I stepped into the room.

"Luke?" I whispered, a slight tremor in my voice.

Then there was movement in the darkness, the light from my candle just catching a fleeting glimpse of something that darted across the room in front of me.

"Luke, is that you?" How I hated that wavering sound in the back of my throat.

The sound of movement came again, but this time from behind. Spinning around so fast that my candle almost flickered out, I could see that the door to the room had now been closed.

"Luke?" I whispered again.

"Why have you come here?" a voice said from within the darkness. Even though I couldn't see him, I knew that the voice belonged to Luke.

"From what Murphy and that clown Potter told me, you guys brought *me* here," I said into the darkness. "You didn't really think that you could all keep this pretence up, did you? It was only going to be a matter of time before I figured out what -"

"I mean, why have you come to this room?" his voice came again from the blackness, and it sounded almost angry.

"They told me you were hiding here," I told him. "And I wanted to see you, Luke."

"I don't want to see you," he said, his voice almost a growl which made me want to cringe away from it.

"What are you scared of?" I said, trying to keep my voice even.

"I'm scared of nothing!" he snapped.

"You're scared of me seeing you," I told him, taking a step closer to his voice.

Sensing my movement, Luke shouted, "Keep away from me, Kiera!'

"I can't," I said, moving closer still. "I haven't been able to stop thinking about you since leaving The Ragged Cove. My life isn't too good either at the moment if I'm to be honest. I became obsessed with finding you – that's all I thought about. Night and day I watched the news for any reports that might suggest you had come up from The Hollows. My flat looks like a frigging newspaper, it's covered with so many -"

"Go away, Kiera," his voice broke over mine. "Forget about me and don't come back."

"Then why bring me here?" And it was my turn to sound angry.

"To protect you – to keep you safe while we deal with -" he started.

"Deal with what?" I demanded. "I'm part of this, Luke; don't you think I know that? I've changed since the Cove. I have nightmares almost every night, I wake up crying blood and I *see* things. You're not the only one who's suffering. But I figure you're too wrapped up in your own self-pity to see that!" Then with my candle held out before me I raced back towards the door. Just as my fingers curled around its cold handle, I felt a hand reach out of the darkness and grip my shoulder.

"What do you *see*?" he whispered, his breath hot against my ear.

"Terrible things," I whispered back, not turning to face him. "I've seen the world overrun with…"

"*What?*" he hissed.

"Vampire bats," I said. *"Vampyrus."*

Then, slowly, I turned to face him, and however much I tried, I couldn't hide the gasp of air that slipped from my lips as I looked at his face in the candlelight. The left half of his face was waxy and taut-looking, like Clingfilm that had been stretched too tight. His skin was pale, but the side of his face that had been burnt looked blue and purple – the colour of a ripe bruise. His left eyebrow had been burnt permanently away, and his left ear looked twisted and melted out of shape. My heart ached to see Luke like this.

"Scare you, do I?" he said, and his voice sounded almost resentful – bitter.

"No," I said, pulling him close, hoping this would show that I didn't fear him. "This is all my fault. If you hadn't put your own life at risk to save mine -"

Then, placing one finger over my lips, he told me to hush. "You're not to blame for this," he said, his voice now softening, and I guessed that he must have felt some relief that I hadn't run screaming into the darkness to be away from him.

"Why have you been hiding away up here from me?" I asked, pulling him so close that my cheek rested against his bare chest. "Were you afraid that I would be scared of you – not want to be with you?"

"Some of that is true," he said, holding me tight against him. "But there are other reasons that I've been hiding – why we've all been hiding out at the Hallowed Manor."

"Why?" I asked.

Then, leading me into the darkest corner of the room and sitting me down on a narrow bed that was concealed there, he said, "We're all being hunted and they won't stop until we're all dead."

Chapter Twenty-One

Luke took a lantern from a small table beside the bed and lit it. A milky-yellow light glowed, throwing long, deep shadows up the walls of the bare room. The floor was wooden and the boards looked rough and unvarnished. The walls were cracked and in some places, the plaster had fallen away, revealing the brickwork beneath it. Cobwebs hung from the corners of the room like dusty-looking chandeliers and I wondered how Luke had managed to hide away in such a place for so long. The room creeped me out and I shifted closer to him on the edge of the bed.

In the light from the lantern, I had a clearer view of Luke and his injuries. Apart from the burns on his face, his left shoulder was also marred by a long scar that ran from just under his chin, down his neck and across his chest. Like the burn on his face, the skin looked stretched and pulled out of shape as if someone had poured boiling wax over him. With a trembling hand, I gently reached out and stroked his chest with the tips of my fingers. He flinched and I snapped my hand away.

"Sorry," I whispered. "Does it hurt?"

"No," he said. "I just worry that you will be repulsed by me."

Without saying anything, I placed my hand against his scars. Looking into his sea-green eyes, I could feel his heart thumping away inside of him. "How could I ever be repulsed…scared of you?" I asked. "You got these scars saving me and I can never forget that…or repay you."

Taking my hand, he removed it from his chest, bought it up to his mouth and kissed it. "You don't have to repay me anything," he said, staring into my eyes. He then added, "I haven't saved you yet."

"You said we were all being hunted?" I asked him. "I guess you're talking about Phillips and Taylor."

"Not just them," he whispered as if someone might be eavesdropping. "There is another."

"Who?"

Then placing his head in his hands, he looked ahead and into the darkness. I couldn't ever recall Luke looking so demoralised. I remembered him to be strong and confident but now he just looked beaten and I guessed it wasn't just his disfigurements that troubled him.

Running my hand down the curve of his spine, I said, "What is it, Luke? Tell me what's happened."

In a low, soft voice he said, "As you know, after leaving The Ragged Cove, Sergeant Murphy and Potter took me below ground – back to The Hollows. We stayed amongst our own while I rested and tried to heal. But word spread amongst the Vampyrus about what had happened above ground. It became common knowledge that we had killed Rom and Roland."

"But they were killers," I whispered, tracing small circles with my fingernails across his naked back.

"An emergency meeting was called by the elders of our race in the Great Caverns," he explained. "Vampyrus came from every part of The Hollows. For as far as the eye could see, the caverns were packed tight with Vampyrus, never before in our history had there been such a huge gathering."

"But why now?" I asked him.

"It has been feared for some time that some of the Vampyrus had been unhappy living beneath humans and some of them wanted more. No longer was it enough that they could come above ground and make a life for themselves amongst humans as long as they returned when the hunger was upon them. It wasn't that the elders particularly cared for the human race; they just didn't want attention drawn to our existence. The elders feared that if humans ever discovered us, they would come in search of us – that they would invade The Hollows, and just like they have done above ground, deplete our world of all its natural resources which would eventually result in the Vampyrus' extinction. So a compromise had been made – Vampyrus could live above ground only if they didn't draw attention to themselves and the rest of our race. The elders hoped that this would placate those Vampyrus who wanted more," he explained.

Then turning to look at me, he continued, "But as you know, Kiera, Rom and his kind wanted more. They wanted to live above ground, as true Vampyrus. They believed they were better than humans. So that's why the Sarge, Potter, and me were sent to hunt them. But our mission was to locate them, to gather evidence and report back. It was the elders who were to make the final decision as to their fate – but as you know, it didn't work out that way. As far as the elders are concerned, we took the Vampyrus law into our own hands and in doing so, we risked drawing attention to ourselves and the rest of our race."

"But they were killing people!" I said. "Rom and his merry men were creating vampires – *monsters!* If that isn't drawing attention to your race, I don't know what is!"

"It wasn't just that," Luke said, looking back into the darkness as if somewhere lurking within it were the answers. "Rom, Roland, Taylor, and Phillips are just the front men. Behind them in the shadows is another. He pulls the strings of those that want more."

"Who is this Vampyrus?" I asked.

"Nobody knows his identity." Luke whispered, again as if almost fearing that he might be overheard. "He hides behind his puppets – those who do his dirty work. They go before him, clearing a path. They brainwash and recruit other Vampyrus, telling them that their lives could be so much more above ground if we didn't keep our identities a secret – if we revealed our true selves to the human race. But whoever he is, he is responsible for everything that is turning bad within The Hollows. Every crime that is committed, from murder to robbery, if you look deeply enough, he will be lurking in the background."

"Can't he be stopped?" I asked.

"How can we stop him if we don't know who he is?" Luke said with a tinge of bitterness in his voice. "Assassins have been sent before to infiltrate his organisation but they have each been rooted out and killed. No one has ever got close to him – not close enough to discover his identity. But word got back to the elders via spies that Rom, Roland, Taylor, and Phillips were his four most trusted disciples and we had killed two of them and left the others close to death. Discovering this, he had marked us…issued a death warrant against the Sarge, Potter, and me. Word spread like fire that anyone who shielded us, anyone who offered us shelter, would be dead, too. So fearing that we had brought war and unrest to The Hollows, the elders offered a deal of peace to this faceless and nameless monster."

"So what was this peace offering?" I asked.

135

"We were," Luke said, and his shoulders shuddered in the gloom. "They banished us from The Hollows – the elders and our race washed their hands of us in an attempt to pacify this monster."

"So you can never go back?" I said, shocked by what he had just told me.

"Never," Luke said, his voice sounding broken. "We had to leave then and there. We had no choice. We weren't even allowed to say goodbye to our friends. It wasn't so bad for Potter – he didn't really have anyone. If you hadn't already noticed, he doesn't seem to make friends that easily."

"What about you?" I asked, placing my arm about his shoulder. Cocking his head, he looked into my eyes and said, "I was the lucky one. The person I love lives above ground, Kiera." To hear this and see the intensity of his stare made butterflies swoop about in my stomach. But before I'd the chance to respond to what he'd said, he continued.

"I came above ground too soon, my wounds hadn't healed properly. I can't stand the daylight at all, and to be uncovered in it for a moment makes my skin smoke and blister until it feels raw. My wings are still in tatters and flying is difficult."

"Will it always be this way?" I asked him, my heart aching.

"As long as I keep out of the sun and in near darkness, the scars will eventually heal. That's why this part of the manor is covered in tarpaulin," he explained. "For the first few days, we hid above ground by travelling at night and sleeping the days away in cheap hotel rooms. But the Sarge, Potter. and me soon realised we were being pursued by the agents of the man that had issued our death warrants."

"How did you know?" I asked him.

"In the towns that we left behind, we heard that there had been reports of people being mauled by animals. The Sarge and Potter went to investigate one day, while I rested in the darkness of some hotel room. The authorities believed that the victims had been killed by animals but Murphy and Potter knew better, they could see the signs."

"Signs?"

"Most people killed by animals don't usually spring from their graves a few days later," he said with a grim smile on his face.

"There were Vampyrus behind us and they were feeding and creating vampires in their wake. So one night, when the moon was out and the air was cool, we went in search of these Vampyrus. You could say that the hunters became the hunted that night. Potter was really pumped up. I'd never seen him so agitated. I think he was craving for blood and not being able to go below ground, the flesh of his own kind was going to have to be good enough. There were two of them and we tracked them to a car parked at the rear of a bar. They waited in the shadows for the bar to close for the night and the last of the staff to leave. We waited in the treetops of a nearby park and waited for the hunters to strike. And we didn't have to wait long. I was glad that the wait was short because Potter had begun to twitch and shake with hunger.

" 'C'mon, show yourselves!' " he kept saying over and over. " 'Let's just get this over with.'

"Then we saw her, this petite barmaid locking the door to the bar behind her and stepping out across the desolate car park. Before she even had a chance to reach her car, the hunters had raced in a blur of shadows and were upon her. But just as quick, Potter had raced across the sky and before I'd the chance to blink he had pulled the girl free of her attackers. The Sarge was close behind her, snatching her away and laying her on the ground. With my wings still tattered and torn, I leapt from the tree and see-sawed towards the unconscious barmaid. Making sure that she was okay, I carried her to her car. Finding the keys in her bag, I laid her on the backseat of the car, out of harm's way.

"Turning away from the car, I watched as Potter tore apart one of the assassins sent to kill us. He showed no mercy. I'd never seen Potter like that before. His arms seemed to be pumping up and down in a blur as he pulled away chunks of the hunter beneath him. Then he set about his face with his teeth and in seconds it would have been hard to believe that the creature had ever had a head, let alone a face. With thick lumps of flesh and sinew swinging from his chin, he turned, looking for the other assassin.

"Murphy had hold of him. The assassin was knelt forward, his head cast low like someone about to be beheaded. Potter strode towards him, his thirst for blood still not quenched.

" 'What do you want from us?' Potter roared into the face of the hunter. 'Is it not enough that we have been banished from The Hollows?'

"The kneeling man made no reply, but Potter wouldn't let up.

" 'Tell me what you want?' he screamed, his face only inches from that of the assassin. Again he kept his head bowed and said nothing.

"Then completely freaking out, I watched Potter grab the assassin by the hair and drag him across the car park to the remains of his partner. Leaning in close, so as only the assassin could hear, Potter said something. I don't know what it was, but the assassin began to scream and beg for his life. And as he sobbed like a baby, I heard him say a name that sent a chill down my spine," Luke said.

"Whose name was it?" I asked Luke.
Looking at me, his eyes gleaming like cat's eyes in the gloom, he said, 'Kiera Hudson.' It was your name that he said."

"But why me?" I asked, gooseflesh scampering up my spine. "What did they want with me?"

Ignoring my question, Luke said, "Murphy and me watched as Potter tortured a confession out of the assassin. It wasn't nice to see and I was shocked at Potter's sheer brutality, but he got the assassin to tell him that Taylor and Phillips were coming for you."

"But why?" I asked, and again Luke ignored my question.

Staring into the darkness in the corner of the room, Luke said, "Once Potter had all the information that he was going to get, he ripped the assassin to pieces. Murphy and me were stunned by the sheer ferocity and speed of his attack. Within seconds he had beheaded the Vampyrus sent to kill us, and had his head buried in his chest cavity like a wild dog and eating as if he were ravenous.

" 'We've got to get him some help,' Murphy said to me just above a whisper. 'If we don't, it won't be long before he's attacking humans to satisfy his hunger. Vampyrus blood won't keep him going for long.'

"I argued with Murphy, Kiera," Luke said. "I wanted to come straight to Havensfield and get you. But the Sarge said that we should stay together, not split up. I was still weak and with Potter being driven insane by his hunger, Murphy said we should go into hiding – we wouldn't be able to help you if we weren't keeping it together ourselves," Luke explained.

"So what did you do?" I asked him.

"We came here," he said. "Murphy had some connection to Lord Hunt. They had grown up together in the same part of The Hollows. But Lord and Lady Hunt were reluctant to help us. The news about our banishment from The Hollows had seeped above ground. And knowing that a threat of death had been made to anyone that helped us, they really just wanted to get rid of us. But Murphy spoke to Michael Hunt in private and whatever it was they discussed, he agreed to let us stay, but on the understanding that we helped him."

"How?" I said, wondering what agreement had been made between them.

"His daughter Kayla had gone missing, so in return for sanctuary, Murphy and Potter agreed to track her and bring her home. I was too weak to go and would only have slowed them down. So it was decided that I would hide out in this wing of the house," Luke explained, and he said it as if he'd let his friends down in some way.

"But what about Potter and his thirst?" I asked. "Come to think of it, how are you all coping?"

"Did Lady Hunt tell you what her husband did as a job?" Luke asked me.

"She said he owned a company that was developing renewable genetics," I told him. "But I'm guessing now that that was a lie?"

"Kind of," Luke half-smiled, as if being caught out.

"What then?"

"He was a chemist – a bit like a doctor really. He was working on renewable genetics of a sort. He was developing a synthetic blood that would ease the cravings for human blood." Luke explained. "But it would only have been a temporary substitute if for any reason a Vampyrus couldn't get below ground. The plan was for each of the Vampyrus to carry around a small bottle of the stuff they could use in case of an emergency. Like if you were on a flight that got delayed and you were forty-thousand feet above ground when the cravings started. Instead of feeding on the flight crew and other passengers, the synthetic blood was to hold back the thirst. A bit like giving a heroin addict methadone. It's not the real thing, but it's meant to help for a while. Hunt called it Lot 13."

"And does it?" I asked, wondering how his cravings were doing.

"Does it what?" he asked.

"Help?"

"Yes," he smiled. "You're safe with me. It doesn't totally get rid of the thirst but it helps – it becomes manageable."

"So what about me?" I asked him.

"Sorry?" he said.

"You never answered my question."

"What question was that?" he said, looking away from me again.

"Why were Taylor and Phillips coming after me?"

Luke didn't say anything, he just looked ahead.

Grabbing him by the shoulder and forcing him to look at me, I said, "They've taken, or worse…*killed* anyone that I've had contact with since returning from The Ragged Cove. Some of these people were my friends and they've suffered because of me. I think I have a right to know why I'm being hunted!"

Standing, Luke took me by the hands and said, "Kiera, come with me and I'll show you."

Chapter Twenty-Two

Picking up the lantern, Luke led me from the room where he had been hiding for so long. In the passageway, he turned right, leading me away from the landing and further into the darkness. Even with the lamp held before him, the passageway was dark and suffocating. Being with Luke did nothing to ease the creepiness that I felt.

"Watch your step," Luke whispered over his shoulder as he led me up a narrow staircase. Reaching out with my hand, I brushed the wall for balance. Again, I could feel that sticky, tacky substance on the walls and its smell became almost overpowering as we climbed.

"What is that sticky stuff on the walls?" I asked him. "It stinks."

"Oh, that," he said over his shoulder. "I've gotten used to it. I don't even notice it now."

"Lucky you," I muttered. "But what is it?"

"It's a mixture of garlic and queets, which is a herb only found in The Hollows. Lord Hunt discovered that when the two are mixed together it forms a powerful paste that sends vampires completely nuts. They hate the stuff – won't come anywhere near it."

"But why is it all over the walls?"

"Hunt had every wall, door, and window frame coated with the stuff," he explained. "Should vampires ever get past the moat and into the grounds, then it's a final layer of protection from them."

"What's so special about the moat?" I asked. "It doesn't even look that deep."

"The water's blessed – holy water if you like," he said, and his voiced echoed back down the staircase. "It acts like a ring of steel around the entire manor. The vampires would never be able to cross it."

"Why did Lord Hunt fear an attack from vampires" I asked. "What was he trying to protect?"

Reaching the top of the stairs, Luke stopped outside a door and looking at me from the darkness, he said, "This is what he was trying to protect." Pushing open the door, Luke stepped inside.

I followed him into a vast room, which I guessed was somewhere hidden inside the roof of the giant manor. There were no windows that I could see and the room was lit by many tall candles that had been fixed into silver-coloured candlesticks. There were so many that the light filled the room with a dim orange glow. As I peered around the room, my stomach began to tighten as I saw what looked like several hospital beds running down each side of the room. Beside the beds stood machines that blinked on and off in the gloom. They buzzed and beeped and luminous green monitor screens cast eerie shadows up the walls.

"'What's -?" I started.

"Shhh," Luke whispered placing a finger against his lips.

Leading me down the aisle between the two rows of beds, I counted ten in all, and in each one, to my continuing dismay, I could see a child. Each of them was connected in some way to the machines that stood beside them. Tubes and wires coiled from their nostrils, arms, and fingertips which all fed back into the monitors and strange looking apparatus. Peering through the candlelight at them, I could see that there was a mixture of boys and girls and I guessed they were aged between thirteen years and sixteen years old.

I couldn't remain silent any longer; I had to know what these children were doing, hidden in this makeshift hospital, in the attic of the manor. "What's going on here?" I asked Luke. "Who are these children?"

Luke just looked back at me, and I could see sadness in his eyes. Then from the shadows in the far corner of the room, a voice said, "They are half-breeds, Kiera."

Peering into the gloom, I saw a figure walk from out of the darkness and towards us. As he stepped into the candlelight, I knew at once that he was the doctor who tried to remove the black bony fingers from Kayla. He looked just how she'd described him. He did look like an owl. He wore blue scrubs and latex surgical gloves. His forearms were muscular and covered in so much white hair, that he would have made a polar bear envious.

"My name is Doctor Ravenwood," he smiled and pushed his glasses back onto the bridge of his nose. His voice was deep, but somehow gentle – *caring*. His tone of voice was like all doctors, who had bad news to break to you.

"Half-breeds?" I said, feeling a little startled at his sudden appearance.

"Yes, I'm afraid," he replied, looking at the children lying in their beds. "It's a problem that arises when Vampyrus and humans produce children together."

'Like Kayla?" I asked, reminding myself of how her father had been a Vampyrus and her mother human.

"Yes," he said, looking at Luke, then back at me. "Kayla has told you then?"

"She showed me her wings," I told him. "Kayla told me how you tried to remove them – to stop them growing."

"That's right," Doctor Ravenwood said.

"And these others," I said looking at the children stretched out in their beds, "they are like Kayla?"

"Yes," he smiled weakly, "but with a difference."

"And what's that?" I asked, glancing at Luke, who was standing with his head bowed and looking at the floor.

"She is only one of the few who has managed to live past the age of sixteen," Ravenwood started to explain. "You see, for years – hundreds of years, the Vampyrus have been coming above ground and living in secrecy amongst -"

"She knows all this," Luke cut in, without looking up from the floor.

Ignoring him, the doctor continued. "Anyway, some of the Vampyrus fell into relationships with humans – most of these humans were totally unaware of their lover's true identity. They were naive to the fact that they were in love with and sharing their lives with a breed of vampire bat. Some even married and they had lives that to the world seemed normal. But these relationships were far from normal. They were marriages between two entirely different species. Fortunately, at first, it seemed that those Vampyrus and humans couldn't have produced children. But over the centuries, some females of the two species gave birth and children were born out of these unions. It was a terrible tragedy as these children were born hideously mutated and they lived very short, and tragic lives. Relationships between Vampyrus and humans was therefore forbidden by the elders of our race, but like any forbidden fruit, some find its taste too hard to resist. So over the years these relationships have continued in secrecy and more children...*half-breeds,* have been born."

"The graveyard," I whispered aloud over the doctor.

"I'm sorry?" he said, looking put out that I'd interrupted him. "What did you say?"

"I found a graveyard in the grounds of the manor," I told him. "They were all graves of children – they were the children born out of these relationships that you speak about."

"That's correct," Ravenwood said, very matter-of-factly.

"But some of them lived to the age of sixteen years," I gasped. "You said that they died at a very early age."

Then looking at the rows of beds in the makeshift hospital, Ravenwood said, "As you can see, Kiera, some live longer lives – but there have ever only been three that have grown past the age of sixteen. We do our best to make those who live longer comfortable."

"Comfortable?" I sighed, looking at the figures sleeping all around me. I went to the foot of one of the beds and stared down at the girl who lay on it. She was about fourteen years old and curled on her side. The girl had long blond hair that curled down the length of her back. But between her golden locks I could see a series of black bones sticky out like a rack of ribs. Turning away, I looked at the boy in the bed next to her. He was about sixteen and with his eyes closed, he looked so peaceful. Tubes ran from each of his nostrils and into some type of breathing apparatus beside the bed. The machine made a wheezing sound as it helped him to breathe. The boy's skin was as pale as chalk and had a translucent appearance, and as I stared harder through the candlelight at him, I could see his heart beating beneath his chest. I could see his veins and arteries, his bones and muscles. It was as if I were looking at a human-shaped jellyfish. The sight of him didn't scare or repulse me, it just made me feel incredibly sad for him – for all them.

"Wouldn't they be better off in The Hollows?" I asked Doctor Ravenwood.

"Oh no," he said, coming to stand beside me at the foot of the boy's bed. "We can't take them home. Remember the relationships that these children were born out of are forbidden. Oh no, that wouldn't do at all."

"So what?" I snapped, "You just sit and wait for them to die?"

Looking at me over the rims of his glasses, Ravenwood said, "We are not ruthless, uncaring creatures, Kiera. Even though these children aren't truly Vampyrus – we still want to look after them – to cure them."

"Cure?" I said. "What, make them human again?"

Shaking his head at me, the doctor said, "They will never be truly human or Vampyrus – they are what they are – half-breeds. But that doesn't mean they have to die young, to not live out their lives and realise their true potential – whatever that maybe."

"You said, *we*, who's we?" I asked him. "You and who else are trying to cure these children?"

"Lord Hunt, of course," he said.

"And how are you planning on achieving this cure?"

Pulling the latex gloves from his hands and rolling them into a ball, he looked across the room at Luke, then back at me. "We discovered it by chance. It was after I removed the piece of bone from Kayla's back. We had been wondering why it was that Kayla had grown past the age of sixteen with very few physical problems. It wasn't until she reached that age that she started to show any physical changes at all. To the outside world, she looks just like any other sixteen-year-old human female."

I thought of how Kayla had been called *'stickleback'* by the other girls at her school and wondered if Ravenwood was just deluding himself. Apart from the children lying in the hospital beds, I'd never seen another sixteen-year-old with wings. But then again wasn't that the point that Ravenwood was trying to make – no other half-breed had lived past the age of sixteen.

"We wondered whether the cure lie in Kayla's DNA." The doctor continued. "So after carefully abstracting the marrow from the piece of bone from Kayla's back, Lord Hunt injected it into Alice over there," and he pointed to a girl lying in a bed at the furthest end of the ward. Ravenwood made his way to the foot of her bed and I followed him, all the while, Luke remained silent.

"See her wings?" Ravenwood asked me, pointing at the girl on the bed. It was difficult to see exactly how old she was, as she was lying on her front, her face turned against the pillow. Out of her back hung two long black wings and just like Kayla's, they were jet-black and covered in a fine, sparkly substance which looked very much like glitter.

"They look okay to me," I told him.

Then taking hold of the tip of Alice's wing, it crumbled into a black ash between his fingers. Rubbing the dust from his hands, I watched as the wing reformed where it had only moments ago broken away beneath Ravenwood's touch. "Six months ago, every bone in her body reacted in the same way," he explained. "You only had to brush up against her and her arm would break, her leg would snap, or her ribcage splinter. But after Lord Hunt injected the DNA taken from the bone in Kayla's back into Alice, her bones began to harden – to solidify. They no longer break now when touched, but it's her wings. As you can see, they are still brittle. If she were conscious, Alice would have been in unbearable pain as her wings had crumbled."

"So why doesn't it work?" I asked him.

Looking at me, his eyes almost seeming to shimmer behind his glasses, Ravenwood said, "Remember I said that only a few of these half-breeds had managed to live past the age of sixteen years?"

"Yes,'" I said, nodding.

"Well, Lord Hunt was of the belief that the extracts of DNA from those three survivors would hold the key to a cure," the doctor said.

"Do you know who these three are?"

"Kayla is one, of course," he said. "Another is an eighteen-year-old boy named Isidor Smith."

"And where is he?" I asked.

"He has been very hard to find – but we have managed to locate him. We don't know if this Isidor Smith knows what he is," Ravenwood said.

"A half-breed, you mean?"

"Exactly," he continued. "But we should know soon enough – Lady Hunt has gone to…how can I put this? *Persuade* him to come home with her."

"Like she did to me?" I said, trying to hide the resentment that I felt about being tricked by Lady Hunt. "So who is the third of these surviving half-breed?"

Taking his glasses from the tip of his nose and cleaning the lenses on the hem of his scrubs, he looked at me and said, "For someone who has the ability to *see*, Kiera, you don't *see* very much at all."

"See what?" I asked, the muscle in my stomach beginning to tighten.

"Can't you see the real reason that Lady Hunt got you to come and stay here?" he asked, pushing the glasses back onto his nose.

Feeling numb, I shook my head at him. "She brought me here so Luke and my friends could protect me from Taylor and Phillips."

"And why do you think you would need their protection?" Ravenwood asked.

"Because…because…" I started, but my mind seemed frazzled – confused. Then I remembered what Taylor had said to me in St. Mary's graveyard back in The Ragged Cove. Taylor had told me that I was *unique*! "No!" I whispered backing away from Doctor Ravenwood.

"Yes, Kiera," he said coming towards me. "You are one of the three who can save these children. You are a *half-breed*."

Chapter Twenty-Three

"It's not true!" I snapped, turning on my heels to look at Luke. I was hoping that he would tell me that it wasn't and that there had been some mistake. But he just stared back at me, and again I could see that sadness in his eyes. Running across the ward, I gripped him by the shoulders and said, "Please Luke, tell me that it isn't true!"

Casting his eyes down as if he were unable to look at me, he whispered, "I'm so sorry Kiera."

Letting go of him, I turned, and facing the doctor, I said, "It's not true. I refuse to believe it. My parents were human."

"One of them was," Ravenwood said and his voice had that tone again – the one that told bad news. "Your mother was one of us. She was a Vampyrus."

"Liar!" I roared at him.

"It's true," Luke said from behind me. "Your mother was a vampire bat."

"And how long have you known this?" I hissed, turning on him with tears in my eyes. "You didn't think of telling me this before?"

"I didn't know," he said, coming towards me. "Honestly – I didn't know, Kiera."

"So, how long *have* you known?" I asked, tears now spilling onto my cheeks.

"When I returned back to The Hollows," he said. "The elders told me."

"So where is she now?" I demanded.

"I don't know," he said. "All I know is that Phillips took her like he took Lord Hunt."

"But why?" I snivelled.

"Why do you think, Kiera?" Ravenwood said, coming to stand by my side. "Your mother, Lord Hunt, and Isidor Smith's father are the only Vampyrus who have produced children with humans that have lived past adolescence. Whoever it is that Taylor and Phillips work for, he is the one who believes the parents hold the answer. But he is wrong – we tested Lord Hunt's DNA on the half-breeds and it had no positive results whatsoever. He has realised his mistake now and is therefore in search of their offspring."

"But why?" I said, wiping the tears from my cheeks with the back of my hands. "What possible use could we have? From what Luke has told me about this Vampyrus – he doesn't sound like he would be interested in curing anyone – or any *thing*."

"Cure is not what he seeks," Luke said, placing a hand on my shoulder. "He is interested in your power."

"Power?" I asked. "What power?"

"Kiera, you have the gift of *seeing*, Kayla the gift of hearing, and we've heard that Isidor has the power of smell," Ravenwood said.

"I don't understand," I told him, every fibre of my being feeling alive and on fire.

"Kiera – you've been having nightmares right? But they're more than nightmares – they've become visions. Tell me what you see," he said, fixing his eyes on mine.

Pulling my arms tight around me, I said, "Vampyrus taking over London. Killing passengers on the underground, creating vampires that then feed on humans that, in turn, become vampires until…"

"Until what?" Ravenwood asked me, his voice sounding stern.

"Until there are no humans left," I breathed. "But I saw hundreds…thousands of Vampyrus sweeping over London. There were so many that their wings blocked out the sun."

"What you see, Kiera, is the future…what might happen," Ravenwood explained. "Those Vampyrus you see could very well be an army sent by the elders to protect the human race – to fight alongside them – but that we don't know. The future is not yet set, we have a chance of changing it."

"Kiera, we don't have time to waste – the future of the human race and the Vampyrus balances on a knife's edge," Luke said. "A few days ago, a Vampyrus went crazy on an inbound flight into the UK. At forty-thousand feet, he tore through the plane, gorging himself on the crew and passengers – each one of them becoming a vampire. We can't be sure, but we believe that this Vampyrus' aim was to land a plane at Heathrow, full of bloodletting vampires which would then overrun the airport, sending vampires swarming through London. But the pilot fought back by ditching the plane into the sea, killing all on board before they reached London."

"I saw that on the news," I told him, "the day that Lady Hunt came to visit. So do the government…the authorities know what is going on?"

"The plane has yet to be recovered," Luke said, "So no – they are not aware. But we fear it may only be a matter of time before our existence is known to the wider world. We have people in place – Vampyrus that have worked their way over the years into positions of power within governments around the world, but they will only be able to bury so much of the truth. And if your nightmares are visions of what is yet to come, then it won't be long before those corrupted Vampyrus like Taylor and Phillips start attacking major cities across the globe."

"But I still don't understand how I will be of use to *this* Vampyrus?" I asked, still feeling numbed and confused by everything that I was hearing. "How will I be able to help him?"

Folding his white hair-covered arms across his chest, Ravenwood looked at me and said, "Imagine having an ally that could see into the future – predict what your enemy was going to do next. Someone who can see through darkness – see what others fail to *see*."

I thought back to how I'd seen into the darkness in the crypt beneath St. Mary's church in The Ragged Cove. But that had only happened once. "But it's not a precise thing that I can do," I told Ravenwood. "It's very hit-and-miss."

"Your gift is still developing," he told me. "But you must realise that your abilities are getting stronger each day. You have more and more of these visions – you *see* more. It will only be a matter of time before you have complete control over your gift."

"But my eye, it bleeds – I pass out," I told him.

"That's just a symptom of your developing powers," Ravenwood said. "That will soon pass as you become accustomed to your power."

"But what about Kayla and this other one…Isidor Smith? What do they bring to the party?" I asked him.

"Just like you, Kiera, can you imagine what an asset Kayla would be to our enemy? You could send her forward to spy. From behind closed doors, outside buildings, from miles away she would be able to hear them plotting. To listen in as they planned their next strike – their next move. From great distances she would be able to know from which direction the enemy approaches, their numbers, and the fear in their hearts. Isidor, with his sense of smell, would be able to track the enemy – never lose their scent – hunt them down until they could run no more. Imagine, Kiera, having an army with such gifts – they would be invincible."

"An army?" I asked, raising my eyebrows. "There are only the three of us."

"You don't really think that once our enemy understood what it was that was so special about your DNA, what made you so unique, that he wouldn't use that on the other half-breeds who had been born?" Ravenwood asked me. "Even if they were born sick and feeble like the ones you see in this room, he would be able to heal them like we plan to do and who knows what powers they might have."

"But why do the half-breeds have the potential to be so much greater than a Vampyrus?" I asked the doctor.

"We don't know, is the honest answer," he said scratching his white wiry hair. "It must be something to do with when the two sets of DNA come together. We know that other species of bat have undeveloped eyesight and there are many myths that bats are, in fact, blind. This is untrue – some bats can even see ultraviolet light. So perhaps when human DNA and Vampyrus DNA is thrown into the mix together, it creates an enhanced ability of sight. We know that some bats hear in sonar, and others have an incredible sense of smell – perhaps these abilities are greatly magnified when the two species mix."

"Like some potent cocktail?" I said.

"Perhaps," he said, flashing a thin smile at me.

Then looking at both Luke and Ravenwood, I said, "But even if this were all true and I was some freaky half-breed, Phillips, Taylor, and whoever it is they work for seem to be forgetting that there is no way on Earth that I will betray my own race and fight alongside them."

Then staring at me, Ravenwood said, "You seem to be forgetting two things, Kiera."

"And what are they?" I asked, cocking my head at him.

"You don't actually have a race that you belong to. Secondly, they have the best bargaining tool that your enemy could ever want."

"Which is?"

"They have your mother," he replied with a grim smile. "And the fathers of Kayla and Isidor. I think they'll be able to make the three of you do anything that they want you to do."

With my heart sinking in my chest and wanting to throw-up, I said, "And *you* seem to be forgetting, I don't actually believe any of this shit." Then pointing to the children lying asleep in their beds, I added, "I'm nothing like them, or Kayla. I mean look at me, I don't have wings!"

Taking me by the hand, Luke whispered, "Let us show you."

Following behind Doctor Ravenwood, Luke led me into the shadows in the far corner of the room. Hidden in the darkness was a doorway. Pushing it open, Ravenwood ushered us into a small room at the far end of the ward. The room consisted of a desk that was littered with pieces of paper which were covered with equations and handwritten notes. There were files and medical instruments that I had never seen the likes of before. In the corner, there was an examination couch, and attached to the walls were several x-ray negatives of limbs and I guessed they were pictures of the insides of the kids sleeping in the ward.

Taking a clunky-looking camera from the desk, Ravenwood looked at me and said, "Kiera, take off your top and go lay face-down on the couch over there."

"I'm sorry?" I said, pulling my top tightly about me.

Seeing that I looked uncomfortable at his sudden request, he said, "It's okay, Kiera, I'm a doctor. I just want to examine your back."

"Why?" I said, looking across the room at Luke as he might also have the answer.

"I want to prove to you one way or another that you are a half-breed," Ravenwood said.

"How?"

"With this," he said, holding the huge camera. It looked like something that they would have used in the early nineteen-hundreds. The front of it appeared to have a long protruding lens which stuck out like an accordion, and it had handles on either side. As I looked closer at it, I could see that it wasn't made of plastic or metal, but wood.

"What's that?" I asked him.

"A camera of sorts," he smiled. "You have nothing to fear, Kiera. I'm sure your friend Luke will be watching out for you."

Looking towards Luke again, he nodded and said, "It'll be okay, I wouldn't let anyone hurt you. I promise."

Believing in him, I went to the couch and began to unbutton my shirt. Glancing up at Luke, I asked, "Do you mind?"

Smiling to himself, he turned his back. Once my shirt was off, I climbed onto the couch and laid on my front. Ravenwood came towards me, with the camera-type contraption in his hands.

"This might feel a bit cold," he warned, placing the end of the machine between my shoulder blades. He then very gently moved it down the length of my back to the base of my spine, then up again around both sides of my ribcage. The end of the device did feel ice-cold and I felt the skin on my back tighten with goose bumps.

"Put your shirt back on. I'm all done," he said.

Climbing off the couch, I threw my shirt back on. "You can turn around now," I told Luke. He looked at me and he still had that boyish grin tugging at his lips. "You're so juvenile," I tutted.

Ravenwood placed the camera-thing on his desk and flipped a switch on the side of it. The machine made a purring noise as a cone of brilliant white light shone from the lens. The light shone against the wall and I looked at it. It was like watching an old black and white movie. At first, the moving picture seemed blurred and out of focus. Ravenwood adjusted a few dials on the side of the device and the image on the wall sharpened. And as it did, I could see that it was some sort of x-ray of my spine and ribcage. The camera, or whatever it was, had recorded my insides and was now playing the images back onto the wall. But as I studied the images, I could see that my spine and ribcage looked different – different from pictures that I had seen in human anatomy books. I had way too many bones and there was shading over my lungs.

"That can't be me," I gasped.

Ignoring me, Ravenwood went to the wall and taking a pen from the pocket of his scrubs, he pointed at the images being played out. "This is amazing," he said, and I could sense the excitement in his voice. "I've never seen such a developed set of wings that have yet to break through the skin." Then, jabbing at the wall with the tip of his pen, he said, "Look Luke, can you see the humerus? And look! There's the radius and ulna. The bones are perfectly formed."

"I don't believe it," I trembled, those tears standing in my eyes again. "I would know if I had all those extra bones in me. They would be heavy. I would know that they were there."

"Not necessarily," the doctor said, not being able to take his eyes from the weird-looking x-ray. "You've always had these bones inside you, Kiera. Why would you feel any different? It's all you've ever known. And besides, these bones aren't heavy – they're mostly hollow – you know, to be able to help you fly better."

Pointing at the wall I said, "What are those dark patches over my lungs?"

"Oh that's just the patagium," he beamed.

"In English," I said, tears now running down my cheeks again.

"Your wings, Kiera – that's what they are! My god –this is amazing!" he shouted.

"Well, I'm glad that you think so," I started to sob, holding myself tightly. "But I don't want to be some freaky-flying-rodent. I just want to be human."

Turning on me, totally unaware of my distress, he said with excitement, "Actually bats are more closely related to humans than they are to mice or rats."

"If that's meant to make me feel any better, it doesn't," I said, choking on my tears. "I don't want this! I don't want *any* of this!"

Seeing that I was growing more and more distraught with each passing second, Luke came towards me and snaked his arm around my waist. "Get off of me," I screamed, pushing his arm away. "Don't touch me!"

"Kiera..." he started, but I didn't let him finish whatever it was he was going to say. I just wanted to get out of that room, away from those black and white pictures of my insides. The thought of having black leathery-looking wings hidden beneath my skin made me want to puke. I couldn't bear the thought of it. Part of me wanted to tear myself open and pull those disgusting things out of me. I couldn't even begin to comprehend what all of this meant. The thought of not actually being human but some freaky half-breed made me feel almost insane.

Why hadn't my father told me? I screamed inside. *Had he even known that my mother was a Vampyrus? And why hadn't my mother told me?* I couldn't help but feel an overwhelming sense of hatred for her. *How could she have done this to me?*

Trying again to comfort me, Luke put his hand on my shoulder. Shoving it off, I stood-up. "I hate the Vampyrus," I hissed at him. "I wish I'd never met you Luke Bishop. I hate you!" Leaving him looking stunned and hurt, I ran from the room.

Chapter Twenty-Four

"Kiera!" Luke shouted as he chased me across the ward and down the stone stairs to the passageway. It was dark, and with tears blurring my vision, I stumbled up the passageway. I just wanted to get out of the manor.

"Kiera, hold-up!" Luke hollered, the light from his lantern splashing up the sticky walls of the passageway. Then I felt his cold hand grip my shoulder and spin me around.

"Get off me!" I screamed, struggling against him. But he was too strong and pulled me against him. Luke held me tight against his chest and stroked my hair as if to sooth me.

"Please just let me go Luke," I sobbed into his chest. "I just want to be away from here."

"Running away won't help," he whispered in my ear.

"Please," I cried.

"Where are you going to run to?" he hushed. "Home? You can't go back there, they are looking for you. You'll be safe here – I'll protect you."

"I don't..." I snivelled, unable to finish my sentence.

Pushing open the door to his room, Luke guided me inside and closed the door behind him. Leading me over to the bed, he sat me down then placed the lantern on the table. "I know this has been a shock for you," he started.

"A shock?" I scoffed. "You've got no idea."

"Then tell me," he said. "Tell me what you're feeling, Kiera."

"Why?" I hissed. "What's the point? I've had enough of being analysed over the last six months to last me a life time."

"I want to help you, Kiera," he soothed.

"I don't need your help. I can take care of myself!" I shouted.

Then taking my hands in his, he looked at me and said, "But I need you, Kiera."

"Really?" I said, not wanting to sound sarcastic – but I know I did.

"You told me that you loved me once, remember?" he said, gently squeezing my fingers against his.

"That was a long time ago," I said, looking down so as not to make eye contact with him.

"So your feelings have changed for me then?" and he sounded kind of hurt.

"That's the problem, Luke, I don't know how I feel anymore," and this time I did look at him.

Taking my face in his hands, he brushed my tears from my cheeks with his fingers. "I'm here for you, Kiera. I can help you with this," he said. "You don't have to go through this alone. I know what you're feeling."

"But that's just it," I whispered, "you can't possibly know how I'm feeling. I'm not a Vampyrus, I'm not even *human* – so what does that make me?"

"Something very special," he said, and his voice sounded soft and gentle in the darkness.

"A freak more like," I said back.

"No, *special*, Kiera," he said, stroking the hair that fell against my face. "You have the ability of doing something wonderful now."

"Like what?"

"You could save all those children up on that ward and any others that come after them," he said. "None of them may need to suffer anymore."

"Yeah, but I could also be their nightmare," I told him.

"How do you figure that?"

"Well, if what Doctor Ravenwood says is true, then once cured they could be at risk of being hunted down by Taylor and Phillips and whoever it is that they work for, and be used to destroy the human race," I told him.

"And that's why it's so important that you don't leave this place," Luke said. "This manor is like a fortress, it is protected against vampires."

"But what if Taylor and Phillips come here – what if they bring others?" I asked.

"They don't know that we are here," he explained, "another reason for Murphy's and Potter's disguises. Not even the housekeeper knows who they are – she doesn't even know that I'm here."

"Does Mrs. Payne know about the children hidden away in the attic?" I asked.

"Yes, she's always known about them, but she is kept away," Luke said.

"What about Kayla, does she know?"

"No, she was stopped from coming up here since she was quite small as far as I've been told. What with all the tarpaulin and scaffolding, she just believes that this part of the manor has fallen into disrepair," he said.

"But if Kayla knew that there were others like her, it might make her feel not so alone. She's struggling to come to terms with what she is," I told him.

Then pulling me close so that our faces were just inches apart, Luke said, "She doesn't have to feel alone anymore, she has you, Kiera – you can help each other."

"I doubt I'll be of much support – I don't understand what's happening myself – let alone try and make sense of it for her," I said. "Ravenwood has just told me that I've got wings hidden inside of me – so how does that exactly work? I mean will they just suddenly pop out one day while I'm waiting in line in the supermarket? It could be embarrassing."

Smiling, Luke said, "I never quite thought of it like that. I don't know when they will unfold from inside you. It could be today, tomorrow, next week, next year, or never for all I know."

"But it's the thought of those little black fingers wriggling about inside of me – it's disgusting," I said and shivered at the thought of them.

"These you mean?" Luke said, standing up. Rolling his shoulders back, I heard the unmistakable sound of his skin rippling and stretching and then a flutter as his wings unfolded from inside him. Stretching his arms out on either side, his wings hung down beside him. In the glow of the lantern, I could see what Luke had meant when he said his wings were still damaged from the fire.

They hung limp and tattered looking from his back, whereas I had remembered them to be taut and powerful-looking. At the tip of each wing, I could see those three black bony fingers. Luke looked at me and as he did, the fingers opened and closed as if trying to clutch at the air.

"Come close," he said smiling, making the middle finger at the tip of his right wing curl like a question mark and beckon me forwards.

Standing, I went to him, wringing my hands before me.

"They're just like having another pair of hands," he explained.

"Two hands are enough," I said moving closer still, not taking my eyes off the bony black fingers that wriggled back and forth.

"You weren't like this before, back in The Ragged Cove," he said.

"That's before I found out I had a set of my own curled around my ribcage," I cringed.

"Touch them," he smiled. "Go on – they don't bite."

Raising my hand, I leant forward, and as I did, I could see that the fingers swivelled on what looked like a wrist. The fingers were long and pointed, with sharp nails capping each end.

"They're more like claws than hands," Luke explained. "In fact, the bones in a bat wing are very much like that of the bones in the human arm."

"That doesn't make me feel any better," I told him. "I'm not meant to be human, remember?" Then with my fingertips millimetres from the claw, it reached out and grabbed my hand. I tried to jerk my hand away, but the black bony fingers were strong and held my hand fast.

"Don't panic," Luke laughed. "I'm not going to hurt you – I promise. I just want you to see that what you have inside you isn't so bad. It's not something to be scared of."

Looking into his eyes, then back at the claw that had hold of my hand, I started to relax. Despite how they looked, the skin covering them actually felt soft, just like the flesh covering my own hands. The nails, though, were hard and yellow, like ivory. If mine turned out looking like that, I'd have to do something with them. Give them a trim at least.

Luke relaxed his grip, and the claw released my hand. "See," he smiled. "They're not so bad, are they?"

"I guess not," I said, inspecting his wings. "Will these repair themselves?"

"Eventually," he told me. "As long as I stay out of the light and keep hidden away in the dark, they will heal."

"How much longer will you have to stay hidden away up here?" I asked him.

"I don't know. But each day I start to feel a little stronger," he said, folding his arms around my shoulders and pulling me against him. "But my situation doesn't seem so bad now."

"Oh, and why is that?" I asked, looking up into his face, which glowed pale in the light from the lantern. In the semi-darkness, the scars that covered the left side of his face seemed less defined, as if they weren't there at all.

"Because I have you," he said, leaning forward and kissing me gently on the mouth.

As his lips touched mine, images of Potter came racing to the front of my mind. I pushed those memories of being kissed by him away but it was harder to ignore the warm sensation in my stomach that those images brought with them. Closing my eyes, I refused to think of how Potter had kissed me with such force and passion and those butterflies ebbed away.

Luke must have sensed my hesitation in kissing him back, and whispered, "What's wrong?"

"It's nothing," I said, then kissed him.

At once, I felt those overpowering sensations that I had felt in The Ragged Cove and it was like no time had passed since last being together. Luke ran his hands through my hair and pulled me closer still. I could feel the hardness of his chest against mine and his skin felt cool like marble. He ran his hands down the length of my back, and in my mind's eye, I could see Potter's hands all over me like they had only a few hours before. Screwing my eyes shut, I pushed those memories of Potter away again, and kissed Luke with more passion.

Steering me towards the bed in the corner, Luke laid me gently down, blowing out the lantern. In the darkness, I felt him climb onto the bed beside me. Brushing my long black hair from my face, he covered my ears, cheeks, nose, and lips with the softest of kisses. In that moment, it was like all my fears and worries were swept away. My whole being began to tingle, and with every touch of his, my skin felt as if it were alive. Why my feelings felt so intense and exaggerated when I was with Luke, I didn't know, but the feelings that he stirred within me were overwhelming. *Electrifying with Potter,* a voice said inside my head and I told that voice to shut up and go away.

I could feel Luke's fingers working at the buttons on my top, and the warm breath that came from his mouth made my flesh tingle. I kissed him, and with the tips of my fingers, I caressed the scars on his face, and traced them down his chest and back. I arched my back so Luke could remove my shirt and his wings felt soft like feathers against me. The feel of them made me shudder. Wrapping my hands around his neck, I pulled him down onto me, my lips searching for his mouth. He kissed me back, and for the first time that night, I felt his sharpened teeth nip at my lower lip as his passion heightened. Then, working his mouth down my neck, his lips lingered and I felt his body go tense. His lips closed over my throat forming a tight seal. I could feel the pointed ends of his front teeth scratching against the skin just below my jaw line. His whole body shuddered, his back arched and his wings fanned out on either side of him.

Before I knew what was happening, Luke pierced the flesh on my neck with his teeth. His body locked as if in some sort of a spasm, and he growled in the back of his throat. Fearing that he was going to bite me, I pushed him off with my knees and he staggered to the other side of the room.

"What's wrong with you?" I gasped, blindly reaching for the lantern in the darkness.

"I'm sorry, Kiera," he said, and his voice sounded different – deeper somehow. "I don't want to hurt you."

"Hurt me?" I said confused. Then finding the lantern, I tried to turn it on.

"Don't turn on the light!" he growled.

But it was too late, I'd already found the tiny dial on the side of the lantern that raised the light. Holding the lantern out before me, I swayed it around the room in search of Luke. Then I saw him, huddled in the far corner, his knees drawn up against his chest and his wings folded around him. Getting up from the bed, I started across the room towards him.

"Luke?" I said. "What's wrong? I thought you were going to bite me."

"I was! So don't come over here, Kiera," he warned.

"But I've already told you, you don't scare me," I tried to reassure him.

"I don't want you seeing me like this," he groaned.

"I thought we'd got over all of that?" I said, half-joking.

Standing over him, I hunkered down and pulled back the wing that was pulled around him. Then all at once, those black fingers snatched hold of my wrist and yanked my hand away, but in doing so, his wing opened and I saw the face that stared back at me from behind it. Stumbling backwards in shock, I fell onto my arse and sat staring at him.

"Go away!" he roared so loudly that I flinched backwards and away from him. Not only did Luke have fangs, but his mouth was full of razor sharp teeth. His eyes shone fierce green, and his ears had twisted into points and his nose had turned up into something similar to a snout. Bristly black hair had sprouted from his face, but there was a white-coloured patch of skin shining through where he had been previously burnt.

"What's happened to you?" I gasped, pushing myself back across the floor and away from him.

"I need blood," he groaned as if in pain. "Human blood - and I can't go back to The Hollows."

"But I thought you said that Hunt and Ravenwood had come up with a synthetic…" I started.

"Lot 13," he gasped. "But it just doesn't quite hit the spot. Being so close to you like that – I could smell the human part of you surging through your veins. It was wonderful – you have no idea how *wonderful*."

"What can I do to help?" I asked him.

"Just stay over there," he said gesturing with his hand and I noticed that it was also covered with thick wiry black hair, which glistened in the light from the lantern that now lay on the floor.

"What's happened to you?" I said, my voice wobbling.

"This is what I look like – my true self when living in The Hollows," he said. "I'm a vampire bat, remember?"

"So Murphy, Potter and all of the other Vampyrus look just as you do in The Hollows?" I asked him.

"More or less," Luke said and winced as if in pain.

Then the sudden realisation that I too was half Vampyrus made my head spin and I felt nauseous at the thought that I might too change into something like Luke if I ever went down into The Hollows.

"Do all the female Vampyrus look like that, too?" I dared to ask him.

Guessing what I was driving at, Luke looked at me with his piercing stare and said, "They look beautiful – you don't have anything to worry about." Then he moaned aloud again as if he was hurting in some way.

"What's happening?" I asked him, trying to mask my fear.

"It's passing," he said through gritted teeth. Then rolling onto his side like a drunk, I watched as the hair covering his face faded away, his ears stretched back into shape, as did his nose. The green fire in his eyes faded and his fangs withdrew back into his gums like a cats claws disappearing back into its paws. Crawling across the floor towards him, I helped him up. His skin felt clammy and was covered in a fine sheen of sweat. Brushing his damp hair from his brow, I looked down into his face.

"Are you okay?"

"Never better," he said. Then pointing to the table beside the bed, he added, "In that drawer there is a bottle of Lot 13."

I lead Luke back to the bed where he sat down. Pulling open the drawer, I saw several bottles the size of small test tubes rolling about inside. Each of them was filled with a pale pink gloopey liquid. Taking one, I handed it to Luke. With trembling fingers, he unscrewed the top and tilting his head back, Luke gulped down the mixture. I watched it slide out of the bottle and it almost seemed to cling to the glass sides like slime. Taking the empty bottle from him, Luke shook all over as if caught in a draught and said, "That's better."

"Are you okay?" I asked him.

"Just give me a minute or two," he said, lying back on the bed. "Scared of me yet?" he asked once he had made himself comfortable.

"It will take more than a few scars and some straggly looking whiskers to frighten me away," I said. But deep inside, I did feel scared, but not of Luke, but what I might turn into. Then taking his hand in mine, I added, "How come you didn't worry about scaring Kayla, but you hid away from me?"

Looking at me, Luke said, "I don't know what you mean?"

163

"Well you didn't mask-up when you went in search of Kayla," I said. "She told me that you had scars all down the side of your face. How come you -"

Sitting bolt upright on the bed, Luke stared at me and said, "I don't know what you're talking about. I've never actually met Kayla and I definitely didn't go in search of her."

"You must have gone," I said feeling confused. "Kayla told me that she met a guy in London who said his name was Luke and she described him as having scars…"

"Kiera, I'm telling you I've never met the girl – I've been in hiding up here," he insisted.

"So if it wasn't you, then…oh my god!" I gasped. Pulling on my shirt I raced from the room.

Chapter Twenty-Five

With my hands stretched out before me, I darted down the dark corridor, my heart racing in my chest and beating in my ears. Luke was behind me, his lantern sending eerie shadows up the walls and across the floor. In the dim yellow light, my shadow appeared stretched and elongated, and out of the corner of my eye, my back look distorted, just like I had a pair of wings growing from it. Shuddering, I looked away and the deformed-looking shadow disappeared.

Reaching the top of the stairs I raced down them two at a time. Bolting across the landing, I headed up the stairs towards the corridor that led to Kayla's bedroom.

"Kiera!" Luke said from just over my shoulder, "What's wrong?"

Ignoring him, I pushed open the door and ran into Kayla's bedroom. Scanning the room, I could see that she wasn't there. The window leading to her balcony was open and the cold night air billowed the curtains outwards like a sail.

"Kayla?" I yelled, checking her bathroom. Running back into the room, I could see Luke was standing in the doorway and in the light from the many candles, I could see how pale Luke's face and chest really looked. His skin was almost white and the scars that covered it shone an angry purple and blue. His wings hung from his back, the tips of them nearly brushing the wooded floor and I could see now that the edges of them looked frayed like a piece of lace that had been unpicked.

"What's going on?" Luke asked, his eyes never leaving me as I darted around Kayla's room.

"Kayla told me that she met you in London," I told him, pulling back blankets and kicking aside the clothes that lay strewn all over her bedroom floor. "If it wasn't you, who was it? And why would they pretend to be you? But more than that, she has been meeting a friend in the woods at the summerhouse..." but then I stopped. Something had grabbed my attention.

Crossing the room to her dressing table, lying on top of a pile of used face wipes, perfumes, and lipsticks, I saw a folded piece of paper. Picking it up, I read what was written on it.

Dear Mother,

I know you believe that you have my best interests at heart – but really you don't. If you loved me, you would trust me – the two go hand in hand, don't they?

I know it's been difficult recently for you with father's disappearance, but it hasn't been easy for me, either. We both know that I'm different from other girls my age and the physical changes that I've undergone have really screwed me up inside. I don't know who I am but more importantly, I don't truly understand what I am.

I know you sent Police Officer Hudson to watch over me and keep me safe, and part of me understood your reasons why and it showed me that you loved me despite the problems I have caused you. But when I discovered tonight you had surrounded me with spies – I knew that you didn't trust me, either. I can't even begin to explain how your lack of faith and trust has hurt me.

I know that I am different – different from you – but I am your daughter. I didn't ask to be made like this – I wish more than anything I could be like other girls my age – but I know that I can't and this I have to come to understand and accept in my own time. But I will never be able to do this if you don't trust me, and by surrounding me with your spies to watch over me, I don't believe that I will ever come to terms with what I am.

Therefore I'm going away – far away from here with my friend Luke Bishop. Yes it has been him that you've seen on the other side of the manor walls. But he has become someone that I can trust – he has become a good friend. Before Kiera tells you what has happened (and I suspect she already knows – you were right you can't get anything past that one) I want to be honest with you. I gave Luke the key to the tunnel that leads beneath the moat, he has been secretly meeting me at the summerhouse in the woods and he has been to my room, he was curious to see where I lived and to see inside the manor.

But mother, you are in great danger from these spies that you have enlisted to watch me. Luke told me that there are two Vampyrus that were behind the disappearance of father – Jim Murphy and Sean Potter, and I've discovered tonight that these are the two that have been masquerading as your chauffeur and

handyman. But worse still, Kiera is working with them. You are in
great danger. When you find this note get as far away from
Hallowed Manor as you can – Luke has told me that Murphy and
Potter are soon to overrun the manor with vampires.

Please don't worry about me mother, I'm with Luke and he
has promised to protect me.

Forever in my heart
Kayla

Handing the letter to Luke, he scanned his eyes over it, then folding it in half, he looked at me and said, "I don't understand Kiera, I've never met Kayla, so who has she been meeting?"

"I don't know," I breathed. "But whoever he is, he's tricked Kayla into giving him keys to the grounds so that he can come and go, he's been in her room and the manor and..." but before I'd the chance to finish what I was about to say, snapshots of the nightmares that I'd been suffering from flashed in front of my mind's eyes. The images were so strong that I wobbled backwards, almost losing my balance.

Gripping my arm to steady me, Luke said, "Kiera, what is it? What can you see?"

Opening my eyes and looking at him, I said, "Kayla's been meeting Phillips."

"Phillips?" Luke asked sounding unsure.

"I've seen him in my dreams, Luke," I told him. "He's scarred down the left side of his face. But not from burns, from where Potter attacked him in the graveyard at St. Mary's Church."

"But that means..." Luke started.

"He's tricked Kayla into believing that he is you – her friend. Without ever meeting you, she wouldn't have known any different. Kayla is in danger!" I snapped and raced past Luke and out of her room.

"Wait!" Luke hollered after me.

"We don't have time!" I shouted over my shoulder, charging down the stairs to the great hall. Reaching the foot of the stairs, I could see Murphy and Potter standing by the front door. There was a hazy blue cloud of smoke hovering just above their heads as

Murphy puffed on his pipe and Potter sucked on the end of a cigarette which dangled from the corner of his mouth.

Seeing me come running down the stairs, Potter opened his arms and smirking he said, "Come running back to me, have you?"

Ignoring him, I looked at Murphy and said, "Have you seen Kayla?"

"Not since she discovered us in the gatehouse," he said.

Joining us in the hall, Luke looked at his two friends and said, "Phillips is here."

"Where?" Potter said, standing away from the wall and blowing smoke out of his nostrils.

"Impossible," Murphy growled. "We've been watching this place for weeks -"

"It doesn't surprise me, then, that he's found a way in," I snapped more angrily than I intended.

Knocking the smouldering contents from his pipe into a nearby flowerpot, Murphy eyed me and said, "Listen here, Hudson, you don't know every goddamn thing in the book. We've been watching your back here. There's only been the two of us..."

"Look, I'm sorry, I didn't mean it to sound like that," I told him. "It's just that I'm scared for Kayla – she doesn't know what Phillips is all about. She doesn't realise the danger that she's in."

Then from behind us, somebody said, "What's going on here?"

Spinning round, I saw Mrs. Payne come from the shadows beneath the wide staircase.

Looking at Luke, Potter, and Murphy, she said, "And who might you three be?" Before anyone had a chance to answer her, she looked at Potter and said, "And put that cigarette out. It's a disgusting habit."

Ignoring her, Potter looked at me and said, "Is she related to you by any chance?"

Turning away from his grinning face, I said to Mrs. Payne, "We don't have time to explain now, but these are my friends." Then pointing to Murphy, I said, "This is my sergeant, the smoker is called Potter, but you'll probably know them better as James and Marshal."

With a look of confusion splashed across her face, she said, "The Chauffeur? Marshal?" Then pointing at Luke, she added, "Where's he come from."

Pointing to the ceiling, Luke smiled and said, "From up there!"

"But...but -" Mrs. Payne started.

"Look it's been a pleasure chatting to you old lady," Potter said, grinding the cigarette out with his heel on her polished floor, "but I'm guessing that we have a more pressing engagement to attend. Is that not right, Kiera?"

Staring at him, I said, "Yes," and in that moment I could feel his rough hands on me again and his lips pressed against mine.

"Well?" Potter asked.

"Well what?" I asked, looking into his green eyes.

"Where's the girl, sweet-cheeks?"

Pushing away those images of me and him together in the gatehouse, I pulled open the front door and said, "Follow me."

Chapter Twenty-Six

A thick fog covered the grounds outside the manor house. It had a murky-yellow tinge to it and was so thick that I could only see a few feet ahead of me. It almost seemed to climb over the walls of the manor house and through the trees like dry ice at a party. The night was cold and damp and through the fog, I could barely make out the moon, which hung in the sky like a monstrous Halloween pumpkin. It had a sickly orange glow to it and its many craters looked like eyes and an evil grin that had been smudged.

We made our way across the lawns which stretched out before us and through the swirling fog towards the trees. Almost blind, we stumbled through the woods in the direction of the summerhouse. The atmosphere felt oppressive and my stomach tightened at the thought of what Philips might have done with Kayla. She would have told him about discovering Murphy and Potter. I doubted that he knew they had been here all the while but now that he knew of their existence, would it frighten him into doing something rash?

My train of thought was interrupted by Potter who said, "So tell me, tiger, how did Phillips get his claws into Kayla?"

"She believed him to be Luke," I explained. "She honestly believed him to be a good-guy."

"So if he wants to harm her, why hasn't he done it before now?" Murphy asked.

"He used her to get into the grounds of the manor," I told him. "He wants to get to those children up on the ward…and he wants me, remember?"

"But you're forgetting," Luke said, "he's one of us. Phillips has wings. Why didn't he just fly over the wall?"

"Perhaps he can't?" I told them. "Remember he got attacked by Potter. I know from my nightmares that his face is scarred like Luke's. Maybe his wings are damaged, too?"

"Or maybe there's another reason altogether," Murphy said, his voice thoughtful as if he were talking to himself.

"Like what?" Potter asked, lighting another cigarette revealing his eyes in the darkness like a pair of green headlamps.

"We know that Hallowed Manor is one of the Vampyrus' strongholds above ground. If he could take this place, then that would send a message out to all those other Vampyrus that he is someone to fear – someone not to be reckoned with. The other sacred places above ground would fear his power and some would more than likely cower to him to protect their strongholds."

"But who is he going to launch his attack with?" Luke asked Murphy. "He hasn't been able to gather enough Vampyrus to his twisted way of thinking to commit to an all-out attack against Hallowed Manor."

"Perhaps he's going to attack with vampires," I said.

There was silence for a moment. Then Potter said, "Impossible. sweet-cheeks. Remember this place is like a fortress. There could never be a vampire attack against this manor. It's surrounded by a ring of blessed water that vampires could never cross. The walls of the manor have been permeated with garlic and queets and if Phillips is planning to launch his attack from the summerhouse, then I'm afraid that I personally fitted a crucifix to the wall. Like the rest of the manor, it's been covered in garlic and queets, and just to make sure, there's a chamber hidden beneath the floor that I've filled to the brim with Bibles, crosses, and more bottles of holy water than you could wish for. There isn't going to be any vampire attack."

Turning to face him, I said, "Kayla spoke about giving a key to Phillips that led to a tunnel beneath the moat," then remembering the padlocked door that I'd discovered, I added, "That tunnel wouldn't be hidden beneath a door against the far wall on the other side of the grounds, would it?"

"Yeah, so?" Potter said, the end of his cigarette winking on and off in the darkness as he smoked it.

"Well, I found tracks – lots of tracks - leading from that secret doorway to the summerhouse," I said, the hairs on the nape of my neck starting to prickle. "And the summerhouse isn't covered in garlic and queets any longer. Someone has been out there and covered all your hard work in paint. The crucifix you put up on the wall, it's been removed. As for the Bibles, crosses, and holy water you say you've hidden, I can't be sure if they are still there."

The three of them looked blankly back at me through the fog. Realising that they seemed to be missing the point that I was trying to make, I gasped and said, "You really don't see it, do you?"

"See what?" Potter said. "Maybe if you stopped talking in riddles and tried good old fashioned English for a change…"

"Phillips has been using the tunnel under the moat to bring vampires onto the grounds of the manor. He repainted the summerhouse to cover up the garlic and queets and removed the crucifix from the wall," I explained.

"So what you're saying is," Potter said flicking his cigarette away, "This place is actually teeming with vampires and has been for weeks while he builds his army?"

Slapping my forehead with the palm of my hand, I said, "At last! I think you've got it!"

Then coming towards me through the fog, Potter said, "Well tell me this, sweet-cheeks, where have they all been hiding out all this time? Remember vampires don't like the sunlight."

But before I could even think about answering his question, Luke had gripped me by the shoulder. "Shhh," he said, and pointed ahead of us. We had reached the edge of the circular clearing that the summerhouse sat in. Screwing up my eyes, I peered through the fog and could just make out two figures standing off to one side in the centre of the clearing. Crouching down behind the trunks of some large trees, the four of us stared at the figures. Before he had even spoken, I knew that it was Phillips and Kayla.

"You don't have to hide," Phillips said, and his voice sounded smooth and calm, and I still had difficulty in believing that he had once been my sergeant at training school. He had been a colleague; but more importantly, a friend.

"There is no point in hiding amongst the trees, my friends. Kayla heard you coming the moment you stepped into the woods."

Standing, the four us stepped out of the fog and into the clearing. I stood silently between Luke and Potter, and Murphy stood alone to one side.

"Hello again," Phillips smiled, and his eyes almost appeared to beam through the swirling fog.

Ignoring him, I looked at Kayla, I said, "Whatever he's told you, Kayla, this guy is *not* your friend. His name isn't Luke Bishop – it's Craig Phillips."

Smiling, Phillips said, "Will the real Luke Bishop step forward?" and as his words left his lips, both Luke beside me and Phillips in the clearing took a step forward.

"Kiera is right, Kayla," Luke said, his voice soft. "I'm Luke Bishop. The guy standing next to you only wants to hurt and use you."

"He told me you would say that," Kayla said. "He told me that you would try and mess with my mind – play tricks on me."

"The only person playing tricks here is the man standing next to you," I told her, inching forward. "He tricked me once, Kayla, and I nearly lost my life because of it."

"Liar!" Kayla spat. "I trusted you Kiera! I told you stuff and showed you things that I'd never shown anyone else, and all the time, you were spying on me with your friends!"

"That's not true," I said. "I didn't know who James and Marshal really were."

"Liar!" Kayla said again, but this time her voice wavered as if trying to stop herself from crying. "If you didn't know who Marshal was, why were you making out with him in the gatehouse? I saw you through the window. You looked pretty friendly to me!"

At once, I could almost sense Luke's eyes boring into me. Not taking my eyes from Kayla, and too uncomfortable to look at Luke, I said, "It wasn't what it looked like, Kayla. I thought he was somebody else."

"Oh yeah?" Luke said, from beside me. "Who?"

"You, of course!" I snapped, turning to him. "You don't really think I'd make out with that jerk, do you?"

"Now that's not nice," Potter said from behind me.

Spinning round, I turned on Potter and shouted, "Why don't you just try shutting your mouth for once in your life! You know I thought -"

But before I'd a chance to say anything else, Potter had stuck another cigarette between his lips and said, "Easy, tiger. Stop getting so excited."

"You're impossible!" I hollered back. "Tell Luke what really happened!"

Then, from the centre of the clearing, Philips said to Kayla, "See? How can you trust any of these people, Kayla? They don't even trust each other."

Just as the last of his words left his mouth, Potter had shot across the clearing in a blur of shadows and had Phillips gripped by the throat. Even by his own Vampyrus speed and agility, Phillips looked momentarily stunned at how quickly Potter was upon him. With his fingers digging into the scarred flesh around Phillips throat, and without taking his eyes from him, Potter shouted across the clearing at Luke.

"Kiera loves you, Luke. There is no doubting that. It was an accident. Yes, she did kiss me, but only because she believed me to be you. She saw the bandages and the disguise in the gatehouse and thought you had been hiding yourself from her." Then turning to look at me through the fog, Potter said, "I was to blame for what happened, Luke, not Kiera. I realised her mistake, but instead of pushing her off, I let her kiss me and I kissed her back."

Averting my gaze, I looked down at the ground. I was grateful for Potter's honesty, but it just confused me even more. When I'd thought I'd made up my mind that he was a complete and utter jerk, he then went and did something completely unexpected and nice – like pulling my car from the snow and now taking all the blame for what had happened at the gatehouse.

"But I made two big mistakes, Luke," Potter continued. "The first was believing someone like Kiera could ever be interested in someone like me," then turning to look back at Phillips, he snarled, "and my second big mistake was not killing you back in The Ragged Cove." Within an instance, fangs had protruded from his gums and he was lunging at Phillips' throat.

Raising a hand to her face, Kayla screamed and leapt backward. Seeing this, Murphy shot forward in a haze of shadows and had taken hold of her, bringing her back to me. Before I'd the chance to say anything to her, a figure stepped from the fog on the other side of the clearing.

"Kill Philips if it will make you feel better, Potter. But it will change nothing. You are all going to be dead before dawn," Taylor said, limping forward. On his head, he wore that wide-brimmed hat, he was naked to the waist and his wings twitched and fluttered around his scrawny frame. Limping towards Potter, who still had hold of Phillips, he chuckled and said, "Go on, I dare you. If it makes you feel any better, rip his throat out, tear the lungs from his body."

Lurching forward, still believing that Phillips was her friend, Kayla shouted, "No! Don't kill him! Please!"

Eyeing Kayla, then Potter again, Taylor said, "Go on, Potter, show the girl what a monster you truly are. Go on, kill a defenceless Vampyrus in front of her."

"Please!" Kayla whimpered.

Taking her by the shoulders, I shook her gently and said, "Kayla, he is not your friend. He cares nothing about you…or me."

"Why would he care about you anyway?" Kayla said, her voice angry and confused.

Staring her straight in the eyes, I said, "Kayla, I'm like you. Me and you are the same."

"How?" she sneered.

"I'm half human and half Vampyrus," I tried to convince her. "Phillips and that wizened–up guy, Taylor, over there want the both of us."

"I don't believe that you're like me," she said. "Prove it."

"I can't," I said, shaking my head at her. "But I have wings, just like you."

"Where? Show me!" she spat.

"They haven't come…come *through* yet," I told her.

"How convenient," Kayla said and almost seemed to sneer at me. "Luke just wants to protect me from people like you."

"He doesn't want to protect you," I insisted. "He wants you – us – because we are unique. You and me have special abilities that they want and there is another like us called Isidor Smith. That's where your mother has gone – she's looking for him." But I could see by the way that she looked at me that she wasn't convinced. There had to be some way to prove to her that I was telling the truth.

"You heard that phone call Kayla," I said. "You heard my friend suffering. You saw how much that hurt me. That was another Vampyrus just like Philips and Taylor who hurt him. They were trying to track me down."

"I don't believe you," she said again.

Thinking back to that last conversation I'd shared with Sparky, something suddenly struck me. He had said "texts". *I received your texts*, he had said. But I'd only sent him the one since arriving at the manor. So who had sent the others? Whoever had found my phone when I'd fallen from the wall. Looking at

Phillips still being gripped by Potter, I turned back to Kayla and holding out my hand, I said, "Give me your phone."

"Why?" she asked.

"Just give it to me, Kayla, and I'll prove to you that Phillips was behind the murder of my friend."

Reluctantly, Kayla pulled her mobile phone from her jeans pocket and handed it to me. Taking it, I dialled my own mobile phone. Pressing it to my ear, I turned to face Phillips and waited for the sound of my mobile phone to start ringing from his direction. Within seconds the night was broken with the shrill tone of my mobile ringing – but it didn't come from the direction of Phillips as I'd suspected. The sound of the ring tone came from behind me. As if on cue, all of us turned to face the woods, even Phillips glanced in that direction as Potter gripped him.

My mobile phone still continued to ring from the slices of darkness between the tress and then it stopped as if cut dead. From within the trees and the fog that curled amongst them, I caught sight of a fleeting movement.

"Who's there?" I called out. Then as if in answer to my question, Mrs. Payne stepped from the tree line, my mobile phone held in her hand.

Chapter Twenty-Seven

Mrs. Payne's wings fluttered in the wind, which made the fog swirl around her as if she were a magician stepping onto a grand stage. Still dressed in her grey frumpy dress, thick woollen tights and uncomfortable black shoes, she came towards me and said, "Surprised that I'm one of them?"

"Not really," I said, there didn't seem to be much that would surprise me any longer. Then my head rocked back as images of her hair flecked with white raced to the forefront of my mind. And again I was standing at the foot of the stairs leading up to the *'forbidden'* wing. In my mind's eye, I could see that her hair was coated in tiny white flecks of...*paint*. It was then that I knew it had been her that had repainted the summerhouse to cover up the sticky coating of garlic and queets. It had been Mrs. Payne that had removed the crucifix from the wall and it had been her who had been paving the way for Taylor and his vampires.

"Would you like your phone?" Mrs. Payne smiled, her tone was insincere and full of loathing.

"Just give it to me," I said opening my eyes and holding out my hand.

Placing the phone in my palm, she let her long, ivory nails scrape across my flesh. Yanking my hand away, Mrs. Payne smiled and looked at Kayla.

"Sweet little Kayla," she said, and brushed the girl's hair with her fingernails.

Kayla knocked the old woman's hand away and said, "How come you had Kiera's phone?"

"I found it, that's all," she said.

Searching through my sent messages, I found two that had been sent to Sparky. Both had been sent after I'd fallen from the wall. The first read:

Remind me of your home address Sparky,
I have a surprise that I want to send to you.
Kiera x

The second read:

Thanks Sparky. I've changed my mind,
I'll bring the surprise to you myself.
Be home tomorrow, but make sure you are alone ;)
Kiera x

Reading those texts, I realised how easily they had tricked my friend into disclosing his home address and arranging for him to be alone. Sparky wouldn't have had any reason to suspect that those text messages hadn't come from anyone else but me. Poor Sparky, what had they done to him? I prayed that he hadn't suffered because of me. With rage beginning to swell inside of me, I turned to Kayla, and shoving the phone under her nose, I said, "Go on, take a look, Kayla. See what your precious friend has been up to." Kayla looked down at the screen and read what was written there.

"But Mrs. Payne had your phone – it was her who sent those texts," she said shaking her head as if not wanting to believe that she had been deceived by Philips.

"And who do you think it was you heard at my friend's address?" I snapped. "It wasn't the old-woman – it was your friend over there," and I pointed in the direction of Phillips who was still hanging from the end of Potter's fist.

Looking over at Phillips, her eyes wide, Kayla said, "Luke, is this true?"

But before he could fill her head with more lies, Potter was tightening his grip around Phillips' throat. Even if he'd wanted to reply to Kayla, I doubted if he would've been able to squeeze any words out.

"Oh god, this is all just so tiresome," Mrs. Payne said as she walked across the clearing and went to join Taylor. The two of them stood, half hidden by the fog, their wrinkled skin giving the appearance of two mummified statues. "Can't we just get this over and done with," she said, sounding bored. Then turning to Taylor, she added, "Let's just keep to the plan. You kill Potter, Murphy, and Bishop, and I'll take the two girls."

Hearing this, Kayla inched closer to me.

Then slowly unbuttoning his shirt and stepping forward, Murphy said in a calm voice, "Oh I'm sorry, I thought the plan was for me and the two boys here to rip your throat out, old woman, then feed you in tiny pieces to Taylor and Phillips. And if I'm feeling in a good mood, I'll let them die before Potter starts feeding them small chunks of your brains. Now that sounds like a plan."

"Jim Murphy," Taylor smiled, "You never change, do you? The only people that are going to die tonight are you and your two sidekicks, Potter and Bishop."

"How do you figure that?" Luke said, moving forward to stand next to Murphy.

"Because your friend Kiera won't let us die," Taylor smiled. Then looking at me, he said, "Isn't that correct, Kiera?"

"I don't know what you're talking about," I hissed at him.

"I have some people here that want to say hello to you, Kiera," Taylor smiled, flashing his yellow-stained fangs.

"What are you talking about?" I murmured, my stomach tying itself into knots.

Then looking back over his shoulder into the woods, he said, "You can come out now."

With Kayla standing beside me, I watched as the shadows between the trees on the opposite of the clearing appeared to move. Then I gasped as Doctor Keats stumbled forward out of the fog. The last time I'd seen her she'd looked like a headmistress, now she resembled a bag lady. Her hair was dishevelled and clumps of it stuck out in thick wisps from each side of her head. Her smart tweed suit was covered in dirt and grime, her tights were torn at the knees and her shoes were missing. With her hands secured behind her back, she wandered into the clearing. She was sobbing and her cheeks were covered in thick, black lines where her mascara had run down her face.

"Doctor Keats?" I whispered in disbelief.

"Yes that's right, Kiera," Taylor smiled, "Your doctor."

"What's she doing here?" I said, unable to take my eyes from her. "She has nothing to do with this!"

"Kiera? Kiera, is that you?" Keats croaked as she fought back her tears.

"Yes it's me," I said. I'd never really liked the woman, but I'd never wished her any harm. Stepping through the fog, I moved closer so that she could see me, I didn't want her to feel alone.

"Taylor, let her go," I said.

"Oh you want to bargain?" and he flashed his smashed-looking teeth at me again. "Okay. How about your friend Potter releases Phillips? That would be a start."

With his hands still fixed around Phillips' throat, Potter looked over at Taylor and said, "The doctor means nothing to me."

"But she does to me," I told him. "I can't just let her die."

"She's gonna die anyway," Potter said, looking at me.

"Please Potter," I groaned.

Looking at Keats standing in the clearing, head bowed forward and arms tied behind her, Potter released his hold on Phillips. Dropping to the ground, Philips rubbed his throat with his hands and pulled himself up. Potter sauntered back across the clearing and stood next to Murphy.

"Now let her go," I said to Taylor.

"Oh Kiera, I wish it was as easy as that," Taylor said, his eyes sparkling in the gloom.

"I told you," Potter said, looking at me while lighting another cigarette.

Ignoring him, I stared at Taylor and said, "Please, she has nothing to do with this."

"But she does," Taylor said. "Thanks to you, she knows way too much about us – about the Vampyrus."

"But she never believed a word that I told her," I tried to assure him. "She thought I was mad…making the whole -" but before I'd the chance to finish, Mrs. Payne had sprung through the air as if being launched from a cannon and clung to Doctor Keats' shoulders. Looking like a giant moth, the old woman swarmed around Doctor Keats as she buried her fangs into her neck. With her arms fastened behind her back, Keats wobbled and stumbled then tipped over onto the ground. Mrs. Payne swooped upwards, her wings shining orange in the light from the moon, then darted back towards the ground and her kill. Thrashing her legs out and screaming, Doctor Keats tried to roll away as blood pumped in a black stream from her throat. Her screams sounded as if she was gargling on a throat full of water as blood jetted from her mouth. Smelling the blood, Mrs. Payne lunged at her again, her wings flitting back and forth behind her. Pulling Kayla close to me and turning away, I couldn't help but notice the look of hunger in

Murphy, Potter, and Luke's eyes as they watched the old woman feed.

Within moments, Doctor Keats had stopped kicking out. Her legs twitched once or twice more then fell still. Climbing from her body, Mrs. Payne wiped away the black-coloured blood that swung from her chin and swooped back towards Philips and Taylor.

"I'm sure that was rather unpleasant for all concerned," Taylor said, his voice was soothing as if he actually cared about the way we felt. "So to avoid any further unpleasantness, Kiera, offer up either Murphy, Potter, or Bishop."

"In exchange for what?" I asked, my heart racing in my chest. "For one of these," Taylor smiled, and from behind him, two figures were shoved into the clearing. Like Doctor Keats, the hands of the two people were secured behind their back.

Screwing up my eyes and peering through the fog, I tried to make out the identity of the two people now standing in the clearing. I could see that they were both male, and at first I didn't recognise them. But as the fog cleared a little in front of them, I could see that one of the males was the owner of the pawnbrokers in Havensfield and the other was David Evans, the gardener who had stolen Mrs. Lovelace's wedding ring. Realising who they were, I shouted across the clearing at Taylor and said, "You've got this all wrong. These people mean nothing to me, Taylor. You might as well let them go."

Then without a moment's hesitation, Taylor said to Mrs. Payne and Phillips, "You heard her, they mean nothing to her."

Then just before he fell to the floor under the weight of Phillips, I heard the gardener say, "I'm sorry I took the old woman's ring." Then he was gone in a spray of red, as Phillips ripped his throat almost in two. Just like the gardener, the pawnbroker disappeared behind Mrs. Payne's wings as she brought him to his knees and began to feed on him.

As the two of them fed, Taylor looked at me and said, "Perhaps in time, we will come to someone that you really do care about." Then clicking his bony fingers he shouted. "Next!"

Then it was my turn to drop to my knees as I saw Mrs. Lovelace and Sparky stagger from the tree line. Mrs. Lovelace looked tired and confused, her face drawn and gaunt looking.

Sparky stumbled, then righted himself as he peered through the fog.

"*You can't do this!*" I screeched at the top of my voice. "Taylor, please I beg you – don't hurt them!"

"At last we have someone that you *do* care about, Kiera Hudson," Taylor smiled.

Almost grovelling on my hands and knees, I lurched forwards, my hands held out before me as if in prayer. "Please, I beg you," I cried. "Don't hurt them. They have done nothing to you!"

"Then perhaps you would like to nominate two of your friends to take their places," Taylor said, his voice now cold and demanding.

"But I can't do that either," I sobbed. "They're my friends, too!"

"I'm growing tired of this sentiment…" Taylor started.

"Take me," I pleaded. "Take me in place of all of them. I'm important to you, aren't I?"

Ignoring me, Taylor said again, "Which of your friends is it to be?"

"I can't!" I screeched at him, slamming my fists against my knees. "Please don't make me choose!"

Then I felt a hand against my shoulder, and looking up I could see Luke smiling down at me. "It's okay, Kiera," he whispered.

Realising what he was about to do, I pulled myself up and held onto him. "No! You can't do this, Luke. I won't let you!"

Pulling me tight, he whispered in my ear, 'It's okay, Kiera."

"It's not okay," I sobbed against him.

"It's the only way," he said, pulling from me.

"No!" I cried and held onto his hands, refusing to let him go.

Then pitching out his cigarette, Potter stepped forward, and blowing smoke from the corner of his mouth he said to Luke, "Come on, lover-boy, let's get this over with."

Leaning forward one last time, I kissed Luke gently on the lips as he stepped away, crossing the clearing towards Taylor, Phillips, and Mrs. Payne.

Looking back over my shoulder, I could see Murphy standing with his arm tucked around Kayla's shoulder. He looked suddenly haggard and old as he watched his friends hand themselves over and Kayla's eyes spilt tears onto her cheeks. Turning back, I watched as Luke and Potter knelt down before Taylor.

Chapter Twenty-Eight

"This is all my fault!" Kayla shrieked from behind me and before I'd even the chance to turn round, she was soaring over my head. And as she did, I saw her wings tear through her shirt and ripple out on either side of her back. But to my surprise, they were no longer the delicate butterfly-type wings I'd seen before, but they were now strong and powerful, just like a bird of prey.

Before Philips knew what was happening, Kayla was yanking him back through the air and away from Luke who knelt before him. Philips made a grunting sound as he slammed into a nearby tree.

"You lied to me!" Kayla screamed, and I could see that her mouth was full of razor-sharp teeth. "You said you were my friend but you used me to get at those that really care about me!" Then she was off again, tearing through the fog towards Phillips.

From above, the sky boomed as if being ripped apart. Looking up, I could see Murphy screaming overhead, his shirt falling away in jagged strips. With the force of a rocket, he smashed into Taylor, sending him crashing into the branches of a tree. It wobbled and lurched, its roots ripping from the earth under the full force of Taylor smashing into it.

There was an ear-splitting scream as Mrs. Payne took off into the air like a firework and raced towards Murphy. Seeing my chance, I raced through the dirty fog to Sparky and Mrs. Lovelace.

"Kiera, what's going on here?" Sparky shouted over the sound of falling branches and the roaring of thunderclaps overhead.

"I don't have time to explain now!" I hollered back, unfastening the cable that bound his wrists. "Just get Mrs. Lovelace away from here."

Looking at me while rubbing his wrists, his mouth opened and closed like a fish. Breaking Mrs. Lovelace's bonds, she peered at me through the fog and said, "Is that really you, Kiera my dear?"

"Yes," I told her, trying not to show the panic in my voice.

"This is all terribly exciting," she said, gripping my arm with her liver-spotted hands.

Looking over her shoulder, I said to Sparky, "Just get her out of here!"

"Where to?" Sparky asked, his forehead and cheeks glowing red from the acne that still ravished his face.

"On the other side of the woods," I said pointing into the distance, "you'll find the manor house. Take her there and lock all the doors."

"But what about you?" he asked, his voice as caring as usual.

"Don't worry about me," I said. "I'll meet you back there later – *now go!*"

"We'll have a nice cup of tea waiting for you," Mrs. Lovelace said as Sparky led her away towards the trees. "And that new gardener you got me is marvellous…" But the rest of what she had to say was lost as she disappeared into the fog with Sparky.

Turning around, to my horror, I saw Kayla struggling with Phillips. He had her round the waist and they were tumbling out of the sky towards me.

"*Help me!*" Kayla screamed, as the ground rushed up towards her. Then there was a blaze of shadows as something swooped in and snatched Kayla from Phillips' arms. The shadow rocketed towards the ground, then stopped suddenly just inches above the grass and I could see that it was Potter who had saved her. He held her tight in his thick-set arms and his bare chest looked taut and hard.

"Don't just stand there admiring the view," he snapped at me. "Get her out of here."

"I'm not going anywhere!" Kayla said in defiance. "I caused this!"

Ignoring her, Potter stared at me and said, "Get rid of the kid." Then he was gone, ascending into the sky.

"That guy's such a dick!" Kayla hissed.

"You know it," I said back.

Glancing up into the night, I could just make out a series of shadows racing back and forth through the fog. I couldn't see who was who or what was what. Then taking Potter's advice, I gripped hold of Kayla's hand and we raced together towards the shelter of the trees. But before reaching them, Taylor swooped out of the sky, landing on the ground before us. With his wings unravelled on either side of him, he raised his arms, tilted his head back and called out, "Vampires, wake!"

Then, as if it had all been planned, the trees surrounding the clearing began to shake. Branches bowed and snapped, showering the ground with leaves. Looking up, I screamed as pale-faced vampires leapt from the tree tops and into the clearing. Just like the vampires I'd witnessed in The Ragged Cove and my nightmares, they appeared frenzied and crazed as they sniffed the air and drool ran like goo from their fangs. The vampires' eyes rolled in their sockets like burning coals in black holes. Spinning round, I watched as vampires leapt into the clearing, not only from the treetops, but from the black spaces between them. They screamed and snapped their jaws at the air like rabid dogs. Pulling Kayla close, I heard the sound of groaning behind me.

Spinning round, I watched as the corpses of Doctor Keats, David Evans, and the pawnbroker began to twitch and stir at my feet.

"What's happening to them?" Kayla asked. "I thought they were dead!"

"They were and they are -" I breathed. "They were bitten by the Vampyrus, so now..."

"Now *what*?" she asked, her voice brimming with fear.

"Now they're vampires," I told her.

Doctor Keats sprang up like a jack-in-the-box, her neck making a clicking noise as she straightened her head on her torn neck. Blood ran in thick streams down the front of her tweed suit and splattered Evans' writhing hand. Smelling the blood, Evans stuck his fingers into his mouth and sucked the blood from them like a child with a soother. The pawnbroker dragged himself to his knees, then, as if receiving some kind of electric shock, he jumped to his feet.

"Hungry," he groaned and came forward.

Whichever way I turned, crazed-looking vampires approached Kayla and me. Their eyes glowed red through the fog, their snapping fangs chattering in the dark. Doctor Keats reached for Kayla and like a wild animal, Kayla lunged at her hand, tearing three of her fingers off with her fangs. Scrunching up her face as if her mouth were full of acid, Kayla spat the fingers away, her wings humming beside me.

Raising her hand, Doctor Keats looked at the spaces where she had once had fingers and smiled through the gap at Kayla. Then lunging forward at Kayla, Doctor Keats was yanked backwards into the sky. In her place stood Luke. The scars on his chest and face glowing blue and black, his tattered wings arched high above his back. Throwing out his arms on either side of him, Evans' and the pawnbroker's heads flew from their shoulders, disappearing into the fog. Their bodies stood momentarily as unaware that their heads were now missing. Then they started to spasm and jerk until they collapsed to the ground.

"How we doing?" he asked.

"Not good," I said, scanning the vampires that closed in on us from every direction.

"Nothing's changed there then," he said. Fluttering past me in a spray of shadows, he was tearing to pieces several of the vampires that had drawn near. Blood rained down and spattered the ground.

Through the fog came the sound of thunder. I peered into it and my left eye began to weep red tears. A flash of blinding white light penetrated my skull then everything went black then grey. Tendrils of fog swirled around me, and as I looked into it, I realised that I could see through it. Ahead of me I could see Potter and Murphy cutting their way through the vampires. But it was more than just seeing through the fog, it was like the whole world had slowed down and I could *see* everything in minute detail. It was only then as I watched Potter and Murphy tear the vampires to shreds that I realised their true power and ferocity. In what would have taken place in a blink of the eye, I watched played out in slow time. Potter's arms shimmied as his claws sliced through the bodies of the unsuspecting vampires that made their way towards Kayla and me. Murphy's teeth tore open their faces, ripping their tongues from their throats and spitting them away like bloated worms. Potter punched his fingernails through the chests of vampires, tearing out their hearts. The two of them worked with such speed, that the vampires only realised what had happened to them by the time several others had experienced the same fate. They toppled over like a stack of dominoes in zero gravity.

Then it was gone, as the flash of light popped in front of my eyes again. I toppled backwards as if I'd been punched in the face, and before I knew what was happening, someone had steadied me by taking hold of my arm.

"Easy, tiger," Potter whispered in my ear, then he was gone again, cutting and slicing his way through the never-ending wake of vampires that streamed into the clearing. He was followed by a trail of shadows and I guessed this was Murphy taking out any of the vampires Potter missed.

I'd been so blinded by these visions that I hadn't noticed Phillips and Mrs. Payne swoop down in the clearing and land next to Taylor. The space that Kayla and I occupied became smaller and smaller. We were within touching distance of them.

"Now, let's take what we really came for," Taylor said, stepping closer to Kayla and me.

Taking Kayla's hand in mine, we both flinched as Mrs. Payne threw herself at us. Her fingernails almost seemed to touch my chest and I could feel her stale breath against my face as a spray of shadows appeared behind her. Before I could truly understand what was happening, Kayla had let go of my hand, sprang into the air, got behind Mrs. Payne, and gnawed through her neck with her fangs. I was only aware of what had happened when Mrs. Payne opened her mouth to scream. She made a belching noise as a rush of air shot through the opening that Kayla had made in her throat. Realising that something was wrong, Mrs. Payne glanced back and in doing so, her head swivelled on her neck like an owl, then fell off. With her body still hovering before me and her wings buzzing, Kayla flung it aside.

"Boy did that woman suck," Kayla said, wiping blood from her lips, "but not anymore." She looked at me and winked, and then she was gone, snatched up into the fog by Phillips.

"Kayla!" I screamed, watching her disappear above me.

"Where is she?" Luke said, appearing at my side.

"Phillips has taken her!" I yelled pointing into the sky.

Luke leapt into the air, but wasn't quick enough. One of the vampires that circled us sprang into the air. Sinking its fangs into Luke's leg, it dragged him back to the ground. Within seconds Luke was overpowered by gnashing and shrieking vampires. Helpless to do anything, I watched as he was pulled to the ground, where he disappeared from view beneath the mountain of vampires that swarmed over him.

"So that just leaves me and you," a voice said, and I spun around to see Taylor leering at me through the fog. He came forward, a cluster of vampires behind him. I had nowhere to go. Then I was grabbed from behind. I shrieked and looked around to see Murphy looking at me.

"Run, Kiera!" he boomed, just as a set of vampire claws dug into his bare shoulders and dragged him to the ground. Within moments, like Luke before him, he was drowning beneath a wave of starving vampires. With my knees starting to buckle and the world swimming in and out of focus before me, I turned around to see Taylor reaching for me.

"Come with me, Kiera, my master has been dying to meet you," he smiled. But through the fog in my own mind and the fog that wafted all around us, I saw his smile fade, as a thin stream of blood ran from the corner of his mouth. His eyes rolled back in their sockets, then out onto his cheeks popped two claw-like fingers that wiggled from deep in his eye sockets. Covering my mouth with my hands, there was a sickening squelching sound as the fingers disappeared back into his skull and Taylor dropped forward onto his knees revealing Potter behind him. His fingers were covered in blood and something which looked close to grey-coloured jelly.

"I'm blind," Taylor groaned at my feet. But before he'd a chance to say anything else, Potter had kicked him over then crushed his skull with the heel of his boot. Reaching for me, Potter pulled me close, out of reach of the vampires that circled us.

"Philips has taken Kayla," I said trying to pull away from him. "And the vampires have…have…" I couldn't bring myself to say anymore, as tears ran down my cheeks, washing away the blood that had come from my eye.

"Let's get to the safety of the summerhouse," Potter growled at me, his fangs looking pink where they had been smeared with blood.

"But…" I started.

"We've got to get to the chamber beneath the summerhouse. That's where I buried the crucifixes and holy water!" he reminded me.

"But…" I tried again, looking back over my shoulder at where Luke and Murphy had disappeared beneath a sea of vampires.

"There's too many of them!" he shouted into my face. "We have to get to the summerhouse!"

Then standing in front of me like a shield, he pinwheeled his arms like a set of rotary blades and began to cut a path through the vampires as he led me to safety. The vampires hissed, spat and lunged at us, as Potter carved his way through them. I wondered why he hadn't just picked me up and flown over them, but as I looked at his wings, I could see they had big, gaping holes in them, tears and rips where he had been attacked by the vampires.

Reaching the summerhouse, Potter shoved me forward and up the stairs to the white-painted front door. With his back pressed against mine, Potter lashed and kicked out at the vampires that pursued us up the steps. Grabbing hold of the door handle, I twisted it and the door flew open. Pushing me inside and slamming the door shut behind us, Potter dragged a chair away from the table and wedged it against the door.

"I don't think that's going to hold them for long," I shouted over the shrieks and groans of the vampires that were now circling the summerhouse outside.

"It only has to last long enough for me to get this hatch open!" he yelled back. Throwing the table aside, he pulled back the carpet beneath it and revealed the hatch. Looking back at me and smiling, he said, "Now this is what I call good planning."

Without wasting another moment, Potter yanked back the hatch, looked inside, and immediately closed it again.

"What's wrong?" I shouted, seeing the fear in his face.

"This is not my fault," he said, staring at me, his mouth open in shock.

"What's not your fault?" I screamed at him, the chair holding the door closed now scraping against the floor under the weight of the vampires.

"You know you said that Phillips would have to have kept the vampires hidden somewhere out of the light?" he said.

"Yeah?" I said. Then reading the fear in his eyes, I added, "You're kidding me! Please tell me that you're joking!"

Shaking his head and looking back down at the hatch, Potter shouted, "They're hidden beneath us!"

No sooner had the words left his lips, the hatch started to open. White fingers curled up from beneath the hatch and made a grab for Potter's foot. Ramming his boot down hard, the hatch snapped closed again.

"I'm not going to be able to stand on this forever," he shouted at me.

Then from behind him, the window broke in a shower of glass, as the vampires reached in at us. The door began to buckle against its frame as the vampires charged at the door from outside. Parts of the door had begun to splinter and the hinges had started to come away from the wall. I looked at Potter as he wobbled to and fro on top of the hatch as the vampires beneath us fought their way out. The sound of scuttling from above was almost deafening as vampires clambered over the roof, desperate to find a way in.

"Come away from the door!" Potter shouted, holding his hand out.

Taking it, he pulled me into his arms and wrapped his tattered wings around me. It was as if it was his last attempt at protecting me. As I looked up into his rugged face, I didn't ever think that I would spend my last living moments held in his arms. Pressed against his chest, I could feel his heart racing and mine matched it.

Looking into his blazing eyes, I said, "I want to know one thing before I die."

"Oh yeah?" he said, looking down at me. "What's that?"

"Did you mean what you said out there?" I asked him, as the door started to come away from its frame.

"What did I say?"

"You said that you made a mistake thinking that a girl like me would be interested in a guy like you," I reminded him.

Then smiling down at me, he said, "Don't go getting yourself all excited, sweet-cheeks, I said that for Luke, not for you," and he kissed me.

The sudden sound of screaming came from outside. But it was more than screaming, it was the sound of people crying out in agony. Then the arms that were reaching in through the windows, exploded into chunks of dust and the fingers curled around the edge of the door broke away like ash.

Pulling myself free of Potter, I ran to the window and peered out. Like a shadow fleeting past in the fog, I could see someone or something moving at great speed.

"There's someone out there," I whispered, "and they seem to be slaughtering all the vampires."

"That's impossible," Potter said. "There's too many for just one person to -" but before he'd had the chance to finish, the door to the summerhouse flew inwards and off its hinges. A figure stood in the doorway, a black silhouette against the orange moon.

"Where's Kayla Hunt?" the figure asked, the voice male, but still young.

"Who are you?" I asked, stepping forward in an attempt to get a better look at him.

"Where's Kayla Hunt?" he asked again, his voice flat and even.

"They've taken her," I told him.

"Taken her where?" and now his voice sounded agitated.

"That's the million dollar question," Potter said.

"Who *are* you?" I asked him again.

Stepping out of the shadows so I could see his face, he looked at me with eyes that seemed to penetrate my very soul and he said, "My name is Isidor Smith and I've been sent to rescue Kayla"

Chapter Twenty-Nine

Pushing Potter and me aside, Isidor went to the trap door. Looking back at Potter, he said, "Are you ready for this?"

"Bring it," Potter smirked, egging Isidor on.

No sooner had the hatch been yanked open, Isidor and Potter disappeared into the darkness beneath it. Teetering on the edge of the hatch, I looked down but all I could see was a blur of shadows and hear the ear-splitting sound of vampires dying.

Then silence.

Scrambling from the darkness, Isidor and Potter appeared from beneath the hatch. Both stood and wiped blood from their mouths and I noticed Potter had it smeared across his chest.

Isidor stared at me from beneath a navy-blue baseball cap. His right eyebrow was pierced with a small silver stud and his otherwise sharp and clean cut look was spoilt by a short, stubby beard that hung from his chin. An intricate pattern of black flames tattooed the left side of his neck and licked just beneath his jaw line. His eyes were such a dark shade of brown that they were almost black. He was tall and his frame was lean.

I remembered Doctor Ravenwood saying that Isidor was eighteen years-old, and despite the tuft of beard, piercing and tattoo, he still had a boyish quality about him. Turning his back on us, Isidor stepped back onto the porch and out into the night. As he went, I noticed what appeared to be a strangely-fashioned crossbow slung over his back and a rucksack that was full of wooden stakes. He wore a long dark brown coat that hung just above his knees, blue jeans, and red baseball boots.

As he left the summerhouse, I looked back at Potter who raised an eyebrow at me. Peering out through the splintered doorway, I could see that the clearing was covered in mounds of what looked like snow. But, standing on the porch, I could see that it wasn't snow at all, but a thick blanket of ash that now covered the ground. It was all over the walls and roof of the summerhouse, and some of the chalky remains of the vampires floated in the air like snowflakes.

Realising that the immediate threat of the vampires had gone, I rushed past Isidor and down the porch steps.

"Did you see Luke?" I asked, praying that perhaps he'd managed to escape.

"Be careful," Isidor warned. "There might still be some of those bloodsuckers out here."

Ignoring him, I said, "Did you see Luke – he was out here, the vampires were -"

"Duck!" Isidor shouted, and in a blink of an eye he took the odd-looking crossbow from his back, loaded and fired it over my head. Crouching, I looked back to see a vampire tearing from the woods at me, its teeth violet with blood, eyes crazed and bulging from their sockets. Within touching distance from me, the stake that Isidor had unleashed ripped through the chest of the approaching creature, tearing it back through the air. Clutching at its chest, the vampire exploded into a shower of dust which erupted into the air like a flour bomb.

Even before the powdery remains of the vampire had hit the ground, Isidor had thrown the crossbow across his back and said, "So who's this Luke guy you keep yapping on about?"

"He's my friend," I told him, making my way back through the mist and fog to where I'd seen Luke fall.

"More than a friend, I sense," Isidor said, coming down the porch steps towards me. Then sniffing the air like a wolf he smiled and added, "No, he's more than a friend to you."

"How do you figure that?" I asked, kicking over piles of ash with the tip of my boot in a desperate search for Luke.

"It's your pheromones!" he said matter-of-factly.

"My what?" I asked, not really paying too much attention as I searched the remains of the vampires that littered the clearing.

"They're scents you give off when you're aroused," he explained. "It's a pretty easy concept to grasp. What they do is allow animals to attract each other on a subconscious level. They activate the more basic instincts in animals -"

"I'm no animal," I said without looking back at him.

"Well maybe not, but I can sure smell that you've got it bad for this Luke dude," he said.

Then I remembered Ravenwood telling me that Isidor had a heightened sense of smell just like my sight and Kayla's hearing. Looking back at him, I saw Potter step from the now derelict summerhouse and out onto the porch. Isidor looked at him, sniffed the air, then stared at me.

"What you staring at?" I asked him.

"Jeez, and I thought your hormones were raging – that guy reeks," he said. Then smiling he added, "Perhaps it isn't this Luke dude you've got the hots for…"

"Give me a break," I groaned, looking back at Potter who now had a cigarette dangling from the corner of his mouth while he inspected his wings. "Don't just stand there Potter, help me find Luke and Murphy!"

"What about Kayla?" Isidor chipped in.

Then as if my prayers had been answered, a muffled groaning sound came from somewhere nearby within the fog. "Over here!" I shouted at Potter and waved my arm in the air to grab his attention. Looking up at me, he flittered from the porch in a haze of shadows and was next to me. Making our way towards the sound with Isidor at our heels, my heart began to pound in my chest at what I might stumble across. Ahead, I could just see an outstretched arm sticking up from beneath a mound of silver ash. Running towards it, I shoved the ash away like a broken sandcastle and pulled at the arm.

He's alive! I thought to myself with tears standing in my eyes. Reaching into the ash, Potter grabbed the other arm and pulled Murphy from within it. His hair was covered grey as was his face and bare chest. He looked as if he'd just climbed out of a chalk pit.

"Where's Luke?" I asked, taking him by the shoulders. Rubbing his eyes with the backs of his hands then shaking the vampire remains from his hair, he looked at me and said, "I saw him break free."

Hearing this, my heart leapt into my throat. "Where is he?" I said looking around at the piles of ash.

"Dunno," Murphy croaked and started to cough the dust from his lungs. "He just took off."

"Took off where?" I asked, desperate to know what had happened to him.

"He went after the girl," Murphy explained, shaking the ash from his wings like a dog shaking sea water from its fur.

"Kayla?" Isidor said, stepping forward. "He went after Kayla?"

"Who are you?" Murphy asked, eyeing him with some suspicion.

"Which way did they go?" Isidor asked, eager to get after them.

"Somewhere up there," Murphy said, pointing into the night sky. "Unless you got yourself a set of wings kid, you won't be catching 'em."

"I've got wings," Isidor said, unfastening his coat.

As he pulled it opened, I gasped, but not at the sight of the many sets of rosary beads that hung against his bare chest, nor the many wooden stakes that had been attached to the inside of his coat, but at the sight of his wings. These were nothing like the wings I had seen on any of the other Vampyrus. Unlike their wings, Isidor's wings hung from beneath his arms and were attached to his ribcage. As he stood with both arms extended on either side of him, it looked almost as if he had two large black webs concealed beneath his arms.

Looking at Isidor's wings and the collection of rosary beads that swung from around his neck, Potter said, "Okay, Madonna, I think we get the picture. Now zip your coat up before you catch a cold."

Looking a little hurt, he turned to Potter and said, "I saved your butt, dude, and don't you forget it!"

"I'm sure having you around will be a constant reminder," Potter said flicking his cigarette away.

"And that's another thing," Isidor growled. "I have a very sensitive sense of smell and if we're gonna be on the same team -"

"Team!" Murphy and Potter said together.

"Now don't you go getting any funny ideas, kid," Potter started.

"Who you calling 'kid'?" Isidor said, striding towards Potter.

"Enough already!" I shouted. "Kayla's been snatched, if you'd forgotten, and Luke's gone after her and god only knows how badly injured he maybe and all you two can worry about..." I started and my bottom lip started to tremble.

"It's okay, Kiera," Murphy said, placing his hand over mine.

"It's not okay! If you hadn't noticed, we barely got out of this alive tonight!" Then looking at him, I said, "And how did you manage to escape?"

Uncurling the fingers of his other hand, Murphy revealed the small silver crucifix tiepin that I'd seen him wearing on the very first day that I'd met him in The Ragged Cove. Winking at me he said, "I told you, Kiera Hudson, this little thing will offer you more protection than any gun, Taser, or baton."

"What about Luke?" I asked. "How did he manage to escape?"

"That, I don't know," he said, shaking his head at me. "But he got away somehow and wasted no time in going after Philips and the girl."

"So are we gonna stand here all night yapping or are we going after them?" Isidor said, almost seeming to hop from foot to foot with energy.

"No," Murphy said, walking away and heading out of the clearing towards the woods.

"No?" Isidor said going after him. "You don't seem to understand – I've been sent to rescue her."

"Goodbye then," Potter said, following his sergeant.

But -" Isidor started.

"No buts," Murphy said, turning to look at him. "We need to get back to the manor house."

"Why?" Isidor pushed.

"If you hadn't of noticed," Murphy said, "we ain't in too good a shape. My boy Potter here needs to rest those wings, and I feel like I've been kicked and punched to hell and back."

"But what about Luke? "I asked.

"What *about* Luke?" someone said from over my shoulder.

Turning, I watched Luke step out of the fog that continued to swirl around the trees and clearing. Running, I threw my arms around him.

"Be gentle," he winced. "I'm hurting."

"Sorry," I whispered, but still held onto him as I guided him towards the others. I noticed that as he walked, he almost seemed to shuffle and stoop. "I'm so happy to see you!'

"I'm sorry," he said, using me as a support.

"For what?" I asked.

"For losing Kayla," he said. "Phillips had too much of a head start on me. And what, with my wings in tatters, I just couldn't keep up. I really did try."

"It's not your fault," I told him. "We'll find her."

"When?" Isidor asked, catching the tail end of our conversation.

"Can't you see he needs rest?" Potter cut in, dismissing Isidor and helping support Luke by gripping him under the arm.

"But -" Isidor started again.

"You don't listen too good, do ya kid?" Murphy barked. "We ain't gonna be no good to Kayla like this. But if you think you can do better on your own, so long and good luck."

"I'm not afraid of any vampires," Isidor said puffing out his chest. "Can't you see what I did here tonight?"

Stepping so close to Isidor that their noses were almost touching, Murphy said, "What happened here tonight was nothing compared to what's coming. This was a mere sideshow. You think because you harpooned a few vampires you're ready to take on a whole army? Because that's what's coming, kid – an army – and a war like you couldn't imagine in your wildest hallucinations. So if you want to be on *our* team, as you put it, shut your face and fall into line."

Without waiting for a response, Murphy disappeared into the shadows and fog as he headed back towards the manor. Making sure that Potter had hold of Luke, I went over to Isidor who stood looking glumly at the ground.

"He isn't so bad," I said, remembering how Murphy and Potter had first treated me back in The Ragged Cove.

"The guy's a dick," Isidor muttered under his breath.

"I thought that at first – but he kind of grows on you," I half-smiled. "Even Potter has his moments I guess." Tugging at the sleeve of his jacket, I led him through the woods and towards the manor.

"I want to go after Kayla as much as you do," I told him.

"But Murphy's right, they won't be any good tracking her in their state."

"I guess," Isidor said.

We walked in silence for a while, always keeping Luke, Potter and Murphy in sight as they staggered and limped between the trees. They looked like the last of the Calvary heading home from the battlefield.

We cleared the woods and headed across the vast lawns to the manor. Turning to look at Isidor, I could see that he looked troubled. I guessed he was worried about what Lady Hunt would say to him when she realised he had failed to save her daughter.

Knowing that I had failed her too, I said, "Don't worry about Lady Hunt. I'll tell her what happened."

"Lady Hunt?" Isidor said, raising an eyebrow at me. "She's dead."

"Dead?" I asked, not believing what I was hearing. "How?"

"The guy who sent me to find Kayla – he murdered her," Isidor explained.

"What was his name?" I asked, confused.

"He didn't give me his proper name," Isidor said, "He just told me to call him Sparky."

Chapter Thirty

"Sparky?" I said, believing that I must have misheard him.

"Yeah, some lanky dude, with a face like a pizza," Isidor groaned. "Why, do you know him?"

"Yeah maybe," I whispered, trying to make sense of what he had just told me. "Why did he ask you to come and get Kayla for him?"

"Because, he said if I didn't he was gonna kill my mother," Isidor said. "She went missing a few months ago – then this Sparky showed up out of the blue a few days ago and said that he had her – but I could save her life if I did this one thing for him. Now you can see why I'm so desperate to get this Kayla back for him."

With my knees feeling as if they were going to give way beneath me, I tried to suck in breath. Then as if being hit by a freight train my head rocked back and there was a brilliant flash of white light and all I could see was those half-breed children lying in their beds clutching at the air as their breathing apparatus was unplugged. I could see broken images of Doctor Ravenwood as if he was being reflected back at me in a thousand broken pieces of glass. He looked asleep – unconscious – dead? These were followed with crystal-clear memories of sitting in my flat with Sparky, as he listened intently to what had happened to me in The Ragged Cove. And in my heart I now realised why he was the only one who had believed me – because he was one of them – sent to befriend me, hoping that I would lead him to my friends. That's how Phillips and Taylor knew who I'd had contact with since returning from the Cove. Their names and addresses. And the phone call – what were the chances of me ringing on the very same day and time that Phillips was sent to capture Sparky? Taylor and Phillips had wanted me to fear for his safety so Sparky could use himself as a bargaining tool when the time was right. I had seen everything but had *seen* nothing at all.

While my friends and me were fighting for our lives at the summerhouse, Sparky was to sneak away back to the manor and….those images of the half-breed children swam before my eyes again…I could see myself pointing Sparky in the direction of the manor and telling him to go and hide there. But what was it Sparky wanted...?

"Are you okay?" someone said in my ear. "Kiera, wake up!"

Opening my eyes, I could see Luke, Potter, Murphy, and Isidor looking down at me.

"Kiera, what's wrong?" Luke asked, kneeling beside me.

"Her eye's doing that bleeding-thing again," Potter pointed out.

"He just wants a way inside the manor," I mumbled.

"Who does?" Murphy said. "Who are you talking about?"

"Sparky," I said, trying to get up.

"Who in the hell is Sparky?" Potter grumbled.

"I thought he was my friend!" I cried and ran towards the manor.

"Kiera!" Luke shouted behind me. "Kiera, what's going on?"

Pushing against the big oak door, I stumbled into the great hall. "Sparky!" I screamed. Then looking to my right I could see that the door to the drawing room was open. "What have you done?" I whispered, seeing the crumpled body of Mrs. Lovelace lying on the floor. Racing into the room, I dropped to my knees and rolled her over.

"Mrs. Lovelace," I said, my voice trembling. Feeling something warm and sticky covering my fingers, I pulled them free of Mrs. Lovelace and winced at the blood that covered them. Her eyes stared blankly up at me, but it wasn't her eyes that made my heart almost stop, but the look of sheer horror engraved into her face and the opening that ran from just beneath her wrinkled chin to her chest bone. From behind me, I could hear the sound of footsteps as the others came running into the hallway. Holding Mrs. Lovelace's cold hand in mine, I stroked the tissue-thin skin that covered it.

"I'm so sorry," I sobbed. "I'm so sorry."

Feeling a hand fall upon my shoulder, I looked up to find Luke next to me. "What's going on here?"

"I was tricked, Luke," I cried. "I thought he was my friend – but all he really wanted was to get..."

"You," he said, helping me to stand and taking me in his arms while the others looked from the doorway.

"No, not me," I said. "If it was me that he wanted then he had plenty of opportunities. He wanted something else."

"But what?" Luke asked, wiping away my tears.

"The half-breeds on the ward," Murphy said, his voice low and grim. Then turning in the doorway, he limped as fast as he could towards the stairs.

Letting go of me, Luke ran towards the door, his wings trailing behind him like a torn cape. Looking at Potter, he said, "How you feeling, my friend?"

"Pissed off! I was ready to die for that loser." Then glaring at me, he added, "Some friend he turned out to be."

"It's not my fault!" I hissed and raced up the stairs after Luke and Murphy.

"Can someone tell me what in the hell is going on here?" I heard Isidor shout as he stood alone at the foot of the stairs.

"Why not tag along and you might find out!" Potter hollered back at him.

Reaching the foot of the stairs that led to the *'forbidden'* wing, Luke snatched up a lantern from the small table on the landing and we ran as hard and as fast as we could along the passageway to the narrow staircase that led to the secret ward in the attic. With my heart pounding in my chest and lungs burning, I followed my friends through the door at the top of the stairs and into the ward. The sight that Luke captured in the glow of the lantern made me want to scream.

Covering my face with my hands, I stumbled back against the wall of the attic. It was too late, the sight of those half-breeds lying half in and out of their beds would haunt me forever. Some were lying on the floor as if they had crawled after the oxygen tanks that had been taken from them. Others lay like alabaster statues, their hands clawing at their throats as they had struggled for breath, their tortured looks of pain forever engraved on their faces. These images seared themselves into my mind and I doubted I would ever be rid of them.

Isidor was last to enter the room and stumble across the devastating scene. He stood motionless, his mouth wide open in shock. Stepping over the lifeless bodies, Murphy made his way to the room at the far end of the ward where Doctor Ravenwood had examined me.

"Ravenwood?" he called out opening the door to the examination room. Then within seconds, he was back in the ward again. "He's been taken," he informed us. "But by the mess in there, it looks as if he put up a fight."

"But why would they want Doctor Ravenwood?" I asked him.

"He was working on a cure with Lord Hunt that would have helped these half-breeds," he explained. "They've already taken Lord Hunt so they've come for the other part of the team."

Looking about the room, I suddenly noticed something missing, but it wasn't just something – it was two of the half-breeds that Ravenwood had earlier introduced me to while they had slept– the girl, Alice, and the boy.

"Two of them are missing," I breathed.

"What?" Potter snapped.

"Alice and the boy, they're gone," I told him. "There were ten beds and ten half-breeds. There are still ten beds but only eight bodies."

"You're right, Kiera," Luke said.

"Can someone tell me what's going on here?" Isidor asked again.

"Shut it!" Potter barked at him.

"They must have taken the two of them," Luke said, looking at me then at Murphy.

"But why only two?" Murphy wondered, combing his grey hair from his brow.

"Perhaps they only wanted the half-breeds that might survive," I said. "After all, they would need to test this cure on a living half-breed – wouldn't they?"

"That's why they wanted Kayla," Isidor said from the doorway. Turning, we all looked at him and in the glow of the lantern that Luke held up before him, Isidor's young and boyish looks appeared to have faded and he now looked old – almost haggard.

"What did you say?' Potter asked.

"He's right,' I said, my heart feeling like a lump of stone inside of me. "Think about it. Kayla is sixteen, about the same age as the two other half-breeds who have been taken. But unlike them, she isn't ill. Kayla has just started to develop her abilities. Doctor Ravenwood has already taken DNA from her and this has had some results in helping the others. That's why they wanted Kayla; they want to force Lord Hunt and Ravenwood to continue their tests on her."

"To find the cure," Luke said.

"But you and Van Helsing over there," Potter said eyeing Isidor, "are both half-breeds. Why not take you two as well?"

I thought about this for a minute and Isidor stood and stared at me. I guessed he was surprised to learn that I was like him and Kayla.

"We need to talk," I half-smiled.

"I know the reason," Isidor said.

"Speak up then," Murphy grumbled.

"Because they know we will go after Kayla and try and bring her back," Isidor said. "They don't have to come looking for us any longer, as we'll go looking for them. They know we'll want to bring her back."

Stepping away from the examination room doorway, Murphy fixed us all with a cold stare. His eyes seemed to blaze beneath his eyebrows that furrowed down and almost touched the bridge of his nose. Then, in a calm but calculating voice that simmered with anger, he said, "We *are* going to find this man who hides in the shadows, this monster who sends his agents to kill our friends and take the people that we love. I tell you this, we won't stop searching, tracking, and hunting until we have brought him to his knees and we have brought those that we cherish home."

Never before had I seen Murphy so grave, his face so ashen and his eyes so keen. "We have learnt that we can trust no one, those we believed to be our friends and allies have betrayed us and we have no one but each other. So get some rest, because we leave tomorrow night and I believe the journey which lays ahead for each of us will test the nerve of our very souls, take us to the brink of our sanity, and I fear not all of us will return."

Without saying another word, Murphy limped over to one of the dead half-breeds lying on the floor, knelt, gently raised them into his arms and placed them back onto one of the beds. With his back turned to us, he whispered, "Please, I just want to be left alone."

Closing the door behind us, we made our way down the stairs, and reaching the bottom, I heard the unmistakeable sound of Murphy sobbing from above us.

I sat on the edge of the balcony which led from my room. The fog had started to clear, leaving behind a moon that shone a milky yellow. The sky was star shot and the wind crisp as it blew in off the moors.

Looking down, I watched Murphy carry one of the murdered half-breed children across the lawn and into the woods. Despite his limp, he cradled the child in his arms. He returned a short time later and carried another from the house and he didn't stop until he had carried them all into the woods. On his last journey, Murphy took a spade with him and I knew then that he was going to bury the children along with the others in the tiny graveyard I'd discovered hidden beneath the weeping willows. From my hiding place, I saw Potter step from the shadow that fell across the lawn. Silently, Potter approached Murphy, and taking the spade from him, he wrapped an arm around Murphy's shoulders and hugged him. I watched this unusual display of tenderness by Potter, and again I felt confused by him. I then heard the unmistakeable sound of Murphy weeping again. Potter said something to his friend, but from my hiding place I couldn't hear what. Then with one arm still wrapped around Murphy's shoulders and the spade in his free hand, Potter led him into the woods towards the graveyard.

I didn't want to be alone, so leaving the balcony, I went in search of Luke. As I'd passed Kayla's room, I saw my iPod on her pillow. Taking it, I made my way up to the room that Luke had used as his hiding place. As I reached the landing, I saw Isidor sitting on the top stair. His back was arched, and he rested his head in his hands. Isidor's eyes were closed and swinging from between his fingers was a set of the rosary beads I'd seen him with earlier. Without saying anything, I turned away, leaving him to his prayers.

Reaching Luke's room, I pushed the door open and stepped inside. He had pulled the tarpaulin away from his window, and as I'd been doing, he'd been watching Murphy take the bodies of the half-breeds into the woods. In the eerie light from the lantern, Luke looked back at me.

"I can't sleep," I told him, stepping into the room.

"Neither can I," he said.

Crossing the room, I went to the window and stood beside him.

"Why is Murphy so saddened by the death of those half-breeds?" I asked.

Turning towards me, his face wan and tired-looking, Luke said, "Two of those half-breeds were his teenage daughters." Then blowing out the lantern, Luke said, "Hold me, Kiera."

Lying together in the dark, wrapped in his wings, I knew that for the first time in my life I couldn't *see* anything. As Luke slept beside me, I eased my iPod from my pocket and switched it on. I was curious to know what the last song Kayla had been listening to before racing upset and angry into the arms of the person she believed she could trust. Putting in the earphones, I heard the gentle voice of Annie Lennox singing *'Why'*.

Why? I wondered. Why hadn't my mother told me that she was a Vampyrus? Why had I been born able to *see* more than I should – more than I sometimes wanted to? Why had I been made with wings?

And as I lay in the dark, I felt scared. I was scared of what I really was and what I might become. I wasn't human and I wasn't Vampyrus – I was what Doctor Ravenwood had called a *half-breed*. But I didn't want to be a half-breed and as the darkness seemed almost to press itself against me, I knew that I no longer knew who or what I was.

Tomorrow, I would leave this place with Luke and the others; and while their mission was to find Kayla and the man who was behind the misery we all suffered, I would be searching for someone else – for my mother. In my heart, I knew that it was my mother who had the answers to the secrets that would help me discover who and what I really was.

Unable to sleep, I climbed from beside Luke and went and sat by the window. Looking down at the lawn, I watched Potter step from the tree line of the woods. I guessed he had finished helping Murphy bury the children. Taking a pack of cigarettes from his pocket, he lit one, the end of it winking on and off in the dark.

Looking back at Luke, I heard him murmur in his sleep. Turning back towards the woods, I stifled a gasp as I saw Potter staring up at me from below. His eyes were fixed on mine and those images of us in the gatehouse flooded my mind again. Stepping back into the shadows of the room, my heart racing, I realised that there was something different about those images – something wrong.

Closing my eyes, I could see that we weren't in the gatehouse at all, but somewhere dark as if below ground. He was holding me in his arms and kissing me all over – but I didn't feel the urge to push him off in disgust like I had before. This time I could *see* myself clinging to him and needing him as much as he needed me.

Snapping open my eyes and forcing those images away, I peeked out of the window again at where Potter had been standing, but he had gone. Where? I didn't know. But what confused me more than his sudden disappearance was why I felt so disappointed that he had gone.

Looking out across the moors, I sat and waited for the blood-red glimmer of the sun to slowly rise up over the rugged horizon. I knew that it would bring a whole new day with it. But that's all I knew for certain…my future and the path that stretched out before me was unknown. Where would it lead me? I didn't know…but that was the excitement I craved wasn't it? Why else would I have ever come to Hallowed Manor, right?

And however much the not knowing of what lay ahead scared me…I knew I just wouldn't be able to stop myself from running towards it.

Vampire Hunt
(Kiera Hudson Series One)
Book 3
Now Available

More books by Tim O'Rourke

Vampire Shift (Kiera Hudson Series 1) Book 1
Vampire Wake (Kiera Hudson Series 1) Book 2
Vampire Hunt (Kiera Hudson Series 1) Book 3
Vampire Breed (Kiera Hudson Series 1) Book 4
Wolf House (Kiera Hudson Series 1) Book 4.5
Vampire Hollows (Kiera Hudson Series 1) Book 5
Dead Flesh (Kiera Hudson Series 2) Book 1
Dead Night (Kiera Hudson Series 2) Book 1.5
Dead Angels (Kiera Hudson Series 2) Book 2
Dead Statues (Kiera Hudson Series 2) Book 3
Dead Seth (Kiera Hudson Series 2) Book 4
Dead Wolf (Kiera Hudson Series 2) Book 5
Dead Water (Kiera Hudson Series 2) Book 6
Witch (A Sydney Hart Novel)
Black Hill Farm (Book 1)
Black Hill Farm: Andy's Diary (Book 2)
Doorways (Doorways Trilogy Book 1)
The League of Doorways (Doorways Trilogy Book 2)
Moonlight (Moon Trilogy) Book 1
Moonbeam (Moon Trilogy) Book 2
Vampire Seeker (Samantha Carter Series) Book 1

Printed in Great Britain
by Amazon